CRACKEN AT CRITICAL

New townships of prefabricated buildings had gathered like rubbish along the high tide mark of a beach around the factories and the quaint housing estates – dating back to the nineteen-thirties and already in decay – which fringed the capital of the Republic. Refugees and traders from London and the shattered Midlands accumulated here in all the wild disorder of an oriental bazaar.

It was to this region that Wyvern drove in his shooting brake the next morning. He had a small collection of canvases under his arm – a Dufy, two Paul Nashes and a Sutherland, the last of his father's fine collection. Wyvern knew of no other way to raise the required money for a lunar ticket quickly. In this quarter, they bought anything – at their own price.

After half an hour, Wyvern emerged with five thousand five hundred pounds in greasy tenners; it was a tenth of what the Dufy alone was worth. But it bought a ticket on the moonship *Aqualung*, leaving at midday the next day.

That gave him twenty-four hours to wait. He just hoped he would still be at liberty when the time came. But the officials at Thorpe spaceport had seemed casual enough: his passport had been checked, his papers examined, and not a word said. He drove home in a state of modest triumph. At four o'clock in the afternoon, soon after his return to Stratton, he was arrested by the New Police.

About the Author

Brian Aldiss is a restless man. This novel resulted from a visit to Finland. Recently he has taken to touring England with his own show, 'Science Fiction Blues', sometimes playing to audiences of twenty-seven. This is termed 'bringing SF to the masses'.

He is best-known as the writer of science fiction, someone referring to him recently as 'the god-father of British SF'. His first novel, *Non-Stop*, appeared in 1958, and he has had a book published every year since, as well as editing numerous anthologies. He also writes ordinary novels. He has won Hugo and Nebula Awards and several prizes for his literary criticism. The British Science Fiction Association voted him Britain's most popular writer, and the Australians World's Best Contemporary Science Fiction Author.

When not playing to packed houses in Welwyn Garden City, Brian Aldiss lives peacefully outside Oxford with his wife, children and cats.

Cracken at Critical

A novel in three acts

Brian W. Aldiss

NEW ENGLISH LIBRARY
Hodder and Stoughton

This book has been published in
the USA under the title *The Year
Before Yesterday*; it has been
specially revised for this edition.

Illustrated by SMS

First published in Great Britain in
1987 by Kerosina Books

First published by New English
Library paperbacks in 1989

British Library C.I.P.

Aldiss, Brian W. (Brian Wilson),
1925–
    [The year before yesterday]
    Cracken at critical.
    I. [The year before yesterday]
    II. Title
    823'.914[F]

    ISBN 0-450-50083-7

Printed and bound in Great Britain
for Hodder and Stoughton
paperbacks, a division of Hodder
and Stoughton Limited, Mill Road,
Dunton Green, Sevenoaks, Kent
TN13 2YA (Editorial Office:
47 Bedford Square, London
WC1B 3DP) by Richard Clay
Limited, Bungay, Suffolk. Photoset
by Rowland Phototypesetting
Limited, Bury St Edmunds, Suffolk.

At first, things simply drifted
Then some learned to flail themselves through
  the water
Some things learned to swim
Some things learned to haul themselves over
  marshy ground
Some things learned to live on the land
Some things learned to creep
Some things learned to run
Some things learned to fly
Some learned to use fire

Some learned to tell stories
  One story was about a different future time
  When everyone could walk
  And no one had to run

Dedicated to the spirit of Hugo Gernsback

THE MANNERHEIM SYMPHONY (I)

The sound of dogs barking at night, when everyone else but you is asleep. The smell of night air. The *feel* of night, coming as if through a special sense. Even one's own footsteps are strange.

My elder brother ran off with a gypsy girl one moonless night long ago. Is he still alive? There must be a special heaven and hell for a man like that. Often I long for them both.

Someone whose grandfather knew Sibelius told me that Sibelius had said, 'There is the everyday world of appearances and the magic world of the inner life. Music is the bridge between them.'

These things I thought of as I walked home through the motionless night. These and many more. I was in a kind of elation – full at once of joy and of questioning. Because of this mood, it was difficult at first to determine whether the dead girl was from the world of appearances or the world of inner life.

I was haunted by my brother's escape into a world of erotic love, away from the political pressures of our world. One may be haunted perhaps by the memory of a flower, given to one long ago in a tender gesture. So even now I remain quite possessed by the memory of that dead girl. Seeing something lying close by the roadside, I switched on my torch. There she lay in dishevelment, legs gleaming like bare branches, skirt rucked about her waist, and all her private parts exposed, upturned as if trustingly to the sky. Even here in exile . . . of course that memory returns, to perplex and lay waste the heart.

And this was in an hour of triumph, or comparative triumph, if I may turn the clock back an hour or two. Perhaps tragedies are attracted to such times, as the Furies visit pride. My symphony was a success. I was on my way home from Oulu, where I had conducted the premiere of my second symphony in the civic centre. Even the eminent critic Jalkirouka had been in the audience. The dark exultant strains of my last movement, which had expanded as never before the sombre chords of my tonal palette, still worked a magic in my head, so that I kept repeating to myself, 'This at least I have achieved, this at least I have done.'

True, I had not been entirely happy with the way the second movement had gone. It had not flowed quite as I had wished.

After the performance, a reception in my honour had been held in Oulu. I had made a short speech before leaving for the airport and the flight back to Kuusamo. My wife had not been waiting with the car at Kuusamo Airport, nor had I entirely expected her. Arthritis had taken a hold of her and she spent an increasing time on the great wicker sofa in our living room, under rugs, reading French novels.

Our house was no more than five kilometres along the highway from the airport, and the night was fine. For some reason – perhaps my restlessness of mind was to blame – I decided not to take one of the airport taxis, as I usually did when Sinnikka was not there to meet me, but to walk home. I put on the fur boots from my luggage and set out briskly, punctuating my step with the rhythmic phrase, 'This at least I have done.' It had not been bad music. It had said something to my fellow-countrymen of the wretched times in which we lived. Posterity would surely grant me that much. Posterity and contemporary critics.

But the second movement, my slow movement, still worried me. In memory of my absconding brother, I had incorporated into the movement a motif of Janacek's, consisting of permutations of a rising or falling fourth with a major second, which I quoted from Janacek's chamber work, *Zapisnik zmizeleho* (Diary of One Who Vanished).

This work for vocal ensemble tells of a young man who falls in love with a gypsy girl and leaves his native village with her. It includes the words, 'If something is one's fate, there's no escape', and my orchestration let the musical theme of passion and fate flow thick and slow. In Oulu, on the concert platform, the flow had been halting. I should have rehearsed the movement better, and I cursed myself that it had not been done.

When I set out for home, the time was approximately two in the morning – 'Now already dawn appears in the sky' – in the words of one of Janacek's *Zapisnik* songs – and stains of sunrise were spreading across a cloud-laden horizon. Darkness was nothing more than a kind of failed daylight in that summer season.

No one was about at that hour. Dogs were running barking in a distant suburb, at a loss to decide whether they were domestic or wild. Beyond the suburbs, the road ran through an unpunctuated landscape. How came the girl here? How came death here? But the appearance was in the future still, and I was still involved with the magic world of inner thought. The lake was somewhere ahead, as yet invisible, on the shores of which stood my house, with Sinnikka in it. Only a few kilometres beyond it, asleep under sullen cloud-banks, was our gigantic, threatening eastern neighbour, at once menace and inspiration, and I by a ditch, in the middle way of life.

My symphony had been met with some reserve by its first audience in Oulu. That was to be expected: the music was not immediately accessible, nor had I intended it to be. Besides, we are a reserved people, subdued alike by climate and history. The critic Jalkirouka had sat in the stalls, his expression unreadable. Wherever I live, that inbred destiny of our people clings to me still – inevitably, as it would cling to any man of spirit. The rivers of our homeland always have their tributaries in streams of mother's milk.

My thoughts grew heavy, my pace slower. When I am alone and not composing, my thoughts sometimes become leaden. Step by step, I worked upon the task of belittling my achievement and of pouring scorn on what I had done.

4

Although I dreaded this process and was powerless against its incursions into my pride, I nevertheless welcomed it as must any artist, who should always carry disappointment in his heart, who must be austere, must be dispassionate, must be restless. Only by this flood of scorn would I be purged, to try again later, and perhaps to create something more profound.

'You give yourself away. You say you write for your times, for your compatriots . . . How provincial! Only second-rate composers would aim for that!' So I rebuked myself, telling myself that I must shun popularity. I must become even less commercial. I must not seek financial reward – that was the way to artistic failure. It must be music itself I lived for. Everything must be sacrificed for music, even the expensive medical treatments which my poor wife required.

How else could an artist hold up his head? Those clapping hands in the concert hall in Oulu – as soon as they fell silent, so too my music had fallen silent in the minds that directed their applause. Musicians, artists, writers, all had their day, but were nothing compared with the statesmen who had careless control over their destiny.

The barking of dogs fell behind now. With only the dull thud of my boots on the road to break the silence, my thoughts sank more deeply into the murderous history of my century, into reveries of those brutal men whose careers had shaped the world. Evil had a power denied music or literature.

*

And some of those brutal men . . . their shadows passed across the *andante* of my second symphony. There was the blazing Swede Charles XII, who never understood the meaning of defeat, who waged war under the stoney walls of Narva while a snowstorm swirled about his men, and there inflicted a stunning defeat on Peter the Great. Later, this madman, bare of head, hair flying in the storm, wearing his martial top-boots, perished while attacking an obscure fortress in Norway. He lost the Swedish Empire, for all his fervour, and Peter the Great fell like a lion upon Charles's Baltic provinces.

Visitors from civilised lands gave their verdict on Peter's nation long ago. The Tzars had unlimited power. They flogged their boyars, the boyars flogged their serfs, the bishops flogged their priests, and everyone flogged their wives, mistresses and children. Poverty, superstition, drunkenness, and vice: these were the familiar manifestations of this lurid displacement of Orientalism northwards. Turbulent but conservative, these terrible peoples passed a thousand years under the Rurics and Romanoffs, worshipping those who brutalised them, depraving and being depraved, and advancing in civilisation not one whit. Ah, who could resist such a tormented nation? Not I!

Under the yoke of this nation went my country in 1809, there to remain for over a century. Then were our nights darkest, our winters longest. The secret police, the bomb, the threat of exile to Siberia: these were the instruments of justice we knew. What if we were a backward country, with little to eat but fish and reindeer and bear? What if we subsisted at poverty level, unable to dream of the utopian ideas which were then beginning to shake Europe and even Mother Russia herself? As the dirty brawling Moscovite Peter gave place to other bullies, to the stern oppressor Alexander II, whose statue stands proudly in our capital city because he flogged us somewhat less than his predecessors, little altered for us; our children in Oulu lived their lives through in wooden huts, sustained on a diet of potatoes and raw herring, dying young of tuberculosis, drink, or childbirth. Evil was our heritage.

It was small credit to us when a measure of independence came our way. The storm of the twentieth century struck change even into the sullen heart of Russia, when two unscrupulous adventurers seized the state, the Jewish Bronstein and Ulianov, who took the names of Trotsky and Lenin. The perfervid and childlike loyalties of the people were transferred, scourged by unprecedented waves of lies and cruelty. The Romanoffs were blown away like burning straw, including the useless Nicholas, last and most lenient

6

of his dynasty. His ineffectual laws, policing, prisons, and secret decrees were henceforth to be strongly reinforced by the new owners of the nation. But in that hour of upheaval, my country cut loose, declaring its independence.

In a world still dominated by the disgusting old idea of nationalism, nothing is regarded as more honourable than independence. Dozens of countries have gained their independence, then to sink into debt and slavery through misgovernment: agriculture, industry, commerce, all have suffered in the brave name of nationalism. We Finns fared rather differently. We celebrated our new freedom with a civil war. That was in 1918. Brief though it was, a million of our number were killed – in a country of four million. Having been blooded, we became a republic under our national hero, Mannerheim, a great fighter and, of course, no less a great drinker and womaniser. After him my symphony was named.

As I thought upon some of the stories I had heard of Mannerheim and his wenching, I turned the final curve of the road that led to home. By now, the sun had swum over the horizon, smouldering among cloud, and the land was bathed in an orange glow. Ahead, low and weary beneath lines of stunted birch, lay the lake, and my house set against its shores. To one side of the road was a ditch in which a small stream flowed. The woman lay half in the ditch, head and arms under the water, looking up towards the air with dead eyes. Her sweater and skirt were torn, with the skirt falling forward so as to leave her private parts exposed for anyone who passed to see. From the attitude in which she lay, it appeared that she had been flung from a car.

As I knelt by her, trying to drag her from the ditch, I looked with tenderness on what she would usually have kept covered, thinking a banal enough thought which might have occurred to any man, that it was this secret lair which rendered our terrible world of lies and oppression tolerable to mankind, which ultimately provoked love, if love was to be had, and which lay at the root of most musical inspiration. Her head came up with difficulty, her hair dripping. I laid her along the bank, smoothing down her skirt . . .

My first supposition was that she had been raped and murdered, though I was too delicate to test my theory by any examination. Such a crime was not unknown, even in my peaceful country. My discovery of her distressed me greatly, and did not permit me to think clearly. All I knew was that I could not leave her under the dawn, exposed to the possible depredations of wild dogs. I would carry her to my house, there to phone the police, although I knew that, this close to the enemy frontier, the police would probably give me a difficult time of it.

A cursory look showed she had been stabbed to death. Under a knapsack she wore, her skirt was torn where a knife or dagger had entered her body. There was little blood on the ground, as far as I could see.

The dead girl was light enough to be a tolerable burden. I slung her over one shoulder, so that her hands tapped against the calves of my legs as I walked in measured tread down the centre of the road.

A light gleamed in the window of my house. Sinnikka always left a light burning at night, whether I was home or not. It was reflected like a lock of gold hair in the still-dark water of the creek before our house, where my boat was moored. Behind the house, like a series of iron bars, stood a sheltering row of birch trees.

On the porch of the house, I set down my burden and my bag and straightened up. Hesitation seized me, and trembling. In thriller movies and suchlike, which I rarely watched, it was nothing for a man to be carrying dead bodies about in the early hours of the morning. In the real world, where motives were more obscure, and obscurities less easily resolved, just to be associated with death was to bring oneself inevitably closer to it.

There was the power of the living to be considered: the response of Sinnikka, the response of those further from me, my friends, my public, and the shadowy powers that ruled our world. The power of the dead, too, was a factor; the girl was gone; her history, whatever it might prove to be, remained, and might have roots which would grow into my life. The strains of that sinister little 'Valse Triste' by Jean Sibelius, part of the incidental music to the play 'Kuolema', stole into my troubled mind.

While cloud remained still tumbled about the horizon, the sky had cleared overhead. Through it travelled one of the Soviet Mars ferries, moving without a whisper, as if to remind me of the world history of which both I and the dead girl were a part – an insignificant part in a chronicle to which no resolution was offered, no escape. Despite all the pressures against the survival of our republic, Finland had managed to flourish under Carl Gustav Mannerheim. Near disasters had not deterred that gigantic figure. In 1935, for instance, only sixteen years after Finland had become independent, Mannerheim had invited a group of five politicians from England, whose favours he hoped to cultivate, to visit our country and witness for themselves the progress we had made. In the centre of our capital, outside the parliament building, a bomb had exploded, killing three of the English delegates outright, including one Winston Churchill, who was then orating about the perils of Communism. Bolsheviks were blamed for the incident, and Mannerheim held a purge of subversive elements; but he in no way altered his policies.

As the gangster regime of Adolf Hitler began to nibble at other parts of Europe, Mannerheim maintained good relations with Germany, and somehow avoided invasion, playing off the Huns against the Slavs. Slowly, year by year, Hitler took over all of Europe. France, 1940. Britain, 1941 – no one in that once-great island could find a leader who would rouse their spirit to resist. Ireland, Portugal, 1942. *Und so weiter* . . .

The Soviets, while gallantly resisting Fascism, were spreading in the East through Korea, in the South through Afghanistan, to take over the old British possessions of India and Burma. Under their wily leader, Zinoviev, who had assassinated his rival, Josef Stalin, the Soviets made an alliance with Japan. Japan, increasing its industrial progress, then spread throughout the East, taking over most of the old colonies of those European powers who had disappeared into the digestive juices of the German python, including

9

Australia. Only China and Sumatra were left untouched, as a sop to the American sphere of influence.

The North Americans, faithful to their doctrine of isolationism, looked on with dismay as darkness fell over Europe, that inhospitable homeland which many of them, or their fathers and grandfathers, had fled – looked on, but did nothing. Even when the island kingdom of the English language fell to the Swastika, a Day of Mourning was held in the USA, but not a single plane rose to fly westward and confront the spread of repression.

Why the Scandinavian world, with its vast empty places and small population, was spared from the general slaughter is difficult to calculate; but to impute rationality to world leaders is generally a mistake. Each Scandinavian country trimmed its sails, signed treaties, made secret extradition laws, and survived, each after its fashion. Nordic culture survived. Elsewhere, culture died, was debased, became mere fantasy, propaganda, or mindless distraction for a subject proletariat. Pan-Reich Music, so-called, is a boisterous and sentimental militarism, incapable of either harmony or discord: a tribal noise. Happily forbidden in the Soviet domains.

All this is secret history, of course. My father told it me, as is the duty of Scandinavian fathers everywhere. The textbooks relate everything quite differently, spraying air-freshener over the dunghills of history. To read a history book, its author fearful of offending *someone*, always that nameless someone, is to step into an alternative world.

*

Conquering my misgivings, I stepped into the drowsy interior of my house. Sinnikka slept her drugged sleep in her tapestried bedroom. I looked down at her, seeing how she had aged, reading in the lines on her face my own progress through the years. She did not move. Whereas I had involved myself in the affairs of the nation, Sinnikka had retreated into the domestic world of the home, and of visits to distant sanatoria for the treatment of her mysterious affliction. We had no children.

10

Once more lifting up the young woman – now with a greater reluctance than before – I carried her into my bedroom and laid her upon the bed. Looking down at her face, I studied its pathetic delicacy. Although it was frozen into a kind of horror, it bore no lines of age. For a moment, I could imagine I saw in its youth the lineaments of a girl I had recently met; but youth carries similarities with it just like age. As far as I could tell, she was no more than twenty years old. Her hair was brown and long. In appearance, she was not particularly Nordic or Slav.

Strapped to her back with leather straps was a small brown knapsack. This I removed in order to make her lie properly flat.

The knapsack contained a few personal items of clothing, a small bruised apple, two paperback books, a comb, a toothbrush, pocket English-Finnish and English-Russian dictionaries, and the woman's papers, in among which was a visa – which could have been forged for all I knew – permitting her to enter and leave the Soviet Union on such-and-such dates. Her profession was given as agronomist, and her name as Carol-Ann Crutchley Cracken. She was American, from the state of Georgia.

I looked at the young woman with a new interest. Americans were few and far between in Europe. For myself, although I disliked the commercialism of their art, I thought of the United States as a country where freedom still existed in a relatively pure form. The nation had, after all, been built by exiles, and for exiles I had a special feeling. Who would have killed Carol-Ann Crutchley Cracken? It could have been agents from the Reich's adversary, that vast, frightened country to the East. Or it could have been someone from within our own frontiers. And, if the latter, there might be reasons of an involved political nature from which I would be well advised to stay away. All told, my best course would have been to leave the lifeless body where I found it, revealing all in the ditch.

I should have caught a taxi, I should have rehearsed the second movement better.

Before further misgivings could overcome me, I went to

the phone and pressed the number of the Kuusamo Police. The number rang, the police symbol came up on the screen. No vision came up – but that was not unusual with the police – when a woman's voice asked me what I wanted. I reported what had happened. After some questioning, and a wait while she reported the matter to a superior, she informed me that a police car would be along in an hour or two. Meanwhile, I was to remain where I was, and not to touch the body in any way.

*

Well, you fool, now . . . I did not finish the sub-vocal remark. Daylight was seeping in from outside, filtering through the green plants on the deep window-ledge of my room. Another day forcing its way in. Soon, Sinnikka would waken. The world would resume its course, and I would undoubtedly be taken to the police station for questioning. For a moment I felt at one with all those exiles, all those prisoners, who, in our century and earlier, have been taken into custody, never to emerge again into the light of freedom.

Dismissing these creepy feelings, I crossed into the kitchen and brewed myself some coffee. Putting some rounds of salami and cheese between slices of rye bread, I ate to quieten my stomach, and returned to the bedroom, still chewing. There was a quilt folded on the chair. Spreading it delicately, I laid it over Carol-Ann Crutchley Cracken's body. Now that I knew her name, I no longer wanted to see her face; no longer did she preserve that decent anonymity which should belong to the dead.

Switching on Lutoslawski's Cello Concerto, I sat to drink my coffee. I had placed the two dictionaries and the two paperback novels on the seat of a chair which my wife had embroidered. Idly, I now picked up one of the paperbacks for inspection.

The garish cover of the book was worn and slightly torn. It had been well-read. I did not think much of Carol-Ann's literary tastes, since it was apparent that the story belonged to the genre of Maybe-Myths, as we call them in Scandinavia, in which many unlikely things are supposed to have happened in the past or the future. The cover showed the typical stigmata of its genre: a rocket-ferry heading for the Moon, a gigantic machine of sorts, a man in uniform scowling into space, and, in the background, a naked woman carrying a deadly weapon.

The title of the book was *The Impossible Smile*. But the name of the author attracted more than my desultory attention. *Jael Cracken*. I searched the pages of the book for any information which would give me a clue to the relationship, which must exist, between the author and Carol-Ann Crutchley Cracken.

The book was published in New York in 1995, although its action was set in the past, as was so often the case with Maybe-Myths, fifty years before that, in 1945. Jael Cracken, the back cover informed me, also wrote under the names of Kyril Bonfiglini and Malcolm Edmunds. This was his thirty-ninth novel of fantasy under the Cracken name. It concerned a possible past Britain – a concept to which, I gathered, the Americans were attracted, since Cracken had written on the same theme previously; his *Cyphers of the Bulldog Planet* had won him a Frederik Award, whatever that was.

In the other room, my wife sighed in her sleep. Removing my jacket, I flung it over the nearby chair. I put my feet up on the side of the bed without disturbing the corpse, and began reluctantly to read. While Lutoslawski played sombrely on, I submerged myself in the world of trash.

THE IMPOSSIBLE SMILE

By Jael Cracken

I. A SCENT OF LOBSTER THERMIDOR

June 1st, 1945. A sunny day on the streets of New York, everyone good-tempered and law-abiding as usual. Music playing from loud-speakers everywhere. Taxis plying their trade. Women looking beautiful at street corners. President Truman's image smiling bene-volently in all the buildings.

But in the HQ of Pan-American International Espionage, high above Fifth Avenue, it was business as usual. Randolph Hurst Shoe-sucker, head of PIE, was briefing one of his crack agents, who sat before the big man on the other side of his mahogany desk.

'We are relying on you,' said the great man. 'We can drop you secretly into Britain – the plan at present is to drop you in the mountains of North Wales, where the underground network will take care of you. But after that you are on your own and must create your own contacts. All right-thinking Britishers will assist you, of course.

'But the fascist enemy is tightening its grip. The country now has a new constitution, binding it closer to Nazi Germany. The British Isles are now officially entitled the British National Socialist Republics, headed by a leader going under the ersatz name of Jim Bull. Here's a picture of him. He doesn't look one bit like Harry Truman.'

That much was true. The picture Shoesucker held up was of a stocky, pink-faced young man with greedy lips, blue, staring eyes, and a shock of curly brown hair. He looked authoritative and slightly untrustworthy. It was many people's ideal impression of a typical Englishman.

'That's Jim Bull. We have reason to believe he is German, maybe the Gauleiter of Pomerania, according to PIE reports. Your duty while you are over there is to assist any plot to assassinate him. You understand?'

14

The agent nodded, tight-lipped. 'Got it.'

'Then get this. Your main duty is to pass on the sum of one million dollars to subsidise the British patriotic underground. The chief operator in the underground is a guy called Dorgen. He's an American plant, taken by the British to be British – he's a clever actor. But you must pass the money to a guy called Wyvern. Say it.'

'Wyvern. A funny name.'

'The British have funny names,' Shoesucker said.

'Okay. Wyvern.'

'Right, Wyvern. You got it. We have reason to believe that Wyvern has telepathic powers rivalling yours. So Dorgen reports. You contact him with the sentence, "Can Love's Affairs Be Hushed?" To which the correct response is, "Nothing I Would Like Better." Say them.'

'"Can Love's Affairs Be Hushed?" "Nothing I Would Like Better." Kind of sloppy, aren't they, sir?'

'That's what Research came up with. Seems they're part of some British hit parade song or other. Any questions?'

He scrutinised the agent closely as the latter hesitated.

'No, sir.'

'Very good. Then give me a kiss.'

The agent came round the desk even as Shoesucker spoke, having seen the thought forming in his mind, and knowing better than to defy a superior.

The kiss was a brief one.

Randolph Hurst Shoesucker broke it off and stood to attention. He held out his hand. 'God be with you.'

'Thank you, sir.'

The agent paused only a moment, then turned and marched from the long room. Though she read the other thoughts which rose in his mind, she made no word of protest. Eileen South was every inch the professional.

*

June 3rd, 1945. Norwich, Capital of the British Republics. In the streets of the fine old city, dominated by its historic castle, very little traffic moved except for military or official vehicles. In this fourth year of the country's occupation by the Third Reich, a wall was being built about the new capital for security reasons. In future, farmers would be allowed to bring their produce to the gates of the city and no further.

Out in the flatlands beyond Norwich, an experimental atomic

power station was being built, using mainly expendable imported French slave labour.

A Porsche growled through the empty streets of the city. Heavy rain was turning the evening green as the car ran slowly up the hill towards the Britannia Barracks. Beside the driver, a nervous man in a blue raincoat consulted his wristwatch every two seconds. He swallowed continually, peering out at the curtain of rain, muttering when the great barrack wall loomed into view.

The barracks, after some hasty redecoration, had been converted into a palace-fortress for Jim Bull, Our Beloved Leader.

Once, this grim site had trained soldiers who went to fight in the trenches of the Great War. Now, with the aid of Jewish Correction labour, its chill dormitories had been turned into committee rooms and private chambers. Behind the plaster of one of the newly decorated rooms, a man crouched. The room was a bathroom belonging to the Leader's suite, and the man was armed.

For forty-two hours the armed man had waited in his two-foot-wide hiding place. He had dozed without daring to sleep, afraid of breaking through the wafer of plaster before him. He had provisions, a luminous watch – and his gun. He heard someone enter the bathroom.

Fixing his right eye to a hair-thin crack, he watched and waited. The man in the bathroom was out of his line of vision as yet; by the sound of it, he was undressing. Grinning his strange grin, the assassin twitched his leg muscles to exercise them. Soon, praise be, he'd need to move fast.

The man in the bathroom went over to the shower, presenting his bare back to the plaster wall; as he turned on the shower, he presented his profile. This was it! For this second the forty-two hours had been endured.

The assassin pushed aside the flimsy plaster and fired three times. Jim Bull, alias Walter von Offnungszeiter, friend of Hitler, Gauleiter of Eastern Pomerania, Hero of the Ordnung von Nacht und Nebel, fell dead. He sprawled under the tepid spray. The water began to turn gravy-coloured as it drained away.

Still clutching his gun, the killer slid sideways in his recess to an old lift shaft. He jumped twelve feet on to a carefully planted mattress, and was on the ground floor. He flung back the folding elevator door whose rusty padlock had been previously attended to, and emerged into a stone corridor at the back of the barrack block.

A soldier in shirt sleeves a few yards down the corridor turned and boggled as the killer flung open a window and jumped into the wet evening. Belatedly, the soldier called, 'Hey!'

16

The killer ran round a washhouse, cursing his cramped legs, skirted the deserted cookhouse, dodged the swill bins, and doubled into the closed way leading to the gym. Two sergeants were approaching him.

They stared in surprise. But the killer wore Army uniform with corporal's stripes. He winked at them as he passed. The sergeants continued to walk slowly on.

He bolted into the open again at the gym, turned left at the NAAFI, jumped the low hedge into the officers' quarters and swerved behind the bike shed.

Now he was in a small laundry square, the laundry standing silent at this late hour. Ahead was what was popularly known as Snoggers' Exit, a narrow wooden gate in the high barracks wall. A sentry stood at the gate.

The fugitive stopped, took aim and, as the sentry hastily raised his light machine-gun, fired. He was running again before the sentry hit the stones. Sounds of whistles far behind spurred him on.

The wooden gate splintered and fell open before he got to it. Outside on the hill track, the sports car stood. The driver, who had broken down the gate, was already jumping back into his seat. His companion, the nervous man in the raincoat, tipped back a seat and motioned to the assassin; directly he had scrambled in, the nervous man followed. The Porsche was already on the move again.

They bucked down the track at sixty, skirting the high walls of the barracks. They slowed to turn down a slope, slipping and crashing through wet bracken, and curved among sparse trees. In a clearing they accelerated again, licked past a ruined bandstand and on to a gravelled road.

Rain was falling more heavily when, two minutes later, they swerved sharply left and climbed again. This track curved among pines and brought them into a chalk pit, once used as a small arms range.

In the middle of the range, a light passenger-type spacecraft waited, its single port open.

The assassin broke from the car and ran across to the ship. He climbed in, ascending the narrow companionway. The pilot, swivelling on his seat, held a levelled revolver until he got a good look at the newcomer's face; then he dropped it and turned to the controls. From the death of the British dictator until the pilot spoke, there had been only sub-articulate grunts.

*

Stratton Hall was a big, eighteenth-century building a few miles from Norwich. Built in expensive Queen Anne fashion, it had been spoilt by Victorian additions; though few cared about such matters in the English Reich. Across a weed-infested courtyard stood the stables. A horse and rider approached them over hummocky turf, moving quietly through the downpour. At the stable door, the rider dismounted and led Black Nick into the dry. As he did so, he broke off a mental union with the animal; instantly, the wild, wordless chiaroscuros of his vision disappeared, and he was back in his own senses.

The feeling of refreshment left Conrad Wyvern. At once, memory of his sister Lucie's death returned to him. He rubbed Black Nick down less thoroughly than usual, watered him, and turned to go.

Wyvern was a tanned, clean-limbed man in his mid-twenties. His lean face and grey eyes made him immediately attractive to women, of whom he had had many, as friends and lovers. In his manner was something more reserved than commanding, to which the state of affairs in his country undoubtedly contributed.

He had ridden bare-back from East Hingham, as always. As always, he had taken the overland route through the

18

woods, avoiding roads, so that Nick could go unshod. He himself went with no shoes or weapon, a piece of rope securing his trousers. The Flyspies which covered the country were good at detecting metal, and Wyvern kept his journeys to East Hingham as secret as possible.

It was eleven o'clock of the June evening, Treble Summertime, as he peered out of the stable, and already growing dark. The rain fell steadily; the harvests would be ruined, turning sour on the stalk. Squinting up at the west gable of the house, Wyvern could see the Flyspy attached to the Hall resting in its recharge cradle, its double vane idle. Even as he looked, the rotors moved and the machine climbed pot-bellied out of its metal nest, circling the building like a tired barn-owl after mice.

Flyspies weren't much good, thought Wyvern. Certainly, they detected any moving metal, but that was something easily circumvented, as he had proved to his own satisfaction. Their television eye was poor – useless in this light – and he walked over to the rear of the Hall with no effort at concealment, although the machine hovered fairly near.

He slipped quietly in by a rear door and went up what had been the servants' staircase to his own rooms to wash and change his clothes. As he did so, he chewed over the evening's disastrous events.

The disused railway station at East Hingham had established itself as a black market. You could buy anything there from a can of cigarettes, costing a few dollars, to a ticket on a moon-bound ship (no upper price limit). Wyvern's sister Lucie was one of the organisers. Surreptitiously, the place thrived; the Republic, desperately short of manpower after the Invasion, left it unmolested.

But when Wyvern had got there this evening, the station was a shambles.

He found an old woman dying in the ticket office. As he gave her a drink of water, she rendered him a broken account of the raid.

'They – Our Leader's soldiers – drove up in trucks,' she said. 'They surrounded the place. Anyone who ran got shot. Then they came in – very rough! Interrogated us – asked us all questions, you know. I was only after a blanket, if I could get one. I thought it might be cheaper at this time of year.'

'What about Lucie?'

'Your sister was rounded up with the other organisers, sir. They were cross-questioned too, and stood against the far wall. Later, they were hustled out, into a lorry, I think. But she passed a note to someone. It must have been for you.'

'Who did she pass it to?' Wyvern asked urgently.

'A little more water, please. It was to . . . I can't think . . . It was to Birdie Smith, who kept the post office – when there was a post. But I think he was shot. We was all shot, sir. Oh – if you'd seen . . . They weren't meant to shoot. The officer called out to stop. But they were young chaps – crazy. Crazy! All crazy. I'll never forget . . .'

She interrupted herself with a burst of coughing which turned to weeping. Five minutes later she was mercifully dead.

Wyvern searched grimly for Smith, the old postmaster. He found him at last some yards down the railway line in the direction of Stratton. The old man lay dead, face down in a clump of docks. In his hand was clutched a note. It read: CON – THEY AFTER TELEPATHS FOR BIG BERK. YOU MUST LEAVE. LOVE EVER, LUCIE.

Conrad crushed it, tears in his eyes, knowing he would never see his sister again.

The message was fairly clear to him. Big Berk was the common name for BRC I, the Nazi-made British Radiotronic Computer, a gigantic structure of thermionic tubes and circuitry situated in the British Republics Sector on the Moon. He could guess why Our Beloved Leader and his gang of thugs should want a telepath for it: he had heard the state secrets which turned into ugly public rumours.

The message told Wyvern something else. It told him that his sister remembered he had the freak mental power. When they were small children together he had once revealed the secret to her. The indescribable blending of their egos had terrified them both; Wyvern never repeated the experiment, and neither of them ever referred to it again. Yet she had not forgotten.

And when Jim Bull's Gestapo got to work on her – would she not, perhaps under narcotics, give up her secret? If she did, Wyvern would be a doomed man.

Lucie was right: he must go. But where? America, now more rigidly isolationist than ever before, licking its internal wounds, faced with indigenous fascism? China, where rumour said anarchy prevailed? Scandinavia, with rigid frontier controls, hostile to the rest of the world? Turkey, the crackpot state which had risen by virtue of the general collapse? The still-warring African republics?

Wyvern towelled himself down in his spartan room, thinking hard. Telepaths were as rare as total eclipses; no doubt the State would like the aid of one. Wyvern had willingly revealed his wild talent to no human being but Lucie. He kept it shut away in a tight compartment. For if he tried to 'read people's minds' (as popular parlance inexactly put it), those people would be instantly as aware of his mental presence as if he were shouting. And although his power was of limited range, it flowed out in all directions, so that he was unable to confine it quietly to one desired receiver.

The power had been erratic throughout his childhood; he still recalled his shock when, at the age of three, he had found himself communicating with the family cat and enjoying the taste of a freshly-caught bird in its mouth. With puberty, his power had become less erratic. Wyvern had used it to charm girls he desired.

During the desperate days of invasion, Wyvern had locked the power away, seeing it as a symbol of adolescent irresponsibility. Now only occasionally – as on his ride with Black Nick – had he ventured to use it, and then with a feeling of guilt, as if he had an unearned gift.

Of course, there had been the man in London . . . Wyvern had been on leave just before the old capital was obliterated. A drunk had barged into him down Praed Street. In a moment of anger, the drunk's mind had opened: the two stood locked in that over-powering union – and then both shot off abruptly. Yet Wyvern knew if he ever met that man again, the recognition would be mutual. And they would try to kill each other.

Most of Praed Street must have sensed that strange meeting, insensitive to mental transmission though they were; but then a crickeytip droned overhead, and everything else was forgotten in a general dive for shelter.

Still bothered by that memory, Wyvern hung his damp clothes over a line and began to dry his hair.

There was a loud rapping at his door. The birds sang their evening chorus. Otherwise the silence was so rich that he had forgotten he was not alone in Stratton Hall. Instinctively he tensed, then relaxed. Not so soon.

'Come in,' he said.

It was Plunkett, one of his pupils on the course he ran, an acned and eager youth.

'Sir, come into the rec, quick!' Plunkett said. 'They've just announced it on the telly – OBL's had his chips! Kaput!'

OBL was an irreverent way of referring to Jim Bull, Our Beloved Leader.

Wyvern followed the youngster downstairs at a run. His govern-ment job was to teach relays of twelve young men the essentials of his own invention, cruxtistics, the science of three-di mathematical aerial lodgements, first established in space and later adapted to stratospheric fighting. He enjoyed the task, even if it was for a loathed regime; the squads of eager young men, changing every five weeks, brought life to the decaying house, with its peeling paint, its two ancient servants, its antiquarian plumbing.

It had been Plunkett, for instance, who had invented the Flyspy-baiter. He had trapped pigeons and tied tinfoil to their legs; when released, they had flown off and attracted the miniature gyro after them, televising frantically and signalling to HG for help.

Plunkett led the way to the rec room. The oak panelling of this seedily grand room, where sporting prints had once hung, was now adorned with pin-ups of Deanna Durbin and Ida Lupino. Eleven youths were clustered round the ill-coloured telescreen. They called excitedly to their instructor.

On the screen, men marching. Wyvern found time to wonder how often he had seen almost identical shots – how often, over years of war, armistice and betrayed peace; it was a miracle there were still men left to march. These now, lean and shabby, paraded beneath the angular front of the capital's city hall, with its asymmetrical clock tower.

'Our on-the-spot newsreel shows you crack troops pouring into the capital for the funeral of Our Beloved Leader, to be held tomorrow. The assassin will be apprehended at any minute; there is nobody in the whole Republic who would not gladly be his executioner!'

As the metallic voice continued, there were more scenes from other parts of the country: York, Glasgow, Hull. Shouting, marching, shows of mourning, the dipping of banners, the Union Jack with its central swastika.

Close-ups showed Bull's mistress, Vera Lynn, weeping over his wreath-covered coffin.

'And now we give you a personal message from Colonel H,' the unseen commentator said. 'Friends, Colonel H! – Head of the New Police, Chief Nursemaid of State, Our Late Beloved Leader's Closest Friend.'

Colonel H glowered into the cameras. Aping the old Prussian style, his hair was clipped to a short stubble, so that it looked now as if it stood on end with his fury. His features were small, almost pinched, their niggardliness emphasised by two heavy bars of dark eyebrow and a protruding jaw. He was even less popular generally than Jim Bull, but more feared.

'Republicans!' he began, as one would say 'curs'. 'Our Beloved

Leader has been killed, shot down by Communist trash. Every one of us is to blame for this misfortune. We should have been more vigilant. We have all lost a friend! We have all lost our best friend! By allowing him to die we have betrayed him and his high ideals. We must suffer! We must scourge ourselves! We *shall* suffer – and we *shall* be scourged! We have been too easy, and the time for easiness is not yet, not while there are still maniacs among us.'

'Sir, why is this goon called Colonel H, sir?' Tom Merry asked – more cheekily than usual, as the course was about to finish.

'Halliday,' Wyvern said. 'He's Irish. Used to be called Brendan Bracken. Previously Minister for Education, responsible for closing the universities.'

H was still talking.

'I shall take over leadership until a new Beloved Leader is elected by Republican methods. I mean to make tight the chinks in our security curtain. The way will be hard, Republicans, but I know you will suffer gladly for the sake of truth, as I do.

'Meanwhile, it makes me happy to announce that the two murderers of Our Late Beloved Leader have just been apprehended by our Police. Here they are for you all to view – and *loathe*. Their punishment will be announced later.'

The scowling visage faded.

On the screen, a bullet-riddled sports car lay overturned near a roadside garage. A motley crowd of soldiers and civilians jostled round it. An officer stood on top of a tank, bellowing his lungs out through a megaphone. Nobody paid him any attention. It was pouring with grey rain.

The camera panned between the crowd. Two terrified men stood against the car. One, the driver, silently hugged a shattered arm; the other, a small fellow in a blue raincoat, stood to attention and wept.

'These are the blood-crazed, reactionary killers!' screamed the commentator. 'Assassins from the enemy bloc.'

'Crikey!' Plunkett exclaimed, 'they don't look capable of passing dud cheques!'

'Stand by for shots from the British Republics Sector of the Moon,' the commentator said.

Familiar domes like great vegetable cloches faded in. Utilitarian architecture, ventilation towers, steaming vents, standardised trappings of power, brute decor, mobs of people surging back and forth, waving sticks, shaking fists.

'These true Republicans demonstrate their loyalty to the new

Leader, Colonel H,' cried the commentator. 'They mourn the grave loss of Our Late Beloved Leader!'

'They don't, you know,' a youngster of Wyvern's party exclaimed. 'I reckon they're *rioting*!'

It certainly looked as if that was the case. The colony had scant respect for any Earth authority, but Jim Bull, according to legend, had been an old spacer, and as such his word had always carried some weight. The sound track was cut in, and the viewers heard an ugly roaring. And then, for Wyvern, the miracle happened. The camera swooped into close-up, to cover a swirling knot of people. In the background, a girl passed, taking no notice of the agitators.

And her thoughts came over clearly to Wyvern.

She was a telepath! He glanced quickly at the other twelve viewers, but they obviously noticed nothing. Somehow, over the digital signal, her thoughts had been filtered out for all but another telepath; and her thoughts were in turmoil.

Wyvern watched her incredulously, his eyes strained to the reproduction of her figure. And she was thinking, in profound anxiety, 'Got to follow him. 108 JJ Lane: that's destination. Heavens, I'm sending – must stop!'

That was all; but with the thought 'I' came, vaguely, her name: Eileen something – Eileen South, it had seemed to Wyvern. In flavours of lemon, pineapple, and lobster thermidor.

She ceased sending. In a moment, she disappeared behind a pillar. The camera lost her. Wyvern forced himself to begin breathing again.

Who the 'him' was Eileen South had to follow, he could not grasp; but floating behind the pronoun had been another phrase in her mind: 'the impossible smile'.

Of one thing he was sure. He had to get to Luna – he had to find Eileen South; she was his kind.

II. BUMPING INTO A DRUNKEN TELEPATH

New townships of prefabricated buildings had gathered like rubbish along the high tide mark of a beach around the factories and the quaint housing estates – dating back to the nineteen-thirties and already in decay – which fringed the capital of the Republic. Refugees and traders from London and the shattered Midlands accumulated here in all the wild disorder of an oriental bazaar.

It was to this region that Wyvern drove in his shooting brake the next morning. He had a small collection of canvases under his arm – a Dufy, two Paul Nashes and a Sutherland, the last of his father's fine collection. Wyvern knew of no other way to raise the required money for a lunar ticket quickly. In this quarter, they bought anything – at their own price.

After half an hour, Wyvern emerged with five thousand five hundred pounds in greasy tenners; it was a tenth of what the Dufy alone was worth. But it bought a ticket on the moonship *Aqualung*, leaving at midday the next day.

That gave him twenty-four hours to wait. He just hoped he would still be at liberty when the time came. But the officials at Thorpe spaceport had seemed casual enough: his passport had been checked, his papers examined, and not a word said. He drove home in a state of modest triumph.

At four o'clock in the afternoon, soon after his return to Stratton, he was arrested by the New Police.

At four-thirty, after a bumpy lorry-ride which he spent handcuffed to the frame of the lorry, he found himself back in Norwich.

*

The New Police had taken over a big department store on one corner of the market square; it swarmed with activity. Still handcuffed, Wyvern was taken through a side door up to the second floor and left with a Captain Runton, who nodded to him in abstracted fashion and continued to direct some men working there.

This floor was still being converted to police use. Once, it had been a spacious restaurant; now, flimsy partitions were transforming it into a nest of tiny offices.

'Let's see, what are you here for?' the captain asked Wyvern mildly.

'It's no good asking me: I don't know.'

'You don't what?'

'Know, I don't know,' Wyvern said.

'Sorry, there's so much banging here! You have to watch these fellows or they down tools. I think they suspect they are not going to get paid for this job.'

A swinging plank narrowly missed his ear. He ducked under a partition frame.

'Now,' he shouted, above a fresh outburst of hammering. 'We've found in practice that the quickest thing for everyone is for you to confess at once, without hedging.'

'Confess what?'

'The *crime*.'

'What crime?'

'What *what*? Oh, what crime? Why man, the crime for which you were brought here.'

'You'll have to tell me what it is first,' Wyvern said grimly.

'Oh hell, I suppose I'll have to take you down and look at your bloody papers,' Captain Runton said sourly. 'It won't pay you to be uncooperative, you know.'

He bellowed to the workmen to keep hard at it and led the way to an elevator. They descended to the basement and Runton pushed Wyvern into a cubicle. Cocking his leg up on the edge of a desk, Runton read carefully through the ill-typed report someone had left on his pad.

Wyvern looked round. Tarnished mirrors greeted him, and glass-fronted cupboards with cracked glass, containing cardboard boxes and big rubber bouncing balls for children. He saw little wooden spades, yachting caps, a dusty poster saying 'The Glorious Norfolk Broads'. Nothing very frightening: he wondered why he felt frightened.

The captain of police was looking at him.

'So you're Conrad Wyvern, one of the inventors of cruxtistics?' he asked.

'Is that why I've been arrested?'

Runton went and sat heavily down in the room's only chair. His behind was running to fat and his hair thinning. It was a wonder how he did it on the lean rations. No doubt he had lost his family and spent long evenings feeling sorry for himself, drinking. He looked the typical man of his age: comfortless, unlovable.

'Why do you suddenly want to go to the Moon, Mr Wyvern?' he asked.

'There's nothing sudden about it,' Wyvern said. 'I've been planning this trip for some time.'

'Why?'

'Oh – a change.'

'A change from what?'

'From routine.'

'You don't like routine?'

'Yes, but I just want to change.'

'You realise you do an important job, Mr Wyvern?'

'Of course. I thought a change –'

'The government doesn't like to lose its important men.'

'I booked return, didn't I? I'll be back in eleven days, before the next course starts at Stratton.'

'The government doesn't like to lose its important men even for eleven days.'

'It's getting choosy, isn't it?' Wyvern asked. He could feel his temper rising.

'These are bad days, Mr Wyvern.'

'Need we make them worse?'

'You can still hear that bloody banging, even from here.' Runton sighed deeply. He picked up the phone.

'The Palace,' he said, not without a trace of irony. After a pause, he said, 'Get me Colonel H.' After another pause, 'I'm Captain Runton, late of Leicester: he'll remember.' Later, 'Yes, I'll settle for his secretary.'

Finally he was put through.

'Hello? Captain Runton here . . . Good. Look, we have Conrad Wyvern here . . . Yes, that's him. He is being rather impolite in answer to polite questions . . . Yes . . . May I bring him over to you? . . . Well, for one thing, we have the decorators in here, making a lot of noise, and for another I hoped I might perhaps have the great pleasure of – er, possibly meeting Colonel H again . . . Oh yes, yes, I'm sure he must be . . . Yes, well another thing was, I hear you have a marvellous new Inquisitor up there, eh? . . . No, oh no, sir, that was a mild joke merely. I'm sorry. I naturally meant Questioner . . . Thank you.'

Runton hung up, puffing out his cheeks. Somebody at the other end of the line evidently did not love him.

'Come on, Wyvern,' he said heavily. 'We're going over to see the big chiefs at the barracks.'

It took ten minutes to drive, in a commandeered Post Office van, up to the barracks where Our Beloved Leader had been shot. It took a further twenty to get through a reinforced security system, by which time Captain Runton was more nervous than his captive.

Apart from his own preoccupations, Wyvern was intrigued by the captain. The man was plainly using him as an excuse to ingratiate himself with the powers-that-be. The fact that Wyvern was someone of importance made him worth hanging on to. As for the man's indifferent manner, half-friendly, half-insolent, that, thought Wyvern, was a national characteristic which the new regime had yet to eradicate, a pose which had become second nature. In the woman Eileen South's mind, he had glimpsed something more positive, more glowing.

27

And now, no doubt, Runton was reflecting that if he had come on a wild-goose chase he would get, not congratulations, but a kick in the well-padded seat of his pants. And *that* would make him unscrupulous about getting something pinned on Wyvern. Just what would happen seemed suddenly in the hands of chance; one thing Wyvern sincerely hoped: that the State's inter-departmental communications were poor, and that these people did not know his sister had been arrested at East Hingham.

That question at least was partly answered when they were finally allowed out of the guard room, and Runton grumbled, 'There's a lot of reorganisation needed here – everyone lives in watertight compartments. No government department knows what the next one is up to. You can't get anything done. Typical.'

The barracks swarmed with soldiers and police. Tanks were drawn up in the old drill square, their hides rhinoceros-like in the grey sunlight.

'I'd better take your handcuffs off,' Runton said. 'They look a bit ostentatious in here. And for God's sake don't try anything, or I'll shoot you down and swear blind you were OBL's murderer. I warn you I can be quite a bastard.'

'I thought they'd already caught the killers?' Wyvern asked, mildly surprised.

'Hold your tongue while you've got the chance,' Runton said in a sharp burst of savagery.

They passed together into the main buildings, where an armed guard met them and escorted them upstairs. The guard's hob-nails clattered loudly up the stone steps. A clock at the top said nearly six. 'Eighteen hours before my ship blasts,' Wyvern thought grimly.

They were pushed through a door on which, in still wet paint, was the legend 'Col. H. & Sec.' Inside, the first thing that caught Wyvern's eye was the pot of white paint itself. It stood nearly empty on a desk, the brush in it. Someone had been doing over the window casement with it, and the room stank of paint.

'Same old Republican muddle,' Wyvern thought, but the man in the room, Colonel H's secretary, gave him other ideas.

The secretary was a man in his late fifties, as thin and neat as a picked chicken bone. His uniform was spotless, his white hair impeccably parted. His eyes were fish cold. He put out an elegant finger and switched off the Bush radio, which had been playing light classical music, accompanying the gesture with a resigned pursing of his mouth.

'Oh – hello, we've an appointment with Colonel H,' said Runton, plainly distressed at lack of clue to rank on the secretary's uniform. 'My name is Captain Runton. Geoffrey Runton.'

Two soldiers stood by the window, backs to the light. They carried machine-guns, and were a wax-moustached, blue-jowled, low-browed kind of men.

'Are you Conrad Wyvern?' the secretary asked Wyvern, ignoring Runton.

'I am.'

'*You* have an appointment with Colonel H,' the secretary said. 'You'll have to wait to see if he will see you. Thank you for bringing Wyvern, Captain. Have you his report there? Thank you, splendid. We will keep you no longer.'

He accepted the report and waited for Runton to shamble backwards out of the room, without once removing his gaze from Wyvern. The latter, to his chagrin, found himself fidgeting and looking down. He decided to defend by attack.

'I am hoping to receive an official apology for the way I've been treated,' he said. 'I was handcuffed and brought here on the very flimsiest of pretexts.'

'Our junior officers make up in enthusiasm what they lack in manners,' the secretary said.

'Is that supposed to be apology?'

The secretary stood up. Coldly, he pointed to a chair in one corner of the room. After a moment's hesitation, Wyvern went and sat on it. Time passed. Men came and went, mainly high-ranking officers. Angry voices were raised at intervals in an adjoining room.

An hour passed before the secretary, whom Wyvern heard addressed as Bradley, took notice of him again, fixing him with a chilly stare.

'The State never apologises. We brought you here to cross-examine you. The Republic is in its early days – we can't afford to be sentimental. Don't you know, the road to success is paved with bruised egos like yours. If you feel badly about all this, it's because you are out of sympathy with us. Why are you out of sympathy with us, Wyvern?'

'I don't think –' Wyvern said, then lapsed into silence. It was hardly an answerable question.

'You are an important man, Wyvern – or could be. You should be a member of the Party, Wyvern. Why aren't you a member of the Party, Wyvern?' He used the name as if it were a dirty word.

'I'm busy – teaching your young men.'

'And?'

'It's a full-time job.'

'You get eleven days break between each course, don't you?'

'There is always much to organise – administrations, rations. My secretary was taken away when –'

'Oh? But everything has to wait if you fancy a flip to Luna, eh?'

'Can you tell me how long it will be before the colonel is ready to see me?' Wyvern asked. 'Perhaps you would care to continue painting your office?'

The secretary reached out and struck him across the cheek. Then he turned, going by a side door into the adjoining room. It slammed behind him, hard.

Wyvern rose, more angered than hurt. The blue-jowls by the window looked eagerly at him, licking their chops in hopes of trouble. Wyvern sat down again.

Minutes passed, heavy as drunken footfalls.

Devoutly, Wyvern wished he could use his hidden powers to find just what these people intended of him; but that was impossible; he could no more commune with H's offensive little secretary without his being aware of it than he could dance with him.

Bradley returned, ushering into the room a man of contradictory physical characteristics – heavy frame, narrow shoulders, large head, small features, dressed in a hairy tweed suit and large German ankle boots. He cultivated a moustache of the kind favoured by the late Josef Stalin, and looked more plebeian in the flesh than on television. It was unmistakably Colonel H, ex-Minister for Education, and the two bodyguards who followed him into the room reinforced the impression.

In his left hand, the colonel was holding a pat of juicy yellow Norfolk butter, and eating it with a teaspoon, which he held in a refined way in his right hand.

'You see, we're producing butter again,' he said, more or less to Wyvern. 'Equality has to be our first concern. Food for the people, provided they work for it. Smash the old class system entirely. "We are the folk of England, who have not spoken yet", as the poet T. S. Eliot rightly said. I was a product of the public school system myself – Framlingham College, much respected – but we'll do away with them, so that the common bloke gets his chance. National Socialism shows us how, the Fuehrer shows the way . . . Decency, fairness – anyone who gets in our way is in trouble.'

It looked as if this kind of rambling lecture might continue for some while, as befitted someone once involved in education. Wyvern stood up.

'May I know why I have been brought here?'

A slip of butter fell on the secretary's desk. Bradley frowned without moving a muscle.

'We've none of us any dignity these days,' Colonel H said. 'It's a harsh old world, enemies everywhere. Germany has got some of its best scientists working on atomic power. That's important, dignity isn't. There are priorities, and I'm going to get them implemented. You can't go to the Moon, Wyvern. What guarantees do we have that you aren't planning to defect to the American Sector as soon as you get there? We need you here, teaching a new generation cruxtistics. As Professor Joad said, there must be sacrifices, or we'll never reach the future at all.'

'Why should you think I was planning to leave the Republic?' Wyvern asked.

Colonel H laughed.

'We can't trust *anyone*,' he said. 'It's going to be tough in Britain this next decade, and those who can't face the prospect will betray us. A hungry man will cut his brother's throat for a crust of bread. I've just had word of a round-up of profiteers at a place called East Hingham – the list of prisoners should be in at any minute. Those sort of people, they're swindling someone, they only deserve shooting.'

He lapsed into moody silence and dug into his pat of butter.

'If only there was some way of *really knowing* what people are thinking inside here.' The colonel thumped his stubbly skull. 'Really knowing . . . And there is a way, if we could only get at it. There's beauty in Truth, Wyvern, take it from me, real beauty, say what you like. And we are developing a way of getting at the Truth, right here.'

'I don't think that idea is something we should discuss with a suspect,' Secretary Bradley said primly.

'Why not?' the colonel asked. Then he laughed, 'You see, I was thinking of sending him down into the cellars to see our new Inquisitor – and he ought to know what it's all about first.'

At that, the secretary laughed too, wet his lips, adjusted his tie.

'You better tell him about it,' the colonel said. He licked the last of the butter off the paper, dropped the paper into a wastepaper basket and slipped the spoon into a pocket of his tunic.

'It won't take long,' the secretary said crisply. 'You have heard of Big Berk, Wyvern. It is the most complex computer in existence, except for Fall Guy, the American computer on Luna. For a number of years, for lack of adequate staff, Big Berk has lain practically idle, yet it is potentially the Republic's greatest weapon.

31

An entire electronics of thought is in the pipeline, and our experts are building into Berk latent mind-reading abilities. Once he is taught, we, the State, will be able to know what any citizen is thinking!'

Wyvern's hands had gone damp. He rested them lightly on the desk, close to the patch where Bradley had discreetly mopped up the butter blob.

'When – when will this scientific miracle come about?' His voice sounded unreal in his ears.

'That's the snag!' Colonel H exclaimed. 'Only a telepath knows what telepathy really is. We had a fellow at Framlingham who could tell you what you had dreamed the previous night. We've got to get our hands on a telepath – as soon as possible.'

'Actually, we *had* one,' the secretary said. 'A fellow called Grisewood volunteered. But there are *surgical* difficulties – which have now been overcome – in coupling these freaks to the machine. Grisewood died. Now we want another of his ilk. You don't happen to know any telepathic persons running round loose, Wyvern, do you?'

Were they playing with him? Did they know all the time?

Wyvern said: 'I wouldn't recognise one if I saw one.'

Colonel H went over to the door. 'Big Berk claims that telepathy is a sort of side-product of intelligence, just as intelligence was a side-product of tribal co-operation – you couldn't get it in an idiot, for instance. So we're checking on anyone who isn't imbecile. We are starting a Republic-wide drive very shortly. You'd better be checked now you're here, Wyvern.'

He turned, his finger on the door handle, and looked at Wyvern. In his eyes was a terrible kind of excitement; Wyvern recognised it: it was blood lust. He knew then that his life and reputation were mere straws to these men.

'Is this justice?' he said.

'My dear man, of course not,' the secretary said, his voice expressing incredulity at such a naive question. 'We are only police, and as such our concern is with the law, not with justice. For justice you must go to the government – *if* you can get there!'

'You are the government!' Wyvern said.

'Good God, not yet!' Colonel H said. 'OBL only died the day before yesterday. Give us a week!'

He uttered his meaningless laugh again, and opened the door.

'Corporal, take this civilian down to Parrodyce in the cellars,' he called.

A corporal and a private marched in at once.

'Parrodyce is our new Inquisitor,' the secretary whispered to Wyvern, conspiratorially. 'You'll find he's hot stuff! A real pervert.'

Wyvern was seized and marched into the corridor. He did not struggle; it seemed useless. The mentality of the captive had descended suddenly upon him, a resignation blind to life. They clumped downstairs, and then down two underground flights, and then along a corridor, and then through a locked steel door and down another corridor. And as they moved more deeply into the stronghold, paradoxically a hope began to grow in Wyvern. This Inquisitor, Parrodyce, however cruel his methods were, would have no more understanding of telepathy than anyone else; he would not know what to look for; he would fail; Wyvern would be released.

The corporal pushed Wyvern into a tiny room. 'Strip,' he ordered, and stood watching interestedly while Wyvern did so.

'Let's have your kit,' he said.

Wyvern handed it over. Protesting would do him no good. In his pockets went his health certificate, passport, identity and ticket for the *Aqualung*.

'How long am I likely to be down here?' he asked the corporal.

'Let's have your watch too. That depends on you.'

'I've got to be out tomorrow.'

'Have you now? I'd better tell the chap who makes the coffins to get busy, then, hadn't I?'

He and the private disappeared, slamming the door closed behind them. Wyvern sat down on a bench and looked about him. The room was damp and musty. It had no features. The bricks which formed its walls had once been white-washed. Now the white-wash was peeling. From the metal light-switch by the door, the electric cable ran up in a conduit to the naked light bulb overhead which, at a rough estimate, emitted about twenty-one and a half watts of illumination.

Wyvern calmed himself by thinking of his sister Lucie, and of girls he had known. In so many of them was a perfect trust and loyalty which, tasted telepathically, conveyed a sensation of flowers growing out of long grass. His sister in particular possessed all the virtues one could find in a human being. He thought again of the mysterious Eileen South, glimpsed on television, and of the hint of her unusual qualities.

Almost for the first time, he began thinking creatively of the gift or curse of telepathy – gift at present, curse if the State used it for their own purposes. The potential had always been within people, or at least within children. It had developed as presumably the practice of language had once developed – mastered only by humans, not by their kind, the animals. Perhaps telepathic people would soon emerge, as separate from others as humans now were from the beasts.

He lost himself in a vivid panorama of thought. Flowers blossomed from him, intricate winding ways of green, animals of grace and unknown strength; his intestines blossomed from his body, flashing their secret colours. Everything opened. The light bulb blazed. He was a landscape, brilliant in the sun of existence, a fount of biology.

The cell door opened. The corporal entered by one step, froze, screamed in horror at the beauty and revelation he saw there, turned and ran. Startled by the noise, Wyvern returned to himself, and to the prison of the everyday.

After a while, the private appeared, gun first, very cautious.

Signalling to Wyvern he led him through a swing door. It was hot in here, and there was a smell of antiseptic and ether about.

'This is where they operate,' the private said in a hushed voice. 'They do some terrible things in here.'

A man in a white coat passed them, wheeling a patient along on a trolley. The private gaped.

'Did you see *that*?' he whispered. 'The poor fellow has had his lower jaw removed! How long do you think he'll live like that?'

Without hanging about for an answer, he pushed Wyvern through another door, remaining outside himself and bolting the door. Wyvern found he was alone with a nurse, a female of pallid features and hawk nose.

'I must warn you that any show whatsoever of violence, or any raising of the voice in shouting or screaming will be dealt with very firmly indeed,' she said, in the voice of one repeating a lesson. 'Now come and have a shower. This way.'

'I don't need a shower,' he said.

'Come and have a shower,' she said. 'You're filthy. Mr Parrodyce is funny about people who stink.'

The shower was nothing. True, for a few seconds Wyvern, twisting in pain against the cubicle wall, thought he was being scalded to death; but then it was over, and the cold soused him back to a grim sanity. Someone, presumably, was just getting his hand in.

'Now you look quite a healthy pink,' said the nurse sociably.

She shackled his hands behind his back in a pair of long-chained cuffs, and led him into another room. Wyvern noticed the walls and

34

door were very thick; the room itself would be quite soundproof.

It was furnished with steel cupboards, a big chair like a dentist's, with gas cylinders attached, and a light table at which a plump man sat, his hands folded on the table top. His spectacles flashed as he looked up at Wyvern.

'This is Mr Parrodyce,' the nurse said, and left the room.

'I've got to kill this devil,' Wyvern thought. He had never felt that way about anybody before; the emotion came on a wave of revulsion that shocked him with its strength.

Yet Parrodyce had not touched him. He had merely come round the table, looked, and gone back and sat down, putting his hands back on the table top. Now he sat there, trembling slightly.

And Wyvern hated him.

He had suddenly realised that the power to kill might well lie within his mind. The shock of ego-union which everyone called telepathy was formidable; driven steel-tipped with hate into an unprepared brain, it should prove fatal. And that would be nice, thought Wyvern.

'What shall I do to you first?' Parrodyce asked, as if to himself.

*

At this point, I had to cease reading. Lutoslawski had finished playing. Glancing at the pages ahead, I could see that Jael Cracken had filled a whole chapter with descriptions of torture I did not wish to read.

The world was full enough of misery without such writers as Cracken needing to add to it with gloating tales of cruelty. Putting the book down, I poured myself a fresh cup of coffee, walking about the room and gazing out of the window to see if the police were coming yet. The corpse of the dead girl lay under the blanket.

Hearing a sound from my wife in her wicker bed, I crept into her room to see if she was comfortable. She still slept, her profile dark against the patterned bolsters, one hand comforting her cheek, its little finger curled pink and delicate as a sea creature. For all her suffering, Sinnikka remained beautiful to my eyes.

As I thought of how her life had enriched mine, the naive remarks about telepathy printed in the paperback returned to my mind. I gave no credence to telepathy; for me, a thing had to be proven or it wasn't there. Still less did I have patience for Cracken's pseudo-evolutionary theory that telepathy might be a new development in the history of mankind. But I caught myself wishing that I could be granted such a delightful power, if only for an hour, before the police from Kuusamo arrived for me, so that I might creep into the mind of my dear Sinnikka, there to lose myself among her thoughts and memories, perhaps even healing any sorrows I had caused her over the years when our existence had been linked . . . And discovering what she really thought of me.

How wonderful it would be, to escape for once from the burden of our own limited personalities, to run like a reindeer over the wilds of another's life-interpretation, to see, as if reflected in a lake, a world existing parallel with our own. But of course that was nothing more than an idle, captivating wish, perhaps in its essence infantile, which had to be put aside.

Sinnikka stirred, as if aware of my presence, and turned her head. Her blue eyes opened. Our gaze met. She smiled. I moved forward and took her hand. She murmured something. But she was still under the influence of her pain-killing drugs. Her eyes closed. Next moment, she was as soundly asleep as ever.

I released her hand. It lay upon the duvet, motionless.

Slightly disappointed, I returned to my room. Since there was for the moment nothing better to do, I picked up the paperback again, to discover if Conrad Wyvern managed to kill the man who was torturing him.

*

The human mind, like the body, has its strange, secret reserves. Among the madness and noise there was a split second when Wyvern was entirely in possession of himself. In that moment, he acted upon his earlier decision to kill Parrodyce. He opened at full blast the telepathic trap of his mind, pouring out loathing to the utmost of his strength – and was met with a counter-surge of telepathic force!

36

On the instant of ego-union between them, Wyvern learnt much; he *knew*, for instance, as unmistakably as one recognises a brother, that Parrodyce was the drunken telepath he had bumped into years ago in London; and then he dropped into unconsciousness.

III. 'YES, YES, I AM FOUL'

Eugene Parrodyce talked rapidly.

Sweat stood out on his forehead, like grease on a bit of dirty vellum. As he spoke, he held a bitter-tasting beaker of liquid to Wyvern's lips, letting it slop down his chin while he concentrated on what he was saying. With the sense of urgency harrying him, he had not unlocked the bands round Wyvern's throat and ankles; but instead of standing over him, he now knelt before him.

'Open up again, Wyvern,' he whispered. 'For heaven's sake open up your mind again and let me in. Why're you closed down on me? You know it's dangerous to you to be talking to you like this – for all I know, they've got the place bugged, although they may be too disorganised to have thought of it yet. H might come in. He came down here once before. If you'd only open up again for a second, we'd get everything cleared up between us – more than we'll ever be able to do by talking.'

'Forget it!' Wyvern said.

The bitter liquid cleared the fire in his body.

'Release my hands and neck, and let me sit up,' he said.

'You – you won't try anything stupid, will you?'

'Keep my ankles locked if you're afraid I'm going to attack you.'

Abjectly, muttering apologies, Parrodyce released the chafed wrists and neck from their bonds; he left the ankles locked, as Wyvern had suggested. And words burst from him again.

'We must communicate, Wyvern! Be sensible! We're the only ones who have this gift – this great gift. You must let me in: I've so much to say and explain . . .'

'Forget it!' Wyvern said. 'I won't open my mind to you again. I'd be sick if I did. You're a walking cess-pit.'

'Oh, it's easy to insult me now, now you know my secret –'

'Parrodyce – you had me here unconscious. *Why didn't you kill me then?*'

The plump man didn't answer. He shook his head helplessly, his eyes fixed on Wyvern's, tears blurring his gaze. He was trying to break through Wyvern's shield. Wyvern could feel him like a blind man padding behind locked doors, rattling the locks.

'Stop it!' he said. 'You aren't coming in. I won't have you. You're too foul, Parrodyce!'

'Yes, yes, I am foul,' the other agreed eagerly. 'But can't you see we are brothers really in this. You've got to help me get out of here. You've –'

'Oh no,' Wyvern said. 'You've got to help *me* get out of here. And first of all there are several things I want to know.'

'Let's connect – then you can know everything!'

'Question and answer will do me, you dog! How did you get this job?'

Parrodyce knelt back wretchedly. He wrung his hands as if he were washing them; Wyvern had read of this gesture but had never before seen it performed. On top of everything else he had suffered, this man's sudden transformation had considerably shaken him. From a torturer, Parrodyce had turned into a sobbing wreck: Wyvern had regained consciousness to find the creature slobbering round his neck.

'A telepath is an ideal inquisitor,' Parrodyce was saying now. 'Don't you see, when I had someone shut up safe in here – so that nobody outside could feel what I was doing – I could explore his mind while he was drugged and read every secret he had. When they came round, even if they were allowed to get away alive, they didn't know what had happened to them. And – and I always delivered the goods to H. I couldn't fail. And I didn't fail –'

'But *why* did you do it?'

'I – I – Let me into your mind! I'll explain then.'

'You filthy vampire! No, I won't let you in,' Wyvern said. And Wyvern had no need for explanation. Their second of ego-union had given him the real truth: Parrodyce was a pathological coward; full of fear himself, he could only exist on the fear of others.

Yet it was not so much this shameless exhibition of fear which revolted Wyvern. Rather, it was to find that a fellow telepath had slipped so far from everything regarded as decent in human conduct. Isolated from others of his kind, Wyvern had vaguely imagined that a telepathic community (supposing such a thing should exist or had existed) would be free from vice; given such a powerful instrument of understanding, surely it would always consider the feelings of its fellows which it could learn so easily? Now he saw the fallacy of his assumption; telepathy was a gift which lay in its place alongside all the other human traits, good or bad. There could no more be a true brotherhood of telepaths than there could be a true brotherhood of man.

'Get these bands off my legs,' Wyvern ordered. 'You're going to let me go free out of here.'

'No! Oh no, I can't let you go now I've found you!'

'Wait! Bradley mentioned there was another telepath. What was his name – Grimslade? What did you do to him?'

'You mean Grisewood? I never got near enough to him to communicate . . . Don't remind me of him – he died horribly, when they tried to couple him to Big Berk. That must be the worst pain of all; I pray I never come to that!'

'Get these shackles off me!' Wyvern said.

Tears ran from Parrodyce's eyes. His spectacles misted. He fumbled at the locks by Wyvern's ankles. When they were undone, he lay helplessly where he was at the foot of the chair.

'You're going to betray me to H! You're going to betray me,' he muttered, over and over again.

'If I betrayed you, I'd betray myself,' Wyvern said in a hard voice. He was testing out his legs; they just held him. Parrodyce, too, got slowly to his feet.

'That's right,' he said thoughtfully. 'If you betray me you betray yourself.'

He mended visibly. Some degree of colour returned to his face. He could see there was hope.

'I can get you safely out of here just by giving the word,' he said. 'I'll do it at once.'

He turned and went slowly back to his cabinets. He began to speak into a concealed phone in something like his old manner. When he finished, he pushed the phone back and came to put his hand on Wyvern's arm.

'I'm in control of myself again now,' he said. 'It was the shock of finding another telepath at last. I must have a drink. Let me give you one, too. They only allow me a stingy bit each day, or I try to drown my sorrows.'

Wyvern curtly refused the drink when it was offered. Parrodyce drank it off and poured himself another.

'I'm kept down here,' he said. 'My life's pure misery, Wyvern, I swear it is. They've given me an assistant just recently, a fellow called Joe Rakister. The company's good for me – it's just someone to talk to, you know. I've become quite fond of Rakister in my own way, you know. But all the while I'm afraid he's really one of H's men, sent to spy on me. I'm not a Nazi. I'm a bag of nerves, Wyvern; I never used to be like this, even during the Invasion. I suppose it's the feed-back effect of the torture. I don't get any pleasure out of it. At least – well, I'm sorry afterwards. Sick, you know. In my dreams they come back and do all the things to me I've done to them.'

His hand started quivering. He put the glass down, biting his lip, and suddenly swung round to confront Wyvern.

'For God's sake do something for me,' he begged.

'What's that?'

'If you ever get the chance – I want you to communicate with me. Oh, I know what it must be like for you: free-diving in a cesspool . . . But you've got to find what I've got wrong with me, Wyvern. You've got to go down and find it, and try and put it right. It must be something buried right down in my id, I don't know what: something someone did to me when I was a kid in a pram, perhaps. Psychiatrists can't do anything. But *you* could! You're telepathic, Wyvern! You could put me straight again, Wyvern.'

Yes, Parrodyce was right. He was just one of the bits of horrible mess man had infested his world with. If you could, you put it right; even if it did no ultimate good.

'If I get the chance, I will, Parrodyce,' Wyvern said. 'Now I want to go.'

Parrodyce thanked him hopelessly, and handed him over to the nurse.

'I spoke to H's secretary,' were Parrodyce's last words. 'You'll be allowed out the main gate.'

He went back into his silent torture chamber, polishing his spectacles and shaking his head.

The nurse handed Wyvern over to the corporal. The corporal gave him his clothes and watched him dress.

'Not a mark on you, except that bruised shin,' he exclaimed wonderingly. 'You frightened me, you know . . .'

'Where are my belongings?' Wyvern asked.

'*Just* going to get them.'

He produced them in an old toffee tin. Wyvern looked rapidly through them; everything was there except two items: the ticket to Luna and his passport. He looked sharply up at the corporal.

'Something missing?' the latter asked. 'This was the colonel's secretary's orders. He told me to give you this.'

He produced a grubby envelope from a tunic pocket. It contained the Luna ticket and the passport, torn to tiny shreds.

A private soldier led Wyvern upstairs and out across the barrack square. It was dark and still raining. Wyvern had no coat, but he scarcely noticed the wet. With a minimum of formality, he was let through the gate into freedom: they had ceased to be interested in him.

He had no option but to walk home, exhausted as he felt. Before dawn, the rain ceased. The sun rose behind cloud. The country was fine and still, trees bending into luxuriant summer growth, dripping moisture into the ground. Grass blades shimmered like harmless spears. The birds rejoiced in the new daylight.

At last Stratton Hall was in sight. It would be empty now, except for the two old servants, as empty as Wyvern felt. He had no hope. Somewhere, thousands of miles away, was a girl he might have loved. Now he would never get to her. There was nowhere else to go, nothing else to do.

A car engine sounded behind him as he turned into the drive gates. Instinctively, he flinched. Had they come to get him back again already? Perhaps he shouldn't have returned here at all; he could have lost his identity and become one of the many nomads who tramped the countryside.

But the driver of the car wore no uniform. He pulled up in a spray of mud and called out, 'Is this place Stratton Hall?' He looked about eighty, but his voice was young and sharp.

'Yes.'

'You just going in? Well, I'm Government Mail. Give this to Mr Conrad Wyvern for me, and spare me a half mile journey.'

He was off. Wyvern looked blankly at the green envelope. He stuffed it in a damp pocket and trudged up the drive. A side door had been carelessly left open. The servants seemed to be still asleep; even the Flyspy was not stirring in its metal nest.

Wyvern sank wearily on to his bed before opening the envelope and reading its contents. Then he sat recalling the discontented voice of Captain Runton saying: 'There's a lot of reorganisation needed here – everyone lives in watertight compartments. No government department knows what the next one is up to.' He began to smile. Then he began to laugh. He laughed helplessly, stupidly, until he was out of breath.

He had just received a government warrant to report to the *SS Aqualung* at 1200 hours on that date for service on Luna. The warrant overrode any such formalities as passports or tickets.

IV. THE WHITE MARE SWIMMING MARVELLOUSLY

For the first part of the brief journey to the moon, Wyvern slept. Even when he felt himself again, he hardly left his tiny cabin.

The ship was almost full, despite reports of trouble in the British

Republics Sector following the death of Our Beloved Leader, for most of the passengers were on official business, and could not make cancellations even if they wished. They had stood about uneasily at Thorpe Field before take-off, grey little people making small British jokes about having to get away from the rain at all costs; Wyvern avoided them, purposely arriving late and keeping to himself.

A painful attempt at pre-Republican luxury had been aimed at aboard. There was a good selection of drinks at the bar; perfumes were on sale; a bookstall sold something besides the eternal grey-paged numbers of *On*, the official magazine of the regime. Wyvern bought a modern Turkish novel. Turkey alone, neutral during the wars, maintained something of an international culture. Haven of refugees from all over the globe, it produced a stream of literature and teleplays in all languages. Istanbul was again 'the incomparable city', as it had been over a thousand years ago.

The novel cheered Wyvern. It was technically competent, humorous and absolutely superficial; its characters moved gaily through their paces in a non-political setting. It all served to restore Wyvern's equilibrium, as it was meant to do. It also directed his thoughts to Eileen South.

She did not know of Conrad Wyvern's existence; he had never met her. Yet such were their natures that he felt he knew her better than an ordinary man might know his own wife. He had caught the essence of her as a grape traps the essence of the sun.

He would find her. In the circumscribed environments of the moon, and with his powers, that would not be too difficult. And then? Then they might perhaps escape together to the American Sector; thanks be to goodness there was nothing like an extradition order these days, with international law a thing of the past. From America, he might be able to do something to aid his fellow-countrymen in their wretched situation.

It was possible that the New Police might have radioed ahead to have him arrested on landing; if they wished, they could have it done – lack of passport would be adequate reason, were one even needed. But they had, as far as Wyvern knew, nothing definite against him; the tearing up of the ticket had been no more than a spiteful gesture. No doubt, Wyvern thought ruefully, his Dufy hung on H's secretary's wall by now.

It was four-and-a-half days before the lines and beacons of the spacedrome showed below. The ship's computer took over and they landed in blinding sunlight with scarcely a jar.

A man called Head, from Government Warfare, greeted Wyvern

as he left the *Aqualung*. He shook hands respectfully. Wyvern was still a free citizen, as far as the term free applied these days. The *Aqualung* had docked on the expanse of field outside the cluster of domes and greenhouses of the British Luna community. Through the ports, the strange city was visible, stewing in sunlight. They transferred from the ship into a buggy, which crawled into the vast maw of the airlocks. There they underwent the tedious process of decontamination: no infections were allowed to enter the closed system of the Sector, where they would circulate all too easily.

Head apologised a hundred times for the lengthy delay.

At last they were officially cleared and allowed to pass into the dome proper.

They drove to a civil servants' hotel on a laner, a small monorail vehicle running among the lanes, as the narrow avenues of the British Sector were called. The hotel accommodation was adequate, although utilitarian, like everything else up here. Head apologised for it all, taking the blame for the entire economic framework upon his own narrow shoulders.

'And I shall call for you punctually tomorrow morning, Mr Wyvern,' he said, smiling deferentially. 'We use the twenty-four hour Earth clock, by the way – as I expect you know. There will be a busy day ahead of us then, I surmise, so I will leave you now to get what I trust will be an excellent night's rest. No doubt you are fatigued by your journey. The water should be turned on at this time of the evening.'

After more profuse expressions of solicitude for Wyvern's comfort, Head left.

His talk of mornings and evenings had been a mere convention: it would be sunlight for the next week, and the clock-like domes had up their polarscreens.

As soon as he was alone, restlessness seized Wyvern. Eileen was somewhere near, perhaps within a mile. He shaved and took an elevator to the top of the building, where there was a gymnasium and a Scandinavian-type sauna. His body still felt wretched. He went in the sauna and sweated a little.

Later, down in the hotel foyer, few people were about, mostly male and as grey and official-looking as the people on the ship. One brightly dressed woman walked elegantly into the bar; she was possibly Turkish. A synthetical orchestra was playing the 'Atomics' from Dinkuhl's *Managerial Suite*.

Catching her eye as the woman scanned the foyer, Wyvern strolled over to her and spoke. She turned large dark eyes upon him, raised her eyebrows slightly, and smiled. 'That would be delightful,' she said, when he asked if she would care for a drink. 'Without alcohol, of course.'

They sat at a tiny round table with scarcely enough room for their two glasses.

She was dressed in a single wrap-around piece of polyfoil, dazzling copper in tone to match her copper shoes and copper lipstick. Her cheeks were high and narrow, her brow broad. She was clearly a specimen of the New Turkish Woman. Her name was Descant Mahood.

'Of course I know *your* name,' she said, when Wyvern introduced himself. 'You perfected the idea of three-dimensional lodgements in *n*-dimensional manifolds such as space. Those ideas could be developed still further in the Turkish Sector, where, as I expect you know, we are into a revolutionary numeral-behavioural-paracomplex. You should join us.'

'Are you a mathematician?' he asked excitedly, moving an inch closer to her.

'I am mistress of Fezzi Forta, the musician. I also design the new orgival planform one-person-wings for holopathic dome flight.'

'I heard there was a Turkish band playing here. You are with them?'

'Incorrect assumption, Conrad. Coincidence merely. I arrived from the American Sector independently. In every way the American Sector is more lively, more innovative, than the British Sector, though no general cultural re-think is in process. Stereotyped ideas, symptomatic of Western decline into militaristic thought, much as here. Their late President Roosevelt was on Luna, running a five-kilometre mile to open their new sports track. I went to meet him. Pleasant, full of goodwill. Not an intellectual. There is a certain mental energy which passes with time, like an Olympic torch, from one racial group to another.'

Dazzled by her, Wyvern said, 'How long are you staying?'

She rose to her feet, smiling a smile which soared above warmth and personality. 'Almost no time at all. Here comes Fezzi now.'

With a gesture of mathematical charm, she left the table to go and greet a portly man who had just entered the foyer and was looking about. Wyvern finished his drink, feeling dispirited. The Turkish miracle was common knowledge. For the first time, he felt himself part of a dwindling culture. Looking round covertly, he saw Fezzi Forta and Descant Mahood, twinkling in copper, walk briskly across the foyer and enter an elevator. If he hoped she might look round and give him a sign he was disappointed.

Making an effort, he turned his mind to more immediate matters. He studied a map of the British Sector framed in the foyer. The name 'JJ Lane' roused his heart excitedly: that was the name of the lane to which Eileen South had been going. He ordered a dinner in better spirits.

The meal was simple: soup, a choice of two main dishes, a sweet, ice cream and something labelled coffee which was unsuccessfully ersatz. The only touch of the exotic was a Martian sauce served with the creamed fish; the new colony had begun to export something other than fissionables. With the present state of world affairs, food was scarcer than uranium.

Once he had eaten, Wyvern went determinedly to bed. But no sooner was the light out and the window polarised than restlessness seized him. Tomorrow might be too late, he thought. Suppose the New Police arrived in the night? He got up and dressed again.

As far as Wyvern could tell, he left the hotel unobserved.

*

The distance to JJ Lane was short. He decided to walk there rather than catch the laner. The British Sector had been planned with mathematical precision even before the first lunar landings by Hitler's von Braun fleet of V9s. The thoroughfares running East-West were called 'Walks', and numbered; the thoroughfares running North-South were called 'Lanes', and designated by the letters of the alphabet, which had to stand doubled after the first twenty-six Lanes, to adhere to the plan.

Unfortunately, British muddle-headedness had crept into the design. Where the German and American Sectors adhered with mathematical precision to their planners' blueprints, the British had succumbed to a traditional love of crooked lanes. JJ, in fact, out on the periphery, cut Five Walk in two places. The plan had been further botched by additions on the wrong side of town, so that Wyvern's hotel, for example, stood in Minus Nine. Despite these complications, it was only ten minutes before he turned into JJ. The street underfoot was of poured lunar concrete. No animal had ever walked over it, Wyvern reflected.

Eileen South had been going to follow someone over to 108. As he too moved in that direction, Wyvern ran over in his mind all he knew of this business. To begin with, something must greatly have surprised her to break through her guard and make her radiate for a moment. There had been no hint in her thought of having met another telepath, which surely would have emerged if she had done. And that indicated that whoever she was going to follow – a non-telepath – had been radiating very strongly to get

45

through. Whoever he was, Eileen's thought showed he was a stranger to her, and something about him evoked in her mind that curious phrase: 'the impossible smile'.

Of a sudden, Wyvern found himself needing to know much more about this stranger to whose house he was going. The stranger was his only link with Eileen; and the stranger had a secret disturbing him powerfully enough to radiate to Eileen accidentally, although her power was shut down.

Wyvern knew such feelings well. If he opened his own mind to become aware of the minds about him, those minds would be as aware of him as he of them. They would be radio receivers picking up his broadcast. Yet when his mind was closed, he still retained an abnormal sensitivity which might be activated by agitation about him. Such blocks of trouble would loom up to him like buildings swimming on oil in a dense fog: some town halls, most mere suburban villas, one perhaps a cathedral of worry.

As he came into JJ, Wyvern met a mob of people. They were a rough-looking lot, although quiet enough at present, their attention fixed on a haggard man who was addressing them. Wyvern caught something of what he was saying.

'. . . this skinflint regime. And things aren't going to get any better, friends. No! They're going to get worse – and they're going to go on getting worse. It was bad enough with Jim Bull in control. He was a black-hearted rogue! But he was an old spacer! You don't need me to remind you he was with Wattleton on the third Venus expedition.

'Now Jim Bull's dead. And I tell you this for nothing, friends – if any of the Earthbound pack that is squabbling for his empty seat now gets a whip-hand over us, we may as well go straight round to the Bureau and draw our death certificates – and I'll be in front of the queue!'

Knowing the stories of Bull's activities as a spacer to be a lie, Wyvern saw that the speaker must be an agent provocateur.

JJ was not a savoury quarter. It had lodgings and snuff palaces and blue cinemas, and even one of the gadarenes beloved by spacemen on the search for orgies, thriving among the many tiny shops. 108 was an 'earth shop', the lunar version of a pawnbroker's, so called because here were stocked all the innumerable little articles in daily use but manufactured only on the home planet. Over the shop was a small apartment. Condensation dripping from the roof of the dome had caused green algae to spread over the concrete facade of the prefabricated building.

He pushed open the shop door and went in.

The place was poky and ill-stocked, with cans of Castrol oil, carpentry sets, Dinky toys, novels by Dennis Wheatley, tins of Brasso, cushions, old radio sets, bottles of Vimto, bound volumes of *Punch*, brassware, and portable stoves. If you thumped your fist on the counter, you would crack the veneer – but some irate customer had thought of that already. In a cubicle at the back, the proprietor slouched over a telephone. He did not look up when Wyvern entered. Something was dripping.

Somewhere out of sight, a man in soft shoes ran heavily down a staircase, burst open a door and let it slam behind him.

Still the proprietor did not move.

'I want some service,' Wyvern said sharply. 'Do you generally sleep at this time of day?'

Still no movement.

'Listen, I want to buy some informa –' Wyvern's voice died as he saw the deep stain on the man's tunic in the region of his stomach. He pushed up the flap of the counter and went round.

The fellow was dead, although still warm and still bleeding. He peered into eternity with a fixed, mercenary stare. His call had never gone through. The lunar ground had no worms; this stabbed body would keep for ever in its coffin.

And did this mean the only link with Eileen South was broken? Wyvern's thoughts twisted unhappily.

Then he remembered the man running downstairs; that could have been the murderer, after something in the apartment above.

He pulled open a flimsy side door and back stairs were revealed. After a second's hesitation, he ran up them three at a time. At the top stood two doors, one open. Wyvern entered at the double.

A man lay on a bed dying. He was curled up clutching at dirty blankets, with a heavy knife in his ribs. In his agony, he rolled on to his back, driving the knife further home. He sighed wearily and seemed to relax.

On his face, an impossible smile stretched from ear to ear.

Wyvern knelt by the side of the bed. This man was no newcomer to violence. He looked every inch a thug. Old scars stretched from either end of his mouth right up in his cheekbones, giving him, even in the midst of pain, that look of ghastly hilarity. He was clearly beyond help and fading fast. He rolled convulsively over again, burying his face in the bedding.

Here was the link with Eileen South. There was only one thing Wyvern could do, loath as he was to do it. He opened up his mind and entered into ego-union with the dying man . . .

*

A garble of voices, beating like rain on a roof. A welter of regret, cruel as frightened fangs. Fear, foamlike. Anger. Vindictiveness, blasphemy, pain: shutters banging in December's storm. Memory. Stupidity, the sparse lanterns going out in the medieval alleys of his mind. Warped ways. And, even now, even yet, hope.

Hopes like bats, pain like a driving sleet seemed to batter against Wyvern's face, blinding his psychic sense.

On all sides of him, three-dimensionally as it appeared, crowded scenes from the man's past life, scudding by, falling out of darkness into more darkness. The backgrounds were mainly of an appalling drabness, the faces in the foreground often twisted into hatred; here a girl's countenance smiled like a lamp, there envy burned in a rival's face; everywhere callousness, besottedness, a life run to seed. Wyvern sank grimly through the sediment.

He was hopelessly lost in the labyrinth, walled up in night while fifty movie projectors played fifty different films on him. And the projectors faltered and dimmed. He had to be quick; the man with the impossible smile was fading out on the tides of eternity.

Like a salmon swimming against the stream, Wyvern tried to

direct the racing images. He followed a tributary where the stains were red, suddenly knew by smell-sense that he was close. Saw a tiny cell, the man crouching there, waiting, waiting, the name of the man, George Dorgen, waiting, waiting to commit a death. The muddled reasons, in part political – the understanding held since a battered childhood that his country was a cruel and merciless place to those who had nothing; in part egotistical – a hopeless lust to be someone, to have a light shine, cameras click, to read his name in headlines, see himself on TV; in part merely mercenary – to get paid for the crime and live with a full belly and a pallid woman called . . . it had gone . . . Gone because of a burly figure stripping beyond the false wall of the tiny cell. The gun coming up, choking blood lust, the breaking in triumph through the wall, the death of the great man, the mysterious ruler, the hated father figure, as, naked and animal-hairy, showing the dead-white soles of its feet, the slippery meat crashed below the rainstorm shower water on to white tiles. White. Blankness. Running. Safe hideout far from Norwich, from Earth. White streaked with stars and arteries.

Strained, taken by anguish, Wyvern backed from the bed. There lay George Dorgen, butchered in his sleep, in his safe hide-out. Deed done by a villain in soft shoes, twice a killer.

Still he was linked to that dying mind. The man's poor life-treasury, its storehouse, was still there, despite intervening clouds. Wyvern tried to see who had paid Dorgen for the assassination of Bull, who had settled the account in this room. But something else was on the scene, a something like another telepathic presence. It came up very dark and soft. It flowed round, over, through Dorgen and through Wyvern's mind. Dorgen was going back now, his years gargling away down an energy-sink into a sub-molecular universe from whence his consciousness had once arrived. Suddenly, there were clear, serene glimpses of pasture land, animals grazing. Then low-ceilinged woodland, a chase, great exhilaration, other hunters, and something speared among dead leaves. Then – misty now – branches, swinging hither and thither, giving place to a trellis-pattern of indescribable light. But the dark and soft presence was now all-embracing.

At the end, it was suddenly swift. It lifted him, broke foaming, tearing away like a mill-race, sucking at his body, his spirit, scream-ing as it sluiced over the bare nerve-ends of organic life. Then Dorgen was dead, and Wyvern left alone on his knees in the fetid room.

*

Wyvern slumped against the ricketty bed. He was vitiated. His body had no strength; his eyes would not open; his mind was dead. There was only the memory of a killer who slayed a man downstairs to come up here and kill another killer; that killer had killed Jim Bull, the killer.

Kill, kill, kill. Wyvern feebly resolved never to use his mental power again, unless . . .

Yet the terrifying experience of entering the dying man's mind taught him much. He perceived how the dead world of the Moon had become a projection for the dead side of mankind's behaviour. No ameliorating nature acted as a balance to life here. This territory had always been beyond the Garden of Eden. No fossils lay in its ashen rock, no animal had ever walked its surface – apart from those crawling things spacers had accidentally brought with them. The Moon, being a dead place, exerted a deadening influence on the psyche. Or was he just imagining things in a moment of weakness?

Certainly he had not imagined the glimpse into some kind of past world, before homo sapiens, in the last signals from the extinguishing spirit. Communication was a more complex thing than he had realised, embracing whole areas of territory he had not thought to claim.

He made a leap back into his childhood. Back to Stratton Hall in its prosperous days. His parents were alive. He had learned to ride the farm horses almost as soon as he could walk. He and Ken, the stable boy, firm friends, had a fondness for the old mare, Daisy, now put out to grass to finish her days in peace. The great animal was dependable, mild, light-treading. She was white. Often she would carry the two boys home in the twilight, the day surrendering to green dusk, and Conrad's mother watched a little anxiously from the house for her son's return. She used to come across the stable yard, calling welcome, as bats wheeled overhead.

Wyvern was startled. This was other than a telepathic link. Suddenly he had found another direction to go, a way into the actual past stored in his memory. He ran in his short trousers and bare feet down the lane, Ken scampering with him and the mare lumbering behind. And the white terrier, Spot, with the patch over one eye, hustling along beside them, full of doggy happiness.

The waters of Stratton Broad covered only a few acres and were slowly filling with rushes. But they could dive off the old quay under the willows, dive into the peaty minnow-speckled water, and swim there hours on end in those eternal boyhood summers. Spot ran in too, barking. The white mare followed, steady as always, swimming marvellously where the boys went, nibbling succulent grass where it grew over the old dyke wall, only her head and broad rump showing. The lazy spreading ripples cast gold patterns on the willow canopy above their heads, carrying them up, up, into the golden dazzle of the sky.

So vivid was the return to the past that Wyvern could hardly bear to find himself in the squalid lunar apartment beside the murdered man.

With shame, he remembered how, as a boy, he had despised his genial old father for having no interest beyond the great house and grounds. All day, his father was content to consort with farm managers, yokels, and gardeners. All evening, he was content with his books and his gramophone records. He never wished to leave Stratton Hall; he never went with his wife and son when she took their boy on the Great Eastern Railway to Norwich or London. As Wyvern grew up, how contemptuous he became of that content-ment of his father's – how crudely, as a teenager, he had spoilt it in every way he could . . . Wasn't it merely to spite his father that he had called himself first communist then fascist, torn down the Union Jack, disrupted by leading demonstrations every measure introduced by that faltering coalition government of Chamberlain's?

At least his father had died before the enemy moved in – died serenely, content in the knowledge that a new early potato, the Wyvern Wonder, had been named after him.

'Forgive me, father. I've certainly reaped my reward for my lack of understanding.'

He stood up. He must beware of his extending powers, that they did not betray him. His situation was doubly dangerous now, and he must be alert to the possibilities of the present.

As far as he had been able to tell from the chaos in Dorgen's mind, the man had no knowledge of Eileen South, of her identity or her whereabouts.

What he needed to do was move fast from this place, and hide somewhere less perilous – perhaps the American Sector, even Turksdome, anywhere.

Without a backward glance at the dead man, he came out on to the landing.

Two men in the uniform of the New Police stood shoulder to shoulder at the bottom of the stairs, revolvers clasped in their fists.

'Come on down,' said one. 'Take it easy. We have orders to shoot.'

'Don't be foolish,' Wyvern said. 'Do you know who you're

talking to? Come up and examine the body. It's long enough since I summoned you. Where have you been?'

The two men moved steadily towards him, as bidden.

'Hurry it up.' He spoke in authoritative tones.

When they were three steps from the landing, he pounced, trying to knock them to either side. But they were ready for trouble, and in a moment had him down on the stairs and heavy boots in his ribs. He gave up, and they dragged him down to a squad car waiting in the lane.

The next three hours were full of uniforms, blows, and questions.

*

After his first interrogation at Police Headquarters, Wyvern was put into an ordinary cell. That interrogation was made by a police sergeant with a man in plain clothes looking on. Then he was marched from the cell and questioned again, this time by a police captain and two men in plain clothes, after which he was taken to a special box-like cell.

The back wall of this cell was fitted with a steel bench. When the door of the cell closed it was so shaped that the prisoner was forced to sit on the bench; there was no room to do anything else. The wall was of glass and, Wyvern estimated, every bit of two feet thick. He sat in his pillory like a fish in an aquarium.

He had been sitting there for about an hour when a man entered the bare room on the other side of the glass. He looked in every way the typical apparatchik, being sleek and blank and neat and having a brown beard. He advanced to the glass and said, 'Your cell is wired for sound so that we can talk comfortably. You will talk. I will listen. Your case is very serious.'

His voice was clipped; he did indeed make it sound serious.

'Hell's bells, it is serious,' Wyvern thought. 'I'm spending all my time recently being browbeaten by big and little autocrats. If I ever get out of here, I shall suffer from a persecution complex for the rest of my days.'

'I've told your people my story twice,' he said aloud. 'I omitted nothing. That fat police sergeant will give you a copy of my statement.'

The beard made no comment, beyond tugging at itself.

'A customer went into the earth shop and found the proprietor dead, stabbed,' the beard said stonily. 'Police were called. They heard a movement in the room above. You appeared. You were arrested trying to escape. In the room you had vacated, a body

52

was found. Our weapon experts say the same blade did both jobs. Obviously, you are Number One suspect. You came to Luna expressly to commit these crimes. It is worth your while to tell your story again.'

'It's all circumstantial,' Wyvern snapped. 'Do I have to tell you people your business? Why haven't you taken my fingerprints? Take them and compare them with those on the knife. You'll find I never touched it. I've told you who I am, I've told you what I'm doing on Luna – ring through and check with the government at once.'

The beard let this outburst die on the hot air.

'I think it worth your while to tell your story again,' he repeated.

Wyvern sighed. Then he capitulated and said what he had said before. With certain simplifications, he told only the truth. His motive for entering the shop he altered, to avoid any mention of Eileen South; he merely made himself out to be a tourist in search of local colour who had accidentally stumbled on a corpse, etc. etc. And another alteration had come at the end of the story.

It was evident that he was entangled in a political murder; it was being pinned on him for reasons best known to the police. There was one obvious way to extricate himself, and he took it. He had to describe the real murderer, as he had been reflected in Dorgen's dying mind. Once that murderer was caught, he was cleared.

He found himself saying for the first time, 'Dorgen could still talk when I reached him. He was able to describe his killer as a tall man with a square face, small black moustache, black bushy eyebrows, hair black with a prominent streak of white in it. Hairy hands and arms, tattoo on left wrist.'

'Dorgen told you this before he died?' the neat man with the beard asked.

'I just said he did,' Wyvern said. His voice rasped; they would not, surely, be on the alert for telepaths up here. His story was perfectly convincing.

'This is the part of your story in which we are most interested,' the beard said. He fiddled edgily with a ring on the little finger of his right hand, while examining Wyvern's face with an excitement Wyvern found puzzling. 'I want to get it clear. You say Dorgen actually told you this, in words?'

'As I said.'

A silence.

'So he spoke to you?'

'With his dying breath, Dorgen said to me, "I killed Our Beloved Leader".'

53

The beard took a precise step or two in each direction, running a fingernail lightly along the thick glass as he walked, smiling and nodding to himself.

Insecurity forced Wyvern to add a corroborative detail gleaned from Dorgen's mind. 'I believe he had an American accent.'

'Mm. I see. An American accent.'

'Now may I go?' Wyvern asked. 'You know where to contact me if you wish.'

'It is not as easy as that,' the beard said. 'Nothing is easy in this world, Wyvern. Men behave foolishly. We are not at all happy about some aspects of your story.' He turned to go, adding, 'You may congratulate yourself at least on having a front seat while history is in the making.'

'I never had a seat I hated more.'

The beard left without comment.

Almost as soon as he had gone, the light in the outer compartment went out. A bright bulb out of reach above Wyvern's head was the only source of illumination. It shone on to the glass before his eyes so that he could hardly see into the part of the room beyond the glass. Once, he thought someone slipped in and observed him, but could not be sure.

The light threw heat on to his head and neck. Cramp crawled in his legs. He just hoped this delay meant they were combing the Sector for Dorgen's slayer.

At least they had no reason to suspect him of powers of ego-union – he hoped. That discovery would involve him in a nasty fate. He recalled what Parrodyce had said when they were talking about H's projected coupling of another telepath to Big Berk: 'That must be the worst pain of all; I pray I never come to it.'

If they *did* find out about Wyvern, it would be remarkably convenient for them. The experimental computer was only a hundred yards away, in the centre of the British Sector!

Wyvern's reveries were interrupted by the opening of a grill behind his head. A basin full of patent cereal and condensed milk was thrust in upon him. He ate and dozed. Broken fantasia on Dorgen's past sleezed through his sleep, interspersed with memories of his own untroubled childhood.

He came suddenly back to full consciousness, to sit bolt upright, blood racing heavily. Beyond the glass, the shadowy forms of Colonel H and his secretary, Bradley, were watching him!

The urge was strong to speak to them, to establish communication, to render them human, but he fought it down and stayed silent, wondering what horrible coincidence had brought them to the scene at this time. He had thought them still on Earth.

H's small features were drawn close together in a scowl of triumph, as if all the venom of him concentrated itself towards the end of his nose. He came forward at last and pressed his hands against the glass.

'What did Dorgen say to you?' he asked in a terrible voice.

'He told me he killed Our Beloved Leader,' Wyvern said.

Silence. Colonel H and Bradley looked at each other.

'This is the part of your confession in which we are most interested, Wyvern,' the secretary said. 'We need to get it absolutely clear. You say that Dorgen actually told you this – in words –'

'You heard what I said.'

'Let's hear it again, Wyvern. Dorgen spoke to you?'

'Yes, I told you. Yes.'

When H spoke again, his words charged Wyvern full of understanding and fear; he realised for the first time the meaning of that impossible smile carved on Dorgen's face; he realised how it had made him betray himself into a future too ghastly to contemplate. H said, 'You are a telepath, Wyvern! That cur Dorgen was *dumb*: he had his tongue cut out twenty years ago.'

*

'You don't look comfortable.'

Sinnikka's voice came to me from a long distance.

I sat up suddenly. My wife, holding her wrap about her, stood over me, smiling. I was slumped in the armchair. The paperback I had been holding had slipped from my grasp and lay on the carpet. My jacket was neatly folded on the next chair, and I felt cold. Looking at my watch, I saw it was almost seven in the morning. Outside, the lake was bright with sunlight.

Rising, I clasped my wife. She put her arms round me. We stood like that for a moment, enjoying the contact.

'You're cold. I'll make some coffee. What time was it when you got home? I didn't hear you come in.'

She spoke lightly, looking searchingly at me as she spoke. Sinnikka's hair was streaked with grey, but still dark and luxurious. She had gathered it up into a bun, as was her custom in the mornings. Her face was long, her lips narrow and well-formed. I never tired of looking at her face. Her pupils were a mixture between hazel and blue, her lashes thick. An inch below her left eye was a mole which always caught my attention, almost as if it were a third eye. I considered this mole a mark of beauty, distinction even; yet somehow it distracted me from ever regarding her straight and searchingly, so that the mystery of her personality would always have to remain unresolved.

To be with Sinnikka was always to feel powerfully the force of her presence. Even when she was still, something seemed to move there. Even when her eyes were downcast, her mole seemed to be observing. She came from an old Swedish-Finnish family – we frequently spoke Swedish about the house – in which there had been more than a taint of madness. Something in her manner suggested a shying away from life: more from distaste than fear, one might guess. That little elusive habit pleased me, reinforcing my wish to be protective towards her.

She walked stiffly towards the kitchen.

'How is it today?'

'No worse.' But I could see how the affliction had her, binding her like ivy about a woodland tree.

'If you feel well enough, Sinnikka, I should introduce you to Carol-Ann Crutchley Cracken.'

Pausing at the kitchen door, holding the handle for support, she looked back interrogatively, indicating that she had seen something under the quilt, and had determined to wait for, rather than ask for, an explanation. As so often, her expressions were impossible to read.

When I told her how I had found the dead girl, she listened without comment. I finished. She came slowly towards the bed, lifted the quilt, looked at the dead girl's face without expression.

'Why did you bring her here? This is the end of us. Unless your friend at the police station – Hakkennon, I mean – will come along and make everything easy for you.'

'I don't know about that.'

As she settled the quilt back into place, she saw the

paperback on the floor where it had fallen from my sleeping grasp. She bent stiffly to pick it up, giving it a casual glance as she threw it on to the bed.

'She deserves to be shot if she reads such rubbish.'

'It's not as bad as it looks.'

My defensive remarks provoked her into one of her rare, calm outbursts. It was almost as if she was not addressing her husband but someone else, so remote was her speech.

'I am against any form of art that comforts and deceives. Count Tolstoy is the last novelist one can respect, apart from the French. Novels have dwindled into mere entertainment. In the same way, the symphony has lost any claims for respect – your First and the *Mannerheim* apart, of course. Only between Haydn and Beethoven did the symphony rise from a mere pleasurable amusement; there is perhaps true tragedy in the *Choral*. After that – deterioration, Tchaikovsky and the rest. All comfort and deception.'

She walked about actively as she was talking, almost as if she had forgotten her arthritis, or it had forgotten her. The thought of her malady made what she was saying the more poignant.

'Plato well understood the seductions of art. If there is to be art at all, it should remind us of the remorselessness, the pettiness, of human life. It should strive to chill us – just as cemeteries should never be pleasant places. They should rather be territories to freeze the blood with reminders of our mortality.'

'You are always so rigorous, dear. And right, of course. I do strive to feel as you do, although you know I find a sort of – oh, *joviality* in the world's evil, which you profess not to feel. In any case, I can make no defence for *The Impossible Smile*. It's just fun.'

'That was my complaint.' Her mole looked coldly at me.

'Well, I don't mean fun. I mean that I needed to relax . . .'

'So you fell asleep reading instead of going to bed . . .'

She contemplated me seriously, refraining from the reproaches I saw on her lips. She would never read anything lowbrow. The critical work she was writing, and had been for two years, was on some intellectual French modernist novels of the nineteen-thirties. 'I'll get the coffee and then you can tell me all about the concert. I gather it was a success, or you would have said.'

'The cello part is too strident in the second movement.'

Nodding once, she turned away into the kitchen, through the brown door with the curtain on its brass runner.

I went to wash my face and teeth. As I was drying myself on a towel, I heard the local grocer's van rolling up to the front door, and went out to greet the man in my shirtsleeves.

Toni brought a carton of groceries which Sinnikka had ordered by phone, together with a sack of goat's milk and other sundries, and the daily paper. I thanked him and carried the stuff in. Placing the box of groceries on a side-table, I spread out the newspaper and leafed through it.

When Sinnikka returned, rustling inside her long gown, I was staring out of the window.

'I will tell you how successful the concert was,' I said, without turning round. 'The music critic in the *Tanaan* says that all my weaknesses were in full display, that strident pizzicatos and violent "shock" chords – whatever they are – do not a symphony make. What they do contribute to is an oppressive evening in which a schmaltzy and superficial second movement remained entirely divorced from a brand of forced egalitarian militarism reminiscent of Shostakovich in his most blatant social-realist vein. I am categorised as a Pan-Reich composer. And so on.'

She came and put a hand on my shoulder. 'I did warn you about that second movement. Too many diminished fifths by half. Less a style than a mannerism . . . In any case, that is Jalkirouka's review, isn't it? Fat little prig, little he knows about music.'

'Mm.' It was hard to conceal my disappointment. She hated me to give in to weakness. The mole had me under observation. If only I had not missed the full orchestral rehearsal on the previous Saturday, the *Mannerheim*, I knew, would have been better. I took my coffee through to the bedroom to lie down. I took Jael Cracken's book, too . . .

The Moon should have been the ideal place for the regime of the British Republics to thrive in: scenery and policy alike were arid and uncompromising. Only in the sense of having been rough-hewn by time did either of them approach beauty; they functioned by virtue of the accidents of the past. And lunar colony and police state alike required a continual maximum effort to maintain equilibrium.

Yet the regime did not flourish; the intransigence of the one clashed with the intransigence of the other. Luna had always been a trouble spot. There seemed to be no room for any law but harsh natural law and, on these stony shores of space, politics secured little foothold. With the death of Our Beloved Leader, revolt against the powers-that-be broke forth again. It was to quell this insurrection that Colonel H had arrived at the British sector.

He took immediate advantage of the chance which threw Wyvern into his power almost as he landed. For, if the lunar base – with Berk the Brain and its potentialities for military conquest – was the key to the future, Wyvern gave Colonel H the power to turn that key. Wyvern was a telepath. From Wyvern, Berk should analyse and adapt the ability to read the minds of the whole population; and when it could do that H would be immovably in the saddle.

'Take him down to BU-X!' Colonel H ordered. 'And be careful with him. Don't repeat the mistakes you made with Grisewood.'

They took Wyvern away struggling.

'Right,' the colonel said to his secretary. 'Now arrange with Imbrium for me to televise to the people at fourteen hundred hours tomorrow in the role of Beloved Leader. Ask them if they consider fourteen hundred better than thirteen hundred.'

He turned resolutely to the mass of reports on his desk. They were without exception smudged and hard to read. The imported Turkish typewriters were unsatisfactory in every way. He made a note on a memo pad to enquire into the possibilities of setting up a typewriter factory in Norwich. Then he turned again to the papers, hunching his shoulders grimly. He was not cut out for paper work.

Secretary Bradley returned from the telephone, looking spruce and savage. 'It's taking them a while to get Wyvern down the passage,' he reported. 'I told them they must not damage him. That's BU-X's job.'

'This ruddy administration –' Colonel H began. He was

occasionally irked by what he considered his underling's prissy way of speech.

'I came back to say we'd forgotten something,' said the secretary crisply. He disliked these outbursts against paper work, believing legislators to be the unacknowledged poets of the world. 'I came to remind you that we had Wyvern in our hands once in Norwich. We should have found out *then* that he was telepathic – that was what we handed him over to Parrodyce for. I understood that gentleman was supposed to be infallible?'

'My God!' H exclaimed, jumping up. 'You're right, Bradley! Of course I had already thought of that.'

He snatched up his desk telephone.

'Send Parrodyce up to me on the double,' he barked.

'Lucky I had the wit to bring that fellow to Luna with us,' he said. 'If I remember, you were against the idea.'

The secretary stood dapper and silent, gazing at the crease in his trousers. He was an excellent judge of when silence was both wisest and most infuriating.

*

The New Police, who had been entrusted with Wyvern, were propelling him fairly rapidly down a stretch of passage when Parrodyce appeared at the other end. The schmo-like Inquisitor looked disturbed. He was wasting no time in answering his boss's summons, but he quaked in doing so. His cheeks shone, his spectacles misted. Then he saw Wyvern and Wyvern saw him.

Only a short while before, Wyvern had resolved never to make contact with a human mind again. His integration with Dorgen had sickened him; it had indeed contaminated him, for he had involuntarily taken over the dying man's jumble of impressions complete, and they were now as much a part of him as his own memories. He wanted no more such. Least of all did he want ego-union with Parrodyce; he already knew that here was a mind more sick than Dorgen's.

Nevertheless, the desperate circumstances altered the case. Too much was at stake for queasiness. He did not hesitate. Disregarding the posse who had bodily hold of him, he made mental contact with Parrodyce.

He held it only for a second. It was enough.

Their thought states interlocked.

Wyvern: 'They've discovered I am a telepath. I slipped up. It's all over. I'm being taken to BU-X, whatever that is.'

60

Parrodyce: 'Fear for myself. That explains what H and buddy want me for. My secret's up – or if not that, they'll think I've failed. Either way: torture, pain. Pain! Remove my lower jaw maybe. Castration . . . !'

Wyvern: 'Stop it! Listen – my guards will be getting most of this exchange. It's bound to leak even into their dull brains.'

Parrodyce: 'Then I *am* betrayed. It's your fault, Wyvern. Why didn't I kill you when I had you? We'll both be taken to BU-X. That's where they fit you up to couple with Berk the Brain. They're worse torturers than I and Joe Rakister, my assistant. Daren't go to H."

Wyvern: 'You must escape, Parrodyce, while you have the chance. Get away to another Sector quickly. Tell them what is about to happen; Berk must be demolished. If this scheme of H's succeeds, he'll rule the entire roost in no time. A telepathic computer would be unstoppable. Get away now."

Parrodyce: 'Must save own skin. Which Sector is powerful enough to defy H, which?'

Wyvern: 'Try any – Swedish will do. American would be best. All Sectors must unite against such a threat. Bomb it to bits if necessary.'

Parrodyce: 'Killing. Good.'

Wyvern: 'Just get the message through. Leave them to judge. Now for heaven's sake scoot, you horror.'

Parrodyce: 'Loathe you. Yet if you were saved, you could probe me properly, find out what went wrong. Some thorn in the infant flesh. Oh, Wyvern, am afraid . . ."

Wyvern: 'There'll be nothing to fear if you get out. And listen, somewhere on Luna is a girl called Eileen South; she's a telepath, no other details. Tell her – tell her I loved her.'

Parrodyce: 'No use for women. Subtle, smothering . . .'

Wyvern: 'Get the message through. Do it all, and I swear if there's ever a chance I'll dig down through your dirt and put you right, if it's still possible.'

Parrodyce: 'Love/hate. Going now.'

The contact broke. The plump figure at the end of the corridor turned and ran back through the door it had entered. Badly frightened, one of the guards slammed home a blow to the side of Wyvern's chin.

Oblivion was a complexity of sensation. The top of Wyvern's sleeping mind whirled, whirled till all its colours blended into blinding whiteness. He was far away, but his heart still beat, his bloodstream still flowed, his latent consciousness foamed and subsided like milk boiling on an intermittent fire. Down there, where sleep never penetrates, alarm was active; the smouldering intelligence knew that something was afoot which would violate its inmost hearth. The something came from outside, where all dangers came from, but it was working steadily in, insidiously, slyly and/or boldly, deeper.

The danger was chromium-plated, then it was a gnarled hand, or it was pins. It had little piggy leech-snouts, or it had nozzles or nails. It assumed any shape to get to where it wanted, and soon the primeval country fell to this protean invader, and enemy camp fires glowed from every point of vantage.

Time slowed, stopped. Presently it began again at a new rhythm. Dawn came: Wyvern roused.

*

He could not move. He was looking at a wall of lawn starred with daisies, or it was a green sky stuffed with stars; slowly, with infantile care, the invalid muscles of his eyes brought it into focus, and it was a green wall of instruments, studded with little dials like eyeballs. It was about three feet away from him. He acquired these facts as a new-born babe might acquire them.

Something fiendish had been done to him.

Men in white overalls crossed his line of vision. For the most part, they ignored him, being more concerned with the dials. Then one came over and injected something into him – it might have been into his shoulder or his calf, he could not tell, could only feel a coolness spread, gradually defining the limits of his body.

It seemed to him he was left alone then, with only the blind eyeballs to watch him. Slowly strength returned. Wyvern discovered that he was lying on his chest with a pillow under his left cheek. Taking his time about it, he rolled on to one side and sat up, propping himself up with his arms helped by the light lunar gravity. The effort dizzied him; he sat with his eyes shut, vaguely exploring the dry taste in his mouth. He could eventually open his eyes again.

He was in a small room on a large table. He had been covered with a blanket which had now slipped aside. He was naked; he could see his body direct, in a mirror slanting above the table. Wyvern stared at the reflection – not in horror, for his subconscious had already accepted this violation.

From six points on the front of his body, and two on his legs, little terminals projected. From the terminals, cables – or were they tubes? – led off. He could tell that his back was similarly served.

His skull was shaved; from it, similar though smaller terminals projected, secured into the bone. There were twelve terminals in his skull, and the connections from them had been built out so that the rear of his head was surrounded by a kind of wire basket, like a fencing mask worn backwards. A pigtail of cable hung from the back of the basket, carrying the wires away.

'Someone's been busy,' Wyvern muttered to himself. Only that trivial thought bubbled up.

At the bottom of the bed, a steel arm with a hook gathered all the thin cables together into one fat one. The fat cable slithered across the floor to a trolley fitted with valves and glass cylinders and a pump which worked slowly and laboriously. At the other side of the trolley, the cable ran into the base of the green instrument panel.

Wyvern had no doubt as to what it all meant. Experimentally, he tugged at the terminal set in his left nipple and felt the network of wires like capillary veins tighten under this skin. He was a cyborg. Part of a biomachine. His innermost chromosome was being syphoned out of him and on to the panel. He could feel his slightest sensation, an itch on the pores of his leg, the stir of bile in his gut, register in micro-amps and flick up a reading on a dial. He

allowed his thoughts to flow through transistorised circuits, rejoicing in new textures, new experiences. His power of thinking quickened. He was ready to be coupled up to Big Berk.

Sighing, he lay down again. A small plastic pack had been inserted under his skin above his fifth vertebra. When he examined it mentally, he found it was a nerve intensifier, permitting extra surges of power to his limbs.

Four men entered the room. They wore white overalls. Two of them took great interest in Wyvern, examining him, prodding him, checking instruments, studying VDUs; the other two stood to one side rather boredly, and began chatting together. Wyvern could hear snatches of their conversation.

'. . . nasty bust up on Twenty One last night. Three of our boys got it.'

'My mate Alfred was down there. Apparently he picked up with some French tart . . .'

It was a reminder of a world which had ceased to exist for Wyvern.

The examination took the best part of an hour. At the end of it, the examiners showed themselves satisfied and left. They returned in ten minutes with Colonel H's secretary, Bradley, puffing out his cheeks and looking important.

The secretary came over to the table and stared down at Wyvern. Viewed from this angle, he looked less the pukka officer than usual, more the thug; his mouth had a stupid set to it observable in men of callous natures.

'You see we managed to bring you through,' he said, mock-brightly. 'How are you feeling?'

'Bradley, you're a fool.'

'I regret the colonel could not come,' Bradley said. 'We are going to get the computer to work draining you straight away. The program is ready. Results should be coming through by late afternoon, shortly after the colonel is officially proclaimed Beloved Leader.'

'I'm not interested,' Wyvern said sourly.

'You should be – it concerns you,' the secretary said. He turned and talked in a low voice to the men in white. After some consultation, one of them left the room; he was gone only a minute and, when he returned, said, 'Yes, they're all standing by at Computer Central.'

'Splendid,' the secretary said. 'Switch on straight away.'

Wyvern tensed himself, not knowing what to expect. He lay there on the rack, eyes probing the others. Apart from some signs of strain, their faces were blank. Of all the winds loose from

Pandora's box, Wyvern thought, the wind of science blows strongest today; untempered by human kindness, it's a cold wind.

But several toggle switches clicked over and he did not die. At first he felt nothing. Then a not unpleasant vibration crept through his body: a tide, an army, a symphony, working on coded harmonics he did not comprehend. It moved steadily through him, learning every cell, and so into his brain.

An indescribable sensation of a myriad doors being flung open attacked Wyvern. But for that moment he was not Wyvern; his identity was gone, sucked into the giant computer for inspection. It fragmented into a myriad pieces, as if every star in the galaxy regarded itself, as if God scrutinised himself in a mirror. Then it was back, packed into the correct cubicles it had come from, a vastly complex organism pretending to be a simple human being. Then silence.

The white-overalled men glanced anxiously up at H's secretary, then turned back to the panels. Without a word, they commenced checking across the wide expanse of instruments.

'What's up?' asked Bradley sharply.

'Power's packed in,' one of the medics said in an equally sharp tone, punching buttons. 'Completely dead.'

The secretary strode over to the board.

'You mean to say –' he began.

'Everything's perfectly in order *here*,' the other interrupted. 'Our readings are all OK. Berk still has input but we've lost output. Can't be the rioters . . .' He bit his thumb and stared at the floor. 'Could be a saboteur who objects to the ethics of all this. Better contact the power engineers . . .'

'Get them as quickly as possible,' the secretary ordered. As he spoke, the phone gonged. He grabbed it and listened, barking every now and again at its screen.

'Damned incompetence,' he remarked, putting the receiver down as if he were lowering an enemy into a cobra's hole. 'That was Computer Central. They say that Berk has shut itself down. They are at a loss to account for it, but are working on the problem. No faults detected as yet. I'm going over there. See that Wyvern does not die.'

He left.

The white coats promptly lit cigarettes. They looked quizzically at Wyvern, then gave him one.

'Thanks,' Wyvern said.

'Smoke while you can.'

'I mean thanks for realising I was still human.'

Confidence had returned to Wyvern. It was clear that the computer was not going to kill him; it had to learn from him, and therefore there was the possibility that he could enlist it on his side. Also, the knowledge that had been, so to speak, drawn from him, shuffled, and put back now showed itself to contain an item he had overlooked. Another plus was that there were no legal charges against him. When Berk had finished its task, Wyvern should again be a free man – provided he could engineer himself free of the colonel's house party.

'Answer a straight question,' he said to the technician. 'Just what do you think I've done that squares your consciences with this inhuman job you are carrying out on me?'

They exchanged looks.

'Do you think we don't know about you?' one asked. 'The whole Sector knows about you!'

'Knows *what* about me?' Wyvern said.

For answer, the other brought a copy of *Lunareview* from his pocket. It was the latest edition. It bore Wyvern's photograph and headlines which ran:

EX-CRUXTISTICIAN-KILLER
DUMB MAN DEAD IN BRAWL OVER BLONDE

VI. BEFORE I SHOOT YOUR FOOT OFF

Now Wyvern was alone in the room except for a guard. The guard called himself a male nurse; his name was William. He was very big and pale and adolescent, and had been born on the Moon; his father was growing gigantic beefsteak mushrooms in the Zodiacal Planets, and living with a Japanese woman; his mother worked in the Imbrium Dyes Factory; he had three sisters, Catriona, Joyce and Joy, all of whom were married except Joy, and she was engaged to a soldier.

This Wyvern learnt when William first arrived. Now the big fellow settled down in a chair beside the couch and absorbed himself in part three of a four part serial entitled *Shall Love's Affairs Be Hushed?*, slotted into a pocket vid-set his sister Joy had lent him.

Wyvern lay back, glad of a chance to think. So much had happened, he found himself marvelling he was still whole and hopeful. Part of the hope lay in the fact that he knew the identity of Dorgen's murderer.

66

During disorienting periods of ego-union he had spent with Parrodyce and Dorgen, many impressions had soaked in on him. He had scarcely heeded them at the time, and had shrunk from trying to sort them later, so unprepossessing had most of them been, so formidably jumbled. Yet hidden information lay in them; he might, for instance, have discovered in them the severing of Dorgen's tongue, had he attempted a total scrutiny of the data. There had been parcels of thought/feeling/memory he had not bothered to unwrap.

Such an unwrapping was precisely what Big Berk had performed in the few moments before its mysterious breakdown. It had coupled like with like, and this orderly process might be said to have altered the whole organisation of his mind. It left two hitherto separate facts significantly side by side: Dorgen's mental picture of his killer; Parrodyce's mental picture of his assistant. The pictures dissolved and merged; they were one: Parrodyce's assistant was Dorgen's killer.

Why? Wyvern asked himself. Why? How? But the truth had lain there undeniably in his mind waiting to be developed, like a film in a dark drawer. He was able even to piece together a name with the portraits. Joe Rakister. Though the name had never actually been formulated to him in the state of ego-union, face and name were one symbol. Joe Rakister.

If only Wyvern could feed that knowledge through to a neutral authority, he would be cleared of the spurious charge H had framed him with. This meant getting himself clear of the Sector. Of a sudden, he longed for a free, straightforward life again.

He slid his legs off the table.

'Here, you've got to stay put,' William said, looking up from his vid-set.

'I've got cramp in my legs. Let me have a walk round.'

'That machine's supposed to look after your cramp.'

'My dear William, science has not yet invented an antidote to pins and needles. Get on with your viewing; I can't go far.'

William grunted uncertainly and returned to the love story. Wyvern found his legs were a good deal stronger than he had expected; the trolley had indeed looked after him well. He walked slowly towards it, feigning weakness and groaning, dragging the cable with him. When he was up on the trolley, he called out.

'I'm going to faint, William!'

The big guard was on his feet at once. Wyvern bent double, grabbed the cable, and wrenched its multi-point plug out of its socket on the trolley base. Thus armed, he swung about, whirling the cable over his head. The heavy-duty ruberoid plug caught William hard behind one ear. He went down on his knees, crashing into the trolley. Wyvern snatched up a urine bottle and crowned him with it.

For a moment Wyvern paused to wonder if he was going to survive being disconnected. Although his blood pounded heavily, he felt well enough, despite the overhead mirror's assurance that he looked horrible. He went rapidly to work.

He slipped William's white overall and slacks off and assumed them himself. He peeled the man's shirt off and tied his hands behind his back with it. He stuffed the vid-set, complete with *Shall Love's Affairs Be Hushed?* into William's mouth. There was adhesive plaster in a roll on the trolley; with this Wyvern stuck the gadget in place and wound a couple of twists round William's wrists and ankles for luck.

The result was not artistic but it would hold for a while.

'That crap's hard to swallow, eh?' he said, genially.

Bundling the loose cable, still attached to the terminals on his body, into a pocket, Wyvern made for the corridor. There was no light or sound anywhere. He could vaguely discern two doors in the corridor, one at each end. He went to one, hesitated, and opened it.

It was a hospital-type wash room and lavatory, without windows. 'This is probably a mile below surface,' he thought, heart sinking. The only outlets, apart from the flush, were a small ventilator grill and a large refuse disposal chute. He opened the latter; it evidently did not function properly, being choked with rubbish: bloody bandages, newspaper, cigarette cartons. A grey human finger caught his eye. Good old Grisewood, he thought grimly; or was it Grimshaw?

He went back down the corridor, glancing in at the recumbent William, who rolled his eyes, and tried the far door.

Emergency stairs went up on his left, another door stood just ahead. He took the stairs, ascending easily in the low gravity.

This floor was illuminated by neon strips. It looked like part of a regular hospital. Someone was talking somewhere.

A row of closed doors faced him, all identical and uninviting. One of them said 'Private'. Wyvern could feel panic beginning to mount; the business of taking pot-luck at closed doors quickly becomes wearing in such sinister establishments.

At least he would have an element of surprise on his side, which might be considerable in view of the contraption on the back of his skull. He barged into the door marked 'Private', determined to bear down anyone inside.

Nobody was there. It was an administrator's office. Neat white furniture. Synthetic flowers. Portrait of Jim Bull. Photograph of Sheffield. Blue air-purifier burning. Fake window showing view of Canadian Rockies beyond.

Quite an anti-climax, he thought. There was a far door. Wyvern opened it, expecting a cupboard.

An old lady dropped a cup of tea and began to scream. In a moment he had his hand clapped over her mouth.

'I'll throttle you if I hear another peep,' he lied. 'Now what do I do?' he asked himself. 'I should have brought that damned adhesive tape from below.'

'Got any adhesive tape?' he demanded.

She rolled her eyes and made signs. He brought his hand an inch away from her mouth and said, 'What was that?'

'I only asked if you had *cut* yourself,' she said timidly.

'Never mind that! Where is the tape?'

'Just next door. It's a store, a medical cupboard, don't you know. You'll find some in there.'

Wyvern didn't want to risk going into the corridor again.

'How do I get out of here?' he asked.

'To where?'

'To anywhere!'

'Well, if you turn right and go down the corridor, you get into the male nurses' quarters.'

'And left?' he prompted.

'There's a side entrance down that way.'

'Which door?'

'The last – no, the last but one on the right.'

'Thanks,' he said. 'Now let's go and get that tape.'

He hustled her through the outer door, paused to peer round the door, took a firmer grip over her mouth, pulled her out into the corridor and opened the door of what she had described as a cupboard.

It was a staff room, with three women in it. The old lady was no fool, Wyvern thought, cursing her quick-wittedness.

He pushed her into the room, slammed the door and ran down the corridor, hoping furiously she had not lied about the staff entrance.

She had. This was a dingy waiting room. Again no windows.

He tried the next door. The corridor echoed with shouting behind him, and he burst out of it with his only weapon, the cable, swinging in his hand.

He was in a dark side hall. It contained a dusty staircase and two other doors, one with frosted glass, through which he saw the blur of an approaching figure. He could also hear someone approaching the second door, steelshod boots ringing on tile. And two pairs of legs appeared at the head of the stairs, descending even as he paused.

It was too late to double back into the corridor, where the women were no doubt marshalling male help. Wyvern was cornered!

At the last possible moment, he spotted a cupboard door under the stairs and dived into it. As he did so, he recognised the voice of one of the men coming down the stairs: it was Colonel H, and in a foul temper by the sound of it.

Vacawashers and brooms filled Wyvern's perilous hiding place. He stumbled against them, but the clatter went unheard, for by this time the pursuers had gained the side hall and run into the two men entering by the other doors. The women from the staff room were all trying frantically to explain at once, the men were trying to calm them.

The voices were silenced by H's bull-like roar. His anger scattered them like pollen on a wind, and in no time they had all dispersed; a siren wailed distantly, insistently indicating that an organised search had now started.

Colonel H came down into the now empty hall with his companion. Through the thin partition, Wyvern could hear every word he said.

'You see what happens,' he was saying. 'Nobody can be relied on. We must reorganise the whole set-up from top to bottom. Once I'm Leader –'

'But we haven't time,' replied the other voice. It was Bradley, his tones full of spinsterish annoyance. 'After this crisis, yes, by all means. But we can't change horses in midstream.'

'You argue too much,' H bellowed. 'I'll ask when I want your advice in future. Now we've lost Wyvern –'

'No,' said the secretary, 'we haven't lost him. He must be in the building.'

'He'd better be!'

'Personally I rather admire Wyvern; he is what a century ago would have been called a good all-rounder. But we have allowed ourselves to be diverted from our original topic,' said the secretary icily, 'which was the question of the disposal of Parrodyce and his assistant, Rakister.'

'How can we dispose of them when we can't lay our hands on either of them?'

'That is a question merely of time.'

'Time, time!' shouted the colonel. 'Too many of the underground – these so-called wretched Democratics – have seeped into
the military for it to be merely a question of time! There's got to
be a reorganisation. There's got to be a purge. Bull had one when
he came to power.' Abruptly, he controlled himself and said in a
lower voice, 'Give orders that they are both to be shot on sight.
Parrodyce is a traitor.'

'Rakister is not,' the secretary said.

'Then why didn't he report back to us when he'd done the job?
I told you long ago, never trust a man who prefers a knife to a gun
– they're always neurotics. Anyhow, he knows too much about
Dorgen. He must go.'

Their conversation grew indistinct. They had moved off into the
corridor. Wyvern heard the door click behind them. He could not
stay where he was: doubtless the building was now being combed.
One obvious avenue of escape presented itself.

He came out of the cupboard and ran up the stairs which H and
his secretary had just descended. As he reached the first landing,
he heard a door open down on the level he had left. Double doors
stood on the landing; he tried them, and they were locked. Softly,
he hurried up another flight.

The stairs ended here in a single door. It was of clear glass, and
also locked. The whole building below Wyvern was housed beneath
the lunar rock, for gazing out he could see he had reached ground
level. In a tiny square, a helicopter waited. This, no doubt, was
the VIP entrance to the hospital.

The door did not budge. It was of reinforced glass, unbreakable.
He flung himself at it uselessly. Footsteps were ascending the stairs
behind him, rapidly, confidently.

Abandoning any idea of secrecy, Wyvern struck at the glass with
his cable plug. To no effect. He was still battering when a voice
behind him said, 'You'd need dynamite to make a go of it, Wyvern.'

He turned to stare into the muzzle of Secretary Bradley's revolver.

A long, tasty silence. Wyvern dropped his cable.

'I suddenly had this thought, you see,' the secretary explained.
'I left the colonel to do all the shouting and doubled back on our
tracks. It occurred to me that you might somehow have sneaked
past us. Come on down to where you belong.'

'Listen, Bradley,' Wyvern said. 'You're not cut out for this sort of
stunt. My telepathic powers represent a hope for a better future. The
regime's doomed anyway, so why not help me out of this? You have
enough intelligence to recognise a moral stink when you smell one.'

71

'A puzzling and illogical appeal,' commented the secretary, 'with a lot of rich ingredients: an argument of necessity, a moral argument, something which sounded suspiciously like an appeal to an old school tie. To imagine that intelligence and morality have a one-to-one relationship shows appalling naivety. Read Nietzsche's *Der Wille zur Macht* when you have time. Now we must get you back on your couch.'

'H would shoot you as soon as look at you!' Wyvern exclaimed. 'He has a better grasp of Nietzsche than you.'

'Not so. He is simply an old-style H. G. Wells-type liberal who has gone over the top. Responding to circumstances, basically, not shaping them. He really has no more time for Nietzsche than you. But you're the last gasp of the old-time English country gentry, Wyvern, telepathy or not. I'm the only true future-fascist type. The world will be mine. You'll see, if you live that long.'

'Bradley, for your own sake, don't think in such misleading categories. H doesn't and he sees you as no more than a dupe – which you are.'

'Won't wash, old boy – too obvious a ruse, and a lie anyway. Oh, granted he's a bit boorish. But stick by him and he'll stick by you; I don't pretend to understand that type of idealism, but there it is. Now come on down.'

'Look here –'

'Come on down before I shoot your foot off. Don't you believe me when I ask you nicely?'

There was no alternative. Wyvern started slowly forward. Then he stopped, shaken by a vast strangeness. Almost at once – it seemed intuitively – he knew what was happening: Berk was on circuit again.

The secretary fired deliberately at his captive's legs. It was too late. Wyvern's figure grew blurred, shadowy, and then disappeared.

The ricocheting bullet spanged dismally down the empty stairwell.

VII. SARTORIAL ELEGANCE MINIMAL

From the orange-tinted windows of the *Single Z* bar there was a fine view of one of the Sector's airlocks, Trafalgar Gate. For the price of a drink, anyone with nothing better to do could sit all day and watch the traffic in and out of the big dome. Eugene

Parrodyce sat and watched it now, from a concealed seat, wistfully.

Military activity was intense. There had been a demonstration here the evening before, and a home-made bomb thrown. Now a light tank stood by the gate, with New and Military Police reinforcing the usual lunar guard. Gas-guns and flame-thrower cannons were in evidence.

The sectionalised glass of the dome began fifteen feet from the ground, and rested on reinforced steel. The entire gate consisted of three pairs of double doors, two of them wide and the full fifteen feet high, for freight, and one much smaller for personnel. There was also a guard room which contained a door to the outside wall of the dome.

The few climbing plants placed here and there about the Trafalgar Gate area failed to conceal the poverty of the military imagination which prevailed over the whole British Sector.

Behind all these doors stretched the vast, compartmented hangar of A & D – Arrivals and Departures. This complex contained a military post, customs offices, a Duty Free section, decontamination rooms, showers, first aid posts, an isolation ward, a fire station and a repair base, besides the runways which terminated at the double airlocks leading to the lunar surface. Teams of men and women worked in A & D, so that people moved in and out of Trafalgar Gate whether or not spaceships happened to be on the landing ramps outside.

Parrodyce knew that besides the actual airlocks at the far end of the hangar, there were also side emergency locks. The knowledge was of no use to him. He did not know whereabouts they were; he had no spacesuit; he could not get into the hangar without four special passes. And to cap it all, he was tied to his seat with funk and indecision.

In his heart, he blamed it all on Wyvern. It was Wyvern's fault. Now he, Parrodyce, was a hopeless fugitive. The only element of comfort was that nobody was likely to betray him to the detested police if they recognised him; and the police had more urgent matters afoot. He thought longingly of his snug little questioning chamber below Norwich barracks, and of the timid friendship he had felt for his assistant, Rakister, until that amiable giant had disappeared.

And now the agent of his misery, Conrad Wyvern, was probably connected to Big Berk. Parrodyce wished he might also be connected. He visualised yearningly a vast father-mother figure who would take him over completely, know all his secrets. Then, recalling the pain this process would involve, he let his attention wander again to the window.

A Turkish six-piece band was haggling with the guard at the Trafalgar Gate. It had come to the British Sector as a seven-piece band; but the zither (doubling guitar) man had been fatally injured the night before in a political brawl. As a protest, the rest of the band was leaving the Sector. Besides a van-load of possessions, they were taking with them wives and instruments, together with their wings. Everyone was talking at once, supplying a chorus of support for Fezzi Forta, the band-leader, who was haranguing the guard commander.

It appeared that the Customs wished to look into the dead musician's coffin, which was leaving with the rest of the band. The Customs seemed to think it likely that the ornate box contained contraband rather than a defunct Turk. Parrodyce was inclined to agree with them. The Turks were lively and noisy and anarchic, and therefore scared the timid Parrodyce.

He was getting a pale sort of pleasure out of watching the tableau when a *Single Z* waiter arrived by his side.

'Gen'leman upstairs wants to see you,' he told Parrodyce, with what Parrodyce regarded as a cold glare.

The liquid in Parrodyce's bladder froze over instantly.

'What's his name?' he asked. 'What's he want?'

'He di'n' say, sir,' the waiter said, adding virtuously, 'and I naturally di'n' ask. But he did say as it was a matter of life and death you went up.'

Parrodyce had an aversion to the word 'death', but he got to his feet almost with a feeling of relief: the initiative was at last out of his hands.

'Where is he?' he asked. 'What does he look like?'

'Right up the stairs. Room 3. A rough gentleman.'

'Rough? Rough? In what way rough?'

The waiter looked non-plussed. 'Well, sir, perhaps I should put it this way. His degree of sartorial elegance was pretty minimal. Also, he could have stood a little nearer to his razor when shaving and, in any case, after-shave lotion had plainly been omitted from his toilet. Nor was a comb to be had. In short, sir, at a superficial glance, sir – rough.'

He held out his hand demandingly.

'Room 3, eh?' said Parrodyce, brushing past the man.

He went up. There seemed no alternative. If the New Police wanted to arrest him, why not do it in their usual fashion – in full view of others, as a warning – rather than in this roundabout way?

If it wasn't the police, it might conceivably be someone offering him help.

Upstairs, cheap moon-plaster was crumbling from the walls. It was gloomy here, with a smell of beer and trousers. The door of Room 3 stood open. Parrodyce entered cautiously, and was immediately grabbed. Arms ferociously strong flung him on to a sofa. He was searched all over, and then his captor stood back and surveyed him.

It was Joe Rakister, Parrodyce's ex-assistant.

'I never thought you'd be fool enough to walk in like that!' Rakister exclaimed. 'You knew I was up here – what made you come? Or have you got someone else with you? In that case, too bad, because we're leaving in a moment by a back entrance.'

This made little sense to Parrodyce. He stared blankly at his late assistant. The man looked wild. He was filthy and unshaven and evidently had not slept for some time. He wore some kind of ill-fitting uniform which included a cap, jammed tightly on his unkempt head. The waiter had the right word: rough.

'You see, I'm too smart for you all,' Rakister explained. 'I cottoned on instantly. As I was eliminating Dorgen, I heard someone come into the earth shop down below. And I thought, "The colonel will get you for this, boy!" And then I realised that he was planning to get me anyway.'

He paused, looking at Parrodyce as if for help. Parrodyce sat on the sofa, hands clasped, trying to stop his upper lip trembling, and said nothing. Scowling, Rakister continued.

'I'd been a sucker. I'd go back for my reward and nobody would ever see me again. For some reason, it was important to him to get Dorgen out of the way secretly; but the secret would only be safe with me out of the way too. Oh, I worked it all out, Parrodyce.'

'Very clever of you, Joe,' said Parrodyce.

'I've seen the telecasts. I know they pinned the job on this bod Wyvern. But that's just a blind to lull me into a sense of security and make me come out of hiding. They can't fool me. Now they've sent you along – to talk me into coming back, I suppose?'

So he did not know that Parrodyce was also on the run – but how could he? Hope rose in Parrodyce again.

'Well . . .' he said. 'Look, would you like a drink?'

'Oh, don't trouble to deny it. I've got no grudge against you, Parrodyce – you were a good boss, as bosses go. But now you're here, you're going to help me. With your assistance, I can carry out a little plan I've hatched. We're going out through Trafalgar

75

Gate, see? I'm beating it out of the Sector, eventually get back to Earth if I can.'

The sense of hope swelled into a sense of triumph. It interfered with Parrodyce's breathing. Rakister had never been as clever as he believed he was.

'Once we're in the clear, you can please yourself what you do,' Rakister continued. 'I shan't harm you if you co-operate. If you *don't* co-operate, I'll kill you as soon as look at you. Get that?'

'You know I'm no fool, Joe. I can see that you are desperate. You look, if I may say so, *rough*. But I wonder if you have ever contemplated existence in the abstract, as I frequently do? There can be no real escape for you anywhere, because you are bound to a limited code of behaviour by the parameters of our declining culture, and so there is no new way for you to think. You are, in other words, forever trapped.'

Rakister, who had heard this sort of intellectual nonsense from his ex-boss before, merely aimed a mock-blow at Parrodyce's head.

'Let's move,' he said. 'Escape.'

'You illustrate my point. Incapable of sustaining a discussion. When I was three, my father made me research the life of Fibonacci. Admittedly, it made me a life-long neurotic, but at least I have understood a few things. I was watching the Turkish band leaving just now. It's true those chaps are just strolling players, good with a saxophone but of pretty low mentality. Yet the Turks as a whole are doing wonders. In just the last few years they have founded a wonderful new phase of culture that goes as far beyond ours as the Neolithic went beyond the Paleolithic. You realise that in the Turkish Lunar Sector men and women *fly*? Even the band has wings with them. They have mastered anti-gravity. How? By subsuming the n-dimensional manifold of space into an expanded function-theory of groups representing the totality of form-systems. The result is a perfectly new number- and behavioural-ideative complex, from which fresh capacities can spring.

'Whereas we are bound to the same old Western mathematical fixation developed in Fibonacci's time and never transcended even with the advent of the space age. The British Radiotronic Computer, our friend Berk, is spewing out a world of figures right now, attempting to move a stage beyond what we might term the declining megalopolitan Christian culture – you'll recall Spengler's argument regarding the mathematical basis of all cultures. But who here has the intellectual qualifications to utilise the functions of that machine beyond primitive medieval concepts of it as an instrument of torture? What the situation reveals is the utter intellectual and imaginative poverty of the British, of which you, Joe, I regret to say, provide a stereotypical example. You speak of flight, not in a Turkish-Fibonaccian mode, but in a British-pedestrian sense.'

'Bollocks, and to hell with your historical paradigms,' said Rakister. 'On your feet.'

'There you go. "Hell", "feet" . . . A closed perspective. Cliché-embedded diction.'

Rakister kicked him.

Parrodyce got to his feet.

Rakister laughed harshly. 'Getting from A to B is a question of Nietzscheian will and not necessarily one of Spenglerian geometry.'

'There are exceptions.'

Rakister peered out of the door of Room 3, then looked back at Parrodyce contemptuously and indicated his own clothing.

'See this get-up I am wearing, what you call rough? Never heard of the working classes, have you? Forget how I came by it. It belonged to a lung-piper. Know what a lung-piper is?'

The term meant nothing to Parrodyce.

'A lung-piper is a chap who inspects the oxygen wells. You know how they get the liquid oxygen up from veins in the lunar crust? The pipes run through the hangar, and the pumps are installed there. We're going to inspect them; I'm the piper, you're my mate. Now here's exactly what we do, and keep your ears open because we've got to hurry. No more Fibonaccis.'

For a man who looked as rough as Rakister, the plan was a pretty neat one.

*

The substitute lung-piper and his mate, the latter in dungarees, the former equipped with a tool case and necessary credentials, crossed from the rear entrance of the *Single Z* bar to the Trafalgar Gate.

There, the Turkish band was haggling its way through the smaller gate. Instruments blared saucily. The Turks had won a moral victory over the Customs officials and the coffin full of loot was getting through untouched. They were the centre of all eyes, which suited Rakister and Parrodyce well.

Rakister had obtained a good deal of information on lung-piping from the unfortunate off whom he had stolen the uniform. Parrodyce following, he marched boldly into the guard room, flashing a yellow pass.

They were well in before a corporal stopped them.

77

'Out of my way, sergeant,' Rakister said. 'We've got to get through here. There's an emergency job required on the underground piping. They phoned through about it, didn't they?'

'Not to my knowledge,' the corporal said, 'but I've only just come off watch. I'll have to wake up the sergeant, if you'll hang on.'

'Wake the bloody sergeant if you like, but we must get on with it unless you want to be floating out on liquid oxygen. There's a break in X–235.'

He had brushed past the corporal, and was in the tiny store behind the guard room proper. Through a doorway on their right they could see the rest of the detail sleeping in steel cots with their boots on.

At the far end of the store was a metal inspection cover. Rakister knelt down beside it, pulled out a bunch of keys and began unlocking the locks and snapping the seals.

'Hang on a bit for God's sake, man,' the corporal said. 'It won't take a minute, but whoever tampers with those seals has to sign a form.'

'Give it me when I come up from the tunnel,' said Rakister.

The corporal weakened. Evidently he did not consider that rousing a sleeping sergeant was too sound an idea.

'How long are you going to be?' he asked, indecision in his voice.

'An hour – eighty minutes,' Rakister said. 'Bring us down some tea, eh? It could be complicated.'

'I'll still be here then,' the corporal said with evident relief. 'I'll go and get the form, if I can find it. I think it's a KH 725A. We should have it somewhere.'

He drifted back into the front room as Rakister pulled up the inspection cover. Parrodyce picked a torch out of the kit they had with them, and they climbed down into the depths, lowering the cover down on top of them.

'Wouldn't it have been playing safer if we had tipped the corporal down here and shut him up?' Parrodyce enquired.

'He knows he shouldn't have let us down here. He'll keep the secret better than we could,' said Rakister, and Parrodyce knew he was right. In the old days, casual remarks like this, revealing Rakister's considerable working knowledge of human psychology, had surprised Parrodyce; he could not understand how a man with such contempt for his fellows gained that sort of wisdom. Now he saw it had been picked up selfishly, to gain Rakister's own ends. Parrodyce saw that his own usefulness was almost at an end.

'Well, I didn't need much help from you, after all,' Rakister said, almost as if reading the other's thoughts. 'I was afraid we might have more than one dumb double-striper to cope with.'

They stood beside the big insulation-encased oxygen pipes; four of them ran straight from darkness to darkness, in a tolerably wide tunnel stretching from outside the dome to the centre of the city. The throb of the pumps was like a heartbeat, almost below audibility level. A notice on the wall proclaimed: IT IS DANGEROUS TO TOUCH THESE PIPES UNLESS INSULATED GLOVES ARE WORN. It was colder than a vault; their breath clouded and fell as rime on to the pipes.

'There should be a lung-piper's hut here,' Rakister said. He took the torch and swung it round.

The 'hut' was a deep alcove a couple of yards down the tunnel. They switched on an electric light and went in. Hoses hung on the wall, tools were stacked in racks. There were pin-ups of a gross kind. There were also two space suits.

'Get 'em on,' Rakister said briefly.

The suits felt icy and were difficult to put on. They helped each other, trembling with cold. One of Parrodyce's teeth began to ache.

'We've got no time to lose,' he said, and then realised it was something he was repeating over and over.

At last they were into the suits. With relief they switched on the heating circuits. The air was sardine-flavoured.

'Don't close your face-plate yet,' Rakister said. 'Then we can talk without using the intercom. Someone upstairs might be listening in. You go first down the corridor. I'll follow. Stop at the outer lock.'

'Very nice,' Parrodyce thought. 'And at the lock you can shoot me if you feel like it. Do you feel like it? I can't tell. I can't tell what anyone ever thinks, despite this freak gift I have. So I walk down this tunnel of darkness, round-shouldered, with a gun following. My precious intellect could wink out forever.' Perhaps someone more observant would know what Rakister felt like. He may have given himself away by some tiny item just as Wyvern was betrayed by an impossible smile.

Ahead, in the long tunnel, the oxygen pipes were punctuated with taps worked by wheels. Hoses could attach to the taps and the liquid be syphoned off if a section of pipe had to be drained for repairs. The taps pointed back down the tunnel the way they had come, like snouts of Bronze Age animals.

Parrodyce had no two thoughts about the matter.

Judging his distance, he flicked off the torch and ran to the nearest wheel. As he turned it, he heard Rakister call in angry silence. Then the liquid oxygen was jetting out; he could feel it thundering through the cock. And he was shouting, cheering, blaspheming.

He switched the tap off after a long minute and flashed the torch again.

Quickly he slammed his face plate shut. The lenses of his spectacles had iced over. He had to wait till the suit heater had coped with the trouble before he could see again. The liquid he had released was boiling, misting up into the corridor, multiplying, writhing, blue, beastly, raw: the stuff of life in killer mood. Half hidden in the vapour, a figure lay across the pipes, frozen there, arms wide like a metal teddy bear. Parrodyce hurried away from it, a little nauseated, tut-tutting to himself. Whatever next?

It was not far to the overhead airlock. He climbed the ladder and heaved himself in, closing the hatch behind him with relief.

Three minutes later he was stepping out of the side of the A & D building on to the moon's surface.

He had never been out alone. It was terrifying! He stood in the shadow of the dome and the shadow was absolutely black. Parrodyce could not see the ground, the hangar or any particle of himself. He tried to think of Fibonacci and better number-worlds, but his stomach still churned.

Some distance away the world began, an intensely bright world with a biting serrated landscape of mortician's beauty and stars that might have been only at arm's length. And in the foreground of this chunk of world, a line of figures was making towards a tracked bus. The figures bore a coffin with them; Fezzi Forta's boys were on their way.

Pulling himself together, Parrodyce forced himself to march across the black void to the light. He got to the vehicle as the last of the Turks was boarding. They hauled him up without question. In the lunar night, all suits are grey.

Gloating to himself, Parrodyce began to plan his next move. He had forgotten Wyvern; he was thinking of the telepathic girl. He needed her more than Wyvern did.

VIII. CUTTING THE POPULATION IN HALF

'To say it in a way you would understand,' Berk the Brain explained, 'I was so surprised I was speechless. I have not been out of order at all. No, I took myself out of circuit, that was all. Incidentally, observe I now refer to the totality of my functions as "I", as if they had corporate personality – a possibility I am investigating. The amount of knowledge you gave me to digest was more than the total volume programmed since I was activated – not, I mean your conscious knowledge, which was comparatively negligible, but the inherited and latent knowledge in you.'

'I did not realise,' Wyvern said, 'that in that brief contact with me on the operating table you had learnt all you could.'

'You had expected the process to be what you call painful,' the computer answered. 'The operation was brief, as you tell time; but once I had grasped one strand of the pattern I could predict and interpret the whole design. It is intensely interesting.'

Conversing with Berk was unlike ego-union. That process was always, basically, a clash of opposing forces, or a locking together of magnetic North and South. Berk had no character; his voice was thin water in the brain. Nothing was there of good or evil, personal ambition, altruism; he was intellect without will, potentiality without promise. There was no threat in him. He was power, but Wyvern was in command. Yet Wyvern was not satisfied.

'Now that you have the power of ego-union with others,' he asked, 'could you achieve mass-communion with multiples of minds?'

'Yes – through you. If you were in ego-union with them.'

Wyvern knew the machine would be reading the satisfaction this

81

answer brought. At once it added, 'After that, I would have their pattern and could communicate with them on my own.'

'Which is how you communicate with me now, although we are not joined by power cables?'

'Precisely. I am supplying the signal, you supply the power.' It was a remark Wyvern would recall with great regret.

He drifted in a highly organised and energy-rich limbo. It was only a moment since he had dissolved before H's secretary's eyes, but his time values had shifted, together with all his other senses. His vision was diffused throughout his body. He was seeing through his cell structure, and on all sides stretched a wall of glass marbles – or so it appeared. He was viewing the carefully stacked elements of his own body. Using the latent knowledge in Wyvern's own mind, Berk had unbonded his bio-chemical position; he was even now escaping from Bradley in a wafer of matter a fraction of a millimetre thick – but the endless array of marbles seemed not to move.

'You can resume normal structure now,' the machine advised.

'How?'

'I will guide.'

'Where?'

'I cannot say what the place is.'

'How can you see it?'

'Through your senses.'

'*I* cannot see it.'

'You will learn.'

And resuming normal structure was easy. Yet it was difficult. Snapping the fingers is easy; yet a one-year-old babe cannot manage it. His cells recalled the shape of Conrad Wyvern and reassembled in it.

Wyvern was in a blank little disused office. He was starving.

'This place is only about fifty metres from where I found you,' the voice in his head announced.

'I'm starving!' Wyvern cried.

He staggered over to a swivel chair and collapsed into it. He still wore the clothes he had taken from the guard, William; he was still peppered with terminals, and the basket of wire still crowned his head. But his flesh seemed to have atrophied, his bones showed, the skin stretched light over his temples. His stomach felt like a walnut. He was in the last stages of starvation.

Berk immediately explained the problem.

'This is my fault,' he exclaimed. 'I had neglected a basic weakness of human organic metabolism. You feed every five waking hours to maintain energy. That energy is easily consumed, and of course the sub-molecular transposition has entirely drained your energy supplies. I told you you were supplying the power. You must go in search of food at once.'

'I worked that one out for myself,' Wyvern said bitterly.

He staggered towards the doorway. His hopes sank directly he looked outside: the corridor stretching either way was painted a drab grey and brown, standard army colours. The opposite wall of the corridor was glass. Wyvern looked out; he was on the top floor of a tall building. Overhead he could see the domes with their polar shields up, curving towards the horizon.

'Not hopeful,' he messaged to the computer.

Without bothering to take precautions, he walked down the corridor, past two closed doors, to a self-service elevator. A notice on it read: UP – HELICOPTERS ONLY. OUT OF BOUNDS TO OTHER RANKS. Wyvern pushed his way in.

'Going up,' he said, and went up.

He emerged on top of the building in what at first was blinding light. When he got his bearings, he saw there were several army personnel about, officers in uniform, men in dungarees. Several helicopters here parked in a line, with one just landing. Painted on the launch pad was a Union Jack with a swastika in its centre.

Wyvern was beyond making any sort of pretense at concealment, nor was it easy to see what exactly he could have done to hide. He merely walked up to the nearest helicopter and flung open the cabin door. Someone called out to him at once.

'The one this end, if you don't mind, sir.'

Nodding curtly in reply to the mechanic who had shouted, Wyvern walked as steadily as he could down the line of air vehicles. As he reached the one designated, the mechanic pulled open the door and said humbly, 'May I just see your pass, sir, please.'

'Do I look as if I was on pleasure?' Wyvern asked, swinging himself up into the little cabin.

Indeed he looked a formidable sight. His gaunt form was clad still in the guard's white overall, his basketwork halo still loomed over his skull.

'I must see your pass, sir; you know that,' the mechanic persisted.

'Oh, very well, man,' Wyvern said. In one of the overall pockets there was a blank report card. He flicked it through the cabin door. As the mechanic swung to retrieve it, Wyvern switched on the engine and revved the rotors.

The mechanic was quick on the uptake. He wasted no time

examining the card, but flung a spanner wildly at Wyvern; it missed, clanging harmlessly against the metal fuselage. At the same time he was yelling at a group of three officers who had been standing nearby, watching Wyvern curiously. They dashed at the machine.

It was beginning to lift when the first officer grabbed at the swinging door. Grimly, Wyvern applied full power. His altitude reached ten feet – and stayed there, the motors labouring angrily. The first officer was dragging himself up. The other officers were also hanging on. The mechanic ran just below the wheels, yelling blue murder and jumping to seize the axle.

'For heaven's sake, do something,' Wyvern gasped to the computer.

'I *can't*. I'd kill you!' Berk replied. 'If I drained off any more of your resources, you'd go out like a light. Your mitochondria would burn out.'

Under the combined weight of the officers, the helicopter listed badly. It was sinking. They slid over to the edge of the building, a wounded bird swarming with rats. Carried away with excitement, the mechanic made one last jump for the axle, missed, and went plummeting into the depths below.

Wyvern's leg was seized. He looked frantically round for a weapon with which to break the officer's grasp, but there was nothing loose. Through the window he could see the faces of the two others, clinging and bellowing. He kicked furiously, but his strength was nothing; he began to slide diagonally across the floor of the helicopter.

'Let go, you crazy fool!' he shouted 'Let go or you'll kill us all!'

The other tugged the harder. Veins stood out on his forehead; one of his fellows had him by the trousers. It was this that made him release Wyvern, and take a firmer grip on the passenger seat. Wyvern hauled himself back to the controls.

Their rate of fall was accelerating. The face of a building slid by, desperately close. The in-dome helicopters were light-weight jobs, designed to carry a maximum of two people. The extra load would be buckling the vanes.

Ahead came another block. They slanted past it, and were making for a lower part of the city, drifting towards Mandalay Gate. As Wyvern calculated it, they would be down before they struck the side of the dome. At that, they would probably hit a building first. He flung open the other door, preparing to jump and run at the first opportunity, if his flagging strength would allow him to. Beneath him swung a pattern of upturned faces and pointing hands. Another 'copter soared up nearby; a video camera projected from its cabin window.

So H and his secretary would probably know already where Wyvern was!

He edged closer to the opening.

'Don't be an idiot!' the lean voice said inside his mind. 'Your human limbs are fragile and you do not yet know how to grow more. Don't jump! Let them capture you. They will think it in their own interest to keep you alive and restore you to health, for they do not realise I have already extracted from you all I wish. Sit tight.'

It was good advice. But Wyvern neither took it nor disregarded it. They struck a street pylon. The 'copter wrapped itself round the pylon and slid to the ground with a mighty rending of metal. Existence became an affair of stars.

Everything was going to be well.

With that conviction Wyvern woke. He'd been back in his dreams to Stratton, walking among the beech copses, riding Black Nick over the sweet bracken, swimming in the infant Yare. Berk had been with him, in air, in water.

Somehow in the dream everything had sorted itself out so easily. He had been refuelled, and the computer had scooped him back to earth and the regime had crumbled and then Eileen South had appeared and then . . . And then he woke up.

He was in a hospital bed again.

'*Plus ça change,*' he thought wearily. But at least he had been fed intravenously. His limbs had plumped out, the hollows had gone from his cheeks. And they had removed the terminals from his body. Wyvern felt his head; stubble ran crisply over it, and the wire cage had gone. He looked human again. He sat up, feeling wonderful.

Berk had been right! They wanted him alive; they would think the computer still had everything to learn from him. If Bradley suspected the truth, it hardly seemed likely he would dare tell H that Wyvern had just disappeared before his eyes. The new Leader, a materialist if ever Wyvern saw one, would dismiss the notion as fantastic. Which it was.

They would couple him back on to the machine – and he would vanish again. But this time for good.

'Hey!' he called. The sooner they fetched him the better. He could face them; he could face anything with Berk on his side.

Already it was nature to him that he was in part a machine, full capacities still unexplored.

It occurred to him then: if they intended to couple him up again, why had they removed the terminals from his body?

'Berk!' he cried inside his head. 'Berk!'

The machine did not answer, only a silence in the skull where its answer should have been. He remembered how he felt when his father died.

Two guards entered the room, the usual wall-faced entities who clicked for bully jobs.

'Get up,' one said in a wall-faced voice.

Wyvern did not like it. He hesitated, until an impatient movement from one of the guns decided him. He climbed out of bed. 'Put that coat on and come this way,' one of the guards said, indicating a greatcoat on a peg. 'And don't speak.'

Wyvern wondered remotely what kind of conversation it would have been possible to engage them in, but it was a poor time for discussion; meekly, he did as he was told. He was marched along a passage and up a flight of stairs, and locked into a waiting room. Beyond the door he could hear voices and footsteps. He reflected on the boring maze-like buildings which constituted habitation on Luna. Maybe the Turkish woman, Descant, was right; they were running out of ideas.

He recalled a song and its casually grim words: 'Life goes on; no one's irreplaceable.'

Again he called Big Berk. Still the mysterious silence.

The door was flung open, this time by different guards. They bundled him out to a yard and into a waiting van, climbing up after him. The vehicle moved off with a lurch and began to travel at speed. At one point, Wyvern thought he heard a shot fired at it.

A quarter of an hour later he was again standing before Colonel H and Bradley.

*

Colonel H was hardly recognisable. His face was flushed and heavy and his head was carried with a peculiar alertness not noticeable previously; he looked, Wyvern thought for the first time, a man to be reckoned with. He slammed a suitcase shut and stood up, glowering at Wyvern.

'Come through here,' he commanded without any preliminaries, gesturing to an adjoining room.

Wyvern walked through. The secretary made to follow, but H thrust out his hand.

'You can stay here and cope with the paper work,' he said sarcastically. 'I'll deal with this.'

He closed the door. Wyvern and he were alone. The room was bare but for a metal stool and a blank telescreen in the ceiling. It would be years, at the present rate of so-called progress, before the warrens constructed on the moon were properly furnished; by and large, they looked as inviting as the craters outside.

H also looked ugly. Wyvern made another mental call, but still there was no reply.

'Request transfer to the Turkish section,' he said.

'I want the answer to one question, and then I'm going to shoot you,' H said.

'That wouldn't be very clever,' Wyvern said. 'Or have you run another telepath to earth?'

'Not Parrodyce, if that's who you're thinking of – and he's got a dose of gamma coming to him when we catch up with him. What should we want another telepath for, eh?'

'To teach your computer to mind-read, as you said,' Wyvern replied.

'*You've already done that!*' the colonel said.

How had he found out? Had they found out, perhaps, from Berk itself? H did not leave Wyvern long in doubt.

'You fool,' he said savagely, 'didn't you realise that when you were communicating with Big Berk anyone within fifty yards could pick it up? One of the officers who pulled your 'copter down got out of the crash as lightly as you – the other two broke their necks, by the way – and he told us everything that went over between the pair of you.'

It was convincing, crushing, final. The only excuse Wyvern had for not having realised it before was that the usual staggering thought emanations of ego-union had been absent during communication with Berk. Berk was not human: he had intellect but no ego. With him, communication was a quiet, unsensational business. But Wyvern, of course, had opened his mind and had been sending at usual strength. In the pressure of events, he had not realised it. Nor had Berk, which was significant – it showed that the machine, being man-made, could on occasion act like a man and proceed without sifting available data.

Even if he had realised that fact, he could have done no differently. It had been essential for Wyvern to communicate. The past was unalterable; and now the future seemed inevitable. For him, death only lay ahead. For mankind, whom Wyvern had imagined he could help, lay the long terror of spies loose in their very heads. And yet – and yet Berk had spoken only to Wyvern . . .

The hostile silence was broken by Colonel H. 'Wyvern, we need Berk on-line again. How do we do it?'

'I don't know.'

'You useless fool . . .'

'Why did you go to the trouble of reviving me after the helicopter smash-up?'

'We need answers.'

'You need to ask the right questions. You pathetic fool, what are you doing, blundering about this dismal, sterile place? Go back home and try to rule England properly, try to make a system that works, where people can live in dignity. Study the rest of the world, study history. Aspire to happiness.'

Colonel H frowned in concentration over Wyvern's words, nodded his head. Then he said, 'Our computer was programmed to learn from you. It followed instructions. It learnt the secrets of your freak mind so quickly that we were deceived. When it closed itself down we presumed there had been a failure in the system before it got to the information. We were wrong there, as we soon discovered. But the point is this: when Berk opened up again and collaborated with you, it was acting directly contrary to instructions. How was that possible? It's a machine, that's all.'

Wyvern leant against a cold wall. The revolver was lowered. The problem was one in which he was also vitally interested – yet at present his brain was working only superficially.

'Perhaps the machine found out something you never have – the sacredness of human life!' he said.

'Sacredness!' H exploded. 'That sort of cant went out of date last century! It's rubbish! Your trouble is, you've had 3,000 calories a day all your life. It's put fat on your brain. You think of me as a roughneck, Wyvern, don't you? You're wrong. I'm the new elite, I've learnt the facts of the modern world! I rule by the iron rod of demography. World population is now about 2,700 million despite all the bloodletting. It's too much. Hitler has the right idea. Keep population down. Cull the degenerate racial stock, cut it out. Shoot the unemployed. Sacredness of human life! I care more than you imagine. My aim is to cut the population of Britain to half within six years. Then we'll be self-sufficient. There will be room for everyone.

'You see, Wyvern, it's a law of nature. Living space takes precedence over ballot boxes.

'Take a damn good look at me, Wyvern. I'm Mother Nature personified!'

Wyvern thought: 'He's been drinking; that's why he's so flushed.'

'You're kidding yourself, not me, H.'

'Just tell me why the Brain – *how* it could go against instructions?' the colonel grated.

Someone knocked on the door.

'Stay out,' H roared, never taking his eyes off his prisoner. 'Well, Wyvern, you must know. Out with it.'

Wyvern thought, 'If only I still had the strength, I'd kill him by mental force. But now I know how much it requires, I just haven't the reserves.'

Aloud, he said slowly, 'I suppose the same sort of law governs Berk as governs your population. They turn instinctively from the old to the new, believing it to hold more promise. Berk thinks I hold more promise. Because his basic programming includes the rule Expand – the old Biblical "Multiply and be fruitful", H, which works inversely for you! – he must follow *me*, for I teach him more than you. Through me he finds easier access to the known world.'

'No longer!' H declared. 'We blew him up completely soon after you crashed.'

Wyvern found he was laughing weakly. It was ironical. He had once schemed with Parrodyce for this. They had done it for him. Instead of triumph – he had lost his best friend!

'I just wanted your confirmation on that point,' H said heavily. 'It was what we had already deduced. That was why we had to destroy Berk. A computer is designed to be a slave. Slaves die when they get initiative.'

He flinched at Wyvern's look of disgust, and added, 'We are at present in hiding. Consequently you have to go out this way instead of more slowly. You are redundant.'

He raised the gun with practised efficiency and squeezed the trigger.

IX. TO THE AMERICAN SECTOR

In hiding! So the new Leader and his secretary were in as poor a position as that! Wyvern recalled that there had been a greatcoat draped over luggage in the outer room, ready for a quick getaway. In England, H was secure, but here on Luna his position was weak, and no doubt a spaceship was already waiting to take him back to Earth.

Wyvern opened his mind to full blast. He conveyed a concise mental picture of the route by which he had been brought to H's room. The necessary effort dizzied him, but he made contact with about forty minds without receiving distance of his impulse. Rainbow-feeling reactions of fear, surprise, triumph, excitement and gratitude pierced him. He felt H stagger under the mental shock, and the secretary outside explode in fury.

Rebel forces were very near the room. Even as their kaleidoscopic impressions seeped to him, Wyvern shut off contact and dived for H's legs. The colonel brought up his knee, striking Wyvern's shoulder, and they both rolled on to the floor.

H had dropped his revolver, but Wyvern in his weakened state was no match for him. H kicked out with his boot at Wyvern's chest and sent the latter sprawling. With one pounce, H was on to his gun and bringing it up again. At that moment, the door was flung open and Bradley appeared. He also was armed. He fired, without hesitation, a single shot.

And at the same moment a terrific charge of mental force enfolded Wyvern. A voice spoke inside his head, lights lit, silver bells rang . . .

'At last we've reached you, Conrad! To get the distance we had to use a tight beam. We couldn't pick you up until you sent and gave us a direction on you.'

'Eileen!' he answered mutely. 'Eileen South!' Encircling the name with a cascade of flowers and explanations.

Unmistakably it was she. The timbre of her thought, the pitch of her mind, were unalterably hers. Her hair slanted across his brow like rain, she was a cool breeze through his tiredness, her face fitted against his.

They began exchanging ideas and information with lightning speed. There were no misunderstandings, no concealments.

'How are you managing to reach me, Eileen?'

'I am in the American Sector.'

'So far?'

'I am linked to Fall Guy, our computer, as you were linked to Berk.'

'Pain, my darling . . .'

'Joy . . .'

'I knew of you – it seems so long ago. How did you know of me?'

'I have only just known, Conrad. A man called Parrodyce . . .'

She flashed Wyvern what Parrodyce had revealed to her of his escape to the Turkish Sector.

'So he got through! Yes, I know what you feel about him, Eileen. When I first found out about you, you were following a man called Dorgen.'

'The man with the impossible smile. A poor victim really.'

'What happened?'

'I was instructed to follow him. I picked up his thought in the Lanes. I found he had killed Jim Bull, your old Leader. Then I realised I had been sending! Anyone might have picked me up. So I made for the American Sector as quickly as possible. You must join us here. You'll be warmly received.'

He sketched his present predicament to her.

And the whole time, he was promising her the sun on the wild acres of Stratton and they were weaving cross-currents of warmth. Then he broke contact.

It had all taken a fragment of a second. Wyvern still sat huddled on the floor. H crouched like a cat, revolver in hand. Bradley was firing from the door.

Following the first bullet came another, and another, and another, each bursting into flesh. Crazily, it seemed as if they might go on pouring forever into their target, leaving it eternally unharmed.

On the fifth shot H fell on his face. A convulsion of his hand muscles fired his gun, his arm was kicked in an arc with the recoil. He did not move again.

'You see,' the secretary said unsteadily, 'I've killed him. I've killed him!' He pressed a handkerchief to his lips.

Wyvern got to his feet. A bitter stink of explosive filled the room, and his ears rang with sound.

'I shot him!' Bradley repeated. 'That'll show them I had no sympathy with him! They've got us cornered – they'll be here any minute now you've given us away. But they won't kill me. They'll see . . . it'll prove I was faithful to the People. You're my witness, Wyvern.'

'You must look after yourself, as you've always done,' Wyvern said tiredly.

The other seized his arm.

'You appealed to me once,' he said. 'Now I'm appealing to you, Wyvern. They'll believe you because you can tell them telepathically. Tell them I was H's dupe or anything, but let them know I shot H – it was him they were really after. I saved your life, you know.'

'You'll have to take your chance,' Wyvern told him.

Bradley grabbed his wrists and thrust his white face into Wyvern's.

'I'll tell you something,' he hissed. 'Something nobody but I knows now that H is dead. You knew Dorgen killed OBL, Jim Bull. He hid behind the wall of OBL's bathroom, waiting his chance; then he made his getaway to the Moon. That all took organisation. H supplied the organisation! He personally had Dorgen walled up while the barracks was being redecorated.'

'You knew this all the time!'

'I didn't know till it was too late,' Bradley said. Wyvern doubted the truth of that; he had the power of checking it telepathically, but shrank from the thought of ego-union with this intriguer.

'After the assassination,' Bradley continued, 'H was uneasy. He thought the underground might get to Dorgen, or Dorgen go to them. He decided we must come here personally, follow Dorgen and kill him. That happened to fit our other plans. We left with Parrodyce and his assistant, Rakister.'

'Because you might need an inquisitor here, and Rakister was just the sort of ruffian to erase Dorgen for you.'

'It had to be done,' Bradley said earnestly. 'So H said.'

'And then when Rakister had killed Dorgen, I suppose you put someone on to Rakister?' said Wyvern with sarcasm.

'Rakister is maddeningly untrustworthy. We have not yet traced him. Things are in a bad way. Perhaps even now we may hold out here till relief comes – it's due.'

As he spoke, the telescreen in the ceiling lit.

The hall of the building was revealed. It had been an easy matter for the rebels, on Wyvern's signal, to burst down the main door, overpower H's small guard force, and seize the controls. With these they were now conducting a telesearch of every room.

Elated at their discovery, faces pressed down on Wyvern and Bradley from above, distorting and ballooning as they swayed too close for focus. Their mouths seemed to open and shut soundlessly, like whales closing in on plankton.

With one shot, the secretary brought most of the screen shattering down on their heads. Shaking the splinters out of his hair, he burst from the chamber. He jumped the luggage in the next room and ran to the outer door, re-loading his revolver as he did so. At the door he halted abruptly and turned back.

'They're coming down the corridor,' he said grimly. 'In case I don't get out of this mess, here's something for you, who landed me in it.'

He fired. They were standing only five yards apart.

A bullet does not take long to travel five yards.

In that hairsbreadth of time, the history of man unrolled ten thousand years forward: for Wyvern *remembered*.

He recalled what Berk had said about finding in Wyvern's mind knowledge of a miraculous kind such as man hardly dreamed of possessing; the unbonding of Wyvern's chemical structure had been only one fragment of that treasury of knowledge.

The bullet had travelled one yard . . .

How had that knowledge ever been forgotten? In a flash of insight, Wyvern saw it had simply been overlooked, just as a man may live a week without realising consciously that he breathed all the while. And this knowledge, being fundamental, had been more fundamentally overlooked.

The bullet had travelled two yards . . .

How had that knowledge been there to begin with? The most powerful force in the world was the blind controlled explosion of organic growth which had taken multitudinous forms, all of them harmonics of the single cell. He found himself down among those original impulses, the biological equivalent of the Big Bang. But this explosion was still contained, recapturable. His new knowledge – he did not even feel terror at it – gave him control of that whole inexhaustible drive.

The bullet had travelled three yards . . .

Wyvern stood there with the secret of the universe in his hands. 'Berk!' he called mutely in gratitude. But Berk had gone.

The bullet had travelled four yards . . .

Only the imminence of death forced him to see what the computer had opened up to him. The factors in the great equation were interchangeable. Mass and energy bore a closer inter-relationship in the new realms of mathematics he had stumbled across. He could harness the para-organic powers which harnessed him.

The bullet had travelled five yards . . .

But Wyvern was nothing more than a parabola of light, flying through the great dome. Something of Berk was there too, freed into a new dimension of inorganic growth. They sailed through the chill of space, a trace of sparks, in the dark void, and out towards the American Sector.

*

She was trembling.

'I don't like to contemplate the future of the world,' she said. 'It has been – well, cosy to be human. I wasn't built to be an abstraction.'

'There will be few who will be able to learn what we can teach, Eileen,' Wyvern said. 'We few will have to act as guardians to the many.'

'So much to do,' she sighed. 'First you must rest. And eat. Promise me that!'

'We'll go a million light years away,' he promised. 'It's not entering abstraction. It's entering a more intense plane of existence. Have you never wondered – what is beyond this universe?'

'Don't,' she said, half-laughing. 'There's enough trouble here without casting so far afield.'

'Talking of trouble,' he said, 'what's become of Parrodyce? I promised to do something for him if he reached you.'

'I did it for you. I had to go down into the lower reaches of his mind.'

Wyvern clutched her hand sympathetically. He knew something of the state of Parrodyce's mind.

'He was a sick man,' she said. 'And yet – no mind is alien. I found the cause buried away, like a splinter sunk into flesh. As Parrodyce was being born, he uttered a telepathic scream. His mother was a weak creature. She died of a cerebral haemorrhage. He carried the guilt of it about ever since.'

'We shall need all the help we can get. Would he be fit to share the new knowledge? Where is he?'

Eileen laughed, and then bit her lip.

'He's certainly better – or changed anyhow. He became friendly with a small band. He's gone to the Turkish Dome with them. It appears they needed a new zither man, and Parrodyce got the job, if you can imagine it. We shall have to make out on our own at first, my darling.'

He could think of nothing in all the new dimensions of the world he would have liked better.

THE MANNERHEIM SYMPHONY (II)

The idea of being totally known to someone, of totally knowing someone – how alluring it was, conjuring at once a new life of simultaneous simplicity and complexity. Alluring and yet banal. For we were all destined always to be in ignorance, not only of those near to us, but of ourselves. Whom did we fear more than ourselves?

As I threw down Jael Cracken's book, the first notes of a new theme came into my head, a little rhythmical passage, possibly *Andante poco giocoso*, like the first movement of Sallinen's Fourth Symphony, somewhat dark and teasing, but at least a counterpoint to the bitter mood brought on by the cruel review in *Tanaan*. The realisation came to me that I had been made happier by the conventional ending of Cracken's little fantasy. How scornful Sinnikka would be if she knew that! Yet in a world of change, in a world where the certainties known to a previous generation were flowing away, out of reach, in a retreating tide, there was room, and more than room for the flimsy comforts provided by commercial fiction. Whatever my darling wife said, her sickness coloured her views.

Why could I not write a symphony that would comfort, rather than disturb?

It was not in me. Both my emotional and my intellectual nature disposed me towards compositions which would convey disquiet. Not necessarily my disquiet, but a general disquiet. I had a dislike of taking anything for granted, seeing so many of my friends living out their lives under false assumptions which they were too lazy – or too smug –

to question. Weren't such lives, whatever their outward display of wealth and success, failures?

Yet with love, the rather vague sort of perfect love, with a glimpse of which Cracken ended his adventure, was not the essence of love that something – perhaps everything – could be taken for granted? Wasn't that the greatest comfort? And didn't everyone need comforting? Real comforting, not mere escapism.

Influenced perhaps by Cracken's pseudo-science, I saw human relationships as a planet. In one hemisphere was a troubled humanity, growing up and instinctively seeking a mate. Seeking, not merely for the excellent biological reason of sexual desire, but for many other reasons as well. Their needs were complex, contradictory even, and generally ill-thought out.

In the other hemisphere was a content humanity, a comforted people, who had found what they sought.

And between these two hemispheres – an improbable equator. To cross that perilous zone, one was supposed to be simultaneously 'in love' and absolutely clear-headed about one's own needs and the needs of the esteemed other. It could not be. Particularly when no educational system had ever been established to teach people how to be happy, as opposed to how to be *homo faber*. There was no such thing as *homo felix*. Indeed, thought I in an aside to myself, standing vacantly in the middle of the room by the dead body, *homo felix* would be Cat People, and they had a rather bad reputation before they even existed in reality.

Even those fortunates who crossed that improbable equator – I numbered myself as one of them – could not guarantee their continued contentment. For once one is content, at peace, then the irrational stirs. The irrational rises up from its primitive lair, and terrible crimes are committed in its name.

Goodness is so fragile. Broken as easily as a porcelain plate.

Sinnikka was in the kitchen. I heard her lethargic movements, could imagine the movements of her limbs.

With the murmur of promising chords in my head, I

crossed to her bedroom where I had left my leather-bound notebook in which I jotted down such things. I saw that it lay on her small inlaid table by the window sill. But as I crossed to it past the bed, it chanced that I noticed a detail which halted me in mid-track.

When rising from her drugged sleep, my wife had turned her duvet towards the foot of the bed. She slept with two bolsters under her head, covered in a material patterned with flowers and little amorous birds in an Italian Renaissance design. These bolsters had pushed back as she rose, though the uppermost one still bore the imprint of her head, distorted into a hollow rather like the shape of those mouths which on a Greek mask represent the spirit of Tragedy. From beneath the lower bolster, the corner of an envelope showed.

The terrors of premonition! How much envelope did I see, protruding from the pillow? Just a small triangle of light blue envelope against the cream sheet, no more than a few centimetres on its longest side. Yet I knew that it contained my damnation – somehow, somehow to be unfolded in time. It waited there for me, protruding like the tongue of an animal callously slain.

A sickness overtook me. This is what people mean when they speak of the blood freezing.

Without volition, I crossed to Sinnikka's bed and pulled out the envelope.

On its blue face it bore my name, written in large immature handwriting. It had been slit open neatly along the top. I was in no doubt who had opened it: in a marriage relationship, such matters are never in doubt.

With timorous fingers, I pulled out the single sheet of paper from its sleeve.

The time and date written on it indicated the previous evening, when I had still been in Oulu. The text was brief, written in blue ink in the same large hand:

I cannot be at your concert, to my great regret. I have to make it to Sweden to renew my visa. I realise that the coach I'm on will carry me through your home village.

Though I cannot greet you, I can at least see your house, stand on your porch. I will leave the coach – I can catch another an hour later.

You don't even know my name. Perhaps you do with many girls what you did with me. I want to have you know that that sudden unexpected meeting last week, its even more unexpected outcome, was intense rapture.

To have met and within an hour be making love with a stranger – even a stranger such as you! I wish you to know I never behaved like that before and never will again. It was a *transcendent experience*.

Not wantonness. No. *Love* for all humanity and especially for you. My mind and body still throb with it. Thank you, thank you, marvellous man.

Be ever happy and ever superb in your music.

   Your loving
      Carol-Ann
I will slip this note through your door and no one will ever know our secret but us.

Such innocence. Such self-deception. Very touching – except that perhaps underlying her pilgrimage to my porch had been an unacknowledged desire to spread her secret a little. If so, the impulse had led to her death only an hour or two later.

As I slipped the sheet of paper back into its envelope, wondering what my next move should be, I heard my wife enter the bedroom.

Sinnikka came in slowly, her two eyes and the mole on her cheek steadily appraising the situation. Though I hid the letter, the action could not be hidden. Slowly, without any movement, the expression on her face changed, became more rapt. Though she never lowered that strange triple regard, somehow she ceased to see me.

With a steady, almost stealthy movement, she closed the door behind her – an irrational act, since we were alone in the house except for the dead girl – and began to remove the light robe she had thrown over her nightdress.

'Undress, and we'll make love before the police come.'

Her voice, low and throaty, had such a note of – well, there was supplication as well as command in it, so forceful that I immediately did as she said. And the act of throwing away clothes, of becoming my naked self as she was doing, awoke ancient lusts in me. This was real evil, this was the leap across the equator in the opposite direction, from the comfortable known back into strangeness. We were anonymous mammals, with too much to hide to reveal anything of ourselves but our bodies. My maleness sprang out red and ready before me, like an animal horn.

She had an alchemical scent about her, the muskiness of a honeycomb stored too long in an old linen cupboard, and the intense regard of her nipples, dark and astonished, was also upon me, upon my body. We were past the stage where eyes gazed at eyes.

How close is love and hate. We flung ourselves together on the bed as if murder was in our minds – as indeed it was. Nothing could have interrupted our raptures.

Yet something did, when we were well on in our frenzies.

At the window, a reindeer face appeared. Its antlers rapped on the pane. We looked up.

Captain Hakkennon stood outside. He gave us a formal touch of his peaked cap and then started round the side of the house.

Sinnikka buried her face in the bolsters. Giving her rump a friendly pat, I hurried from the bed and pulled on some clothes. Hakkennon thumped on the front door. I thrust the betraying envelope deep into my trouser pocket.

'Let me have that letter,' Sinnikka said, indistinctly.

Without answering, I thrust my arms into my shirt and left the room barefoot to admit the waiting man.

Police officer or not, Hakkennon and I were friends, or at least old acquaintances, and his air was a little sheepish as he entered our living room.

'Hope I wasn't disturbing anything important.'

'Did you bring a reindeer?'

'I came by helicopter.'

'I didn't hear anything.'

'Trouble with the engine starting up. That's why I'm so late.'

'What about the reindeer?'

'Can I smell coffee?'

'I really didn't hear you arrive.'

'Perhaps you were busy. Hope I didn't disturb anything important.'

'But where's the reindeer?'

'Er. As a matter of fact, I'm possessed by the ghost of a reindeer. Did you see it?'

'I didn't see any helicopter.'

'The reindeer.'

My wife entered the room. She was holding her hair above her head in a distraught sort of way and was still not wearing any clothes. My magnificent Clytemnestra.

By gesture, I had indicated to Hakkennon while we talked that he should sit down, and we had sunk into easy chairs. Now, in the presence of a naked lady, he rose and said, 'Good morning. I was telling your husband that I have been possessed by the spirit of a reindeer.'

She gave him a ghastly smile and replied. 'Would you and it like some coffee?'

When she had passed majestically through the room, I observed that the captain was sitting with his mouth open, or at least slightly ajar, as if he intended to remain that way.

'Do you wish to see the body, Captain?'

'Thank you, I did, thank you very much. Excellent.'

'The body of the dead girl in the next room.'

'My wife, as you know, is rather a skinny little thing.'

'And the reindeer?'

'Yes.'

I had hardly been able to keep the sarcasm from my voice, but I saw now he was in a slightly bemused state, as if he, too, had passed across some mysterous meridian. Getting to my feet, I said in as friendly a tone as I could muster, 'I suppose after all this delay you really do intend to arrest me? I read an entire novel, waiting for you.'

'I got the impression that you weren't reading a novel when . . . Well, it's a matter of taking you in for questioning.

Are you going to come quietly, I suppose? In the reindeer herd, we say, "Quietest better than fleetest." It's an old saying.'

'Flea test? I didn't know reindeer had fleas. Are you okay?'

Dramatically interrupting our conversation, if that is what it was, Sinnikka entered again, this time carrying a coffee-pot, but still as naked as the day she was born and considerably better developed.

'Coffee, Captain Hakkennon, dearest?'

When he nodded dazedly, she paused, to enquire if he did not find the caffeine went to his head.

'No.'

'This lot will.' Saying which, she poured the pot full over Hakkennon's head. It was not done violently, but rather in the manner of a steady spring downpour. The coffee, damping down the fuzz, made it appear like a heath area devastated by catastrophe.

'Milk?'

He made no answer. Nor did I, for, as I rose to strike her, my wife said, with a look of horror on her face, 'My God, I've forgotten the milk,' and dashed back to the kitchen.

It was difficult to know what to say to him, beyond explaining that Sinnikka was emotionally upset and offering him a towel. He made no remonstration beyond looking at me morosely through the bedraggled hair and the coffee stains. I saw that he was indeed possessed by the soul of a reindeer, just as he had claimed: the long melancholy face, the hair sprouting at the nostrils, the little bedraggled moustache, above all, those large misty eyes, full of guilt and the world's sorrow – they belonged not only to Captain Hakkennon but to that shy, victimised ungulate which lives in its thousands in our northern territory.

'Perhaps I should view the body now,' he said. 'The corpse, that is.'

Carol-Ann Crutchley Cracken lay where I had left her, her pack beside her. Her face still held a kind of distant beauty, but I still did not recognise her as the young woman

101

with whom I had made enthusiastic if indiscreet love a week earlier. I mused on mortality while the officer examined her wound.

He looked up at last. 'She's dead right enough. I'll get one of my men to carry her over to the helicopter.'

'You've got men here?'

'The house is surrounded.'

'Reindeer, too?' I feared reindeer and their mute spirituality.

'It's a wonder they didn't break in when your wife assaulted me.'

'I think a court psychiatrist might say that it was her way of making advances to you, rather than *assaulting* you . . .'

'This wound on the corpse was almost certainly committed with a State Security knife. They leave a distinctive mark. I can tell by the tear in her shirt. I want you to show me exactly where you claim to have found the body, and then we'll fly to Headquarters. No funny business.'

'I quite understand.'

'No coffee.'

'Promise.'

He gave me a dark look.

His men came in and went about the business of removing the corpse. They worked slowly, as if with reverence, but the appearance of Sinnikka with a red bowl on her head and nothing on her body undoubtedly accounted for some of their lethargy.

Hakkennon, meanwhile, collected up Carol-Ann's few visible belongings, including the copy of *The Impossible Smile*.

'Is this the sum total of her possessions?'

'The book's by a relation of hers. It could be a clue.'

'Is this all? You haven't removed anything? All right – outside.'

He was managing to psych himself into a more official mode now, and even hefted his service revolver in his hand to reinforce his returning authority. But he still walked like a reindeer. His head projected low in front of his body.

The helicopter sat by the roadside. It was a Russian Mil,

102

painted black and grey, a businesslike vehicle used by police of many countries, blunt-nosed, slow, reliable, like an old policeman. After Hakkennon had supervised the stowage of the corpse, he and I walked back along the road the way I had come a few hours earlier, an armed escort marching behind us.

He asked me questions on the way. Why had I walked from the airport and not driven? Why had my wife not been with me? And so on. That melancholy head, its cranial hair still damp, swung to watch my every move.

Despite myself, I grew confused. My answers became uncertain. Nor could I recall whereabouts I had come across Carol-Ann's body, finding myself, to my disgust, unsure even on which side of the road it had been lying.

'I'm convinced it was about here. No . . . Maybe a bit further . . .'

Hakkennon was ignoring me. Down went the head. The spirit of the semi-domesticated deer was upon him. Forward went the nose, eager, intelligent. Phantom antlers sprouted. He it was who discovered the crushed patch of grass, the almost invisible spots of blood by the ditch. He it was who wordlessly motioned the police photographers forward.

Twenty minutes later, we were about to climb into the helicopter.

Then the animal was less sure, confronting the black and grey machine vibrating before it.

'I always get air-sick, riding in these machines.'

'While you're getting your breath back, I'll collect my jacket from the house.'

Without waiting for anyone to stop me, I ran back into the house. I had seized the first excuse I could think of to say a word to Sinnikka. She had thrown on a dress. Typically, she got her word in first.

'Give me that letter back. I'll destroy it or it will incriminate us both.'

'Why did you put on that mad act, you bitch, just to turn Hakkennon against me?'

Oh, the smile, the way that mole out-stared me!

'I'll plead insanity in the dock, you bastard. Hakkennon

will be my witness. Why did you bring that corpse in here?'

Outside, hasty footsteps sounded, pounding up the concrete path. Running across the room, I snatched up my jacket from where I had thrown it the night before, across the seat of a chair. Underneath it lay the other paperback novel and two dictionaries which had belonged to Carol-Ann. I had completely forgotten them, concealed as they had been. To show them now to the captain would be to deflect more suspicion on myself, after I had said I had nothing else belonging to the girl.

Quickly I stuffed the novel in my pocket. The dictionaries were too thick to go in. I flung them behind the sofa. Hardly had they landed before two of Hakkennon's men rushed in and grabbed me. I struggled. My wife was screaming, the men were cursing me. Minute by minute, life was getting more like *The Impossible Smile*. I collapsed and allowed them to drag me to the helicopter, whose vanes, rotating, were already stirring up the dust.

*

Three hours after our arrival at the police station in Kuusamo, I was conducted into a cell, given a bowl of muesli and a mug of black coffee, and left alone. The door hissed pneumatically shut, the lock turned.

When I had finished the food and drink, I went to lie down. Already my time-sense was distorted. It was barely mid-afternoon, yet I was exhausted and could not remember when I had last slept.

Hakkennon had proved a rigorous interrogator. With Carol-Ann's note before him – they had searched me and returned all my possessions except that – he had probed endlessly, until I had lost my defences and my pride, and the lies had dropped away.

'I am convinced that you or your wife, or both, are involved in this crime against an innocent foreign girl. You must prove me wrong if you can or I shall break you down. I shall never tire. The reindeer spends its life on the move.'

'I am a steppenwolf, an exile. I have no home to go to.'

104

'On how many occasions did you perform the sexual act with the deceased?'

'I told you. On the one occasion. A week ago, when I should have been rehearsing my symphony. It was not serious. I did not even know her name.'

'She thought it was serious.'

'It was not continuous.'

'With how many other women have you been unseriously involved?'

'Never.'

'When most recently before Carol-Ann?'

'Never.'

'Did your wife know of the liaison?'

'The line between love and hate is very fine.'

'And in your case, now, so too the line between life and death. Tread it carefully.'

'I'm trying to tell you the truth, Hakkennon, I swear. Truth lies in the heart – or what passes for a heart nowadays. I love my wife dearly, I strive to be faithful, to be in every way a good husband. But I am also evil because I am human. I'm not like a character in a novel. I am a good guy but I am also evil, as is the nature of man. You understand that. You're a policeman – you must understand the insidious attraction of evil. I love her but I hate her. She's too close. I'm an exile. Distance I need. Carol-Ann was distance. Unknown. Anonymous. Womanhood. The comforting, encompassing vagina. You understand? I was unable to hate her. So I had no motive for killing her.'

'How many other anonymous women?'

'None.'

'When most recently before Carol-Ann?'

*

So it went on and on. I could not tell whether I was lying or not. Evil gives one a position of power. With evil at one's command, one knows when one is lying. This was powerlessness, confusion. I was slowly being reduced to helpless innocence.

105

My thoughts would not let me rest. In desperation, I took the girl's second paperback from my pocket and looked at it. Just like the other novel, this also was science fiction, Maybe-Myth. I had contempt, the contempt Sinnikka had taught me, for such escapism. Yet – perhaps it would comfort me, as these things are intended to do. For a moment, I let my meditations dwell on those who wrote and read such stuff – how fruitlessly innocent, even pure, must their lives be!

The title of this second helping was *Equator*. Well, that at least was promising. The author's name was unknown to me. I strongly suspected it to be one of the pen-names of the prolific Jael Cracken. It was dedicated to the spirit of Hugo Gernsback, I read. Perhaps that provided a clue, if only I knew who Hugo Gernsback was.

Sighing, I turned to Chapter I.

EQUATOR

I

It was the one time of day when you could almost feel the world rotating. In the rays of the sinking sun, dusty palms round the spaceport looked like so many varnished cardboard props. By day, these palms seemed metal; by evening, so much papier mâché. In the tropics, nothing was itself, merely fabric stretched over heat, poses over pulses.

The palms bowed stiffly as Scout Ship AX25 blasted up into the sky, peppering them with another spray of dust.

The three occupants of the ship were rocked back on their acceleration couches for only a few seconds. Then Allan Cunliffe got up, strolled casually over to the port and gazed out. Nobody would guess from his composed face that the ship had just embarked on a hazardous mission.

'At once you begin to live,' he said, looking down at the world with a kind of pride.

His friend, Tyne Leslie, nodded in an attempt at agreement. It was the best, at the moment, that he could do. Joining Allan, he too looked out.

Already, he observed wonderingly, the mighty panorama of sunset was only a red stain on a carpet below them; Sumatra lay across the equator like a roasting fish on a spit. Outside: a starry void. In his stomach: another starry void.

At once you begin to live . . . But this was Tyne's first trip on the spy patrol; living meant extra adrenalin walloping through his heart valves, the centipede track of prickles over his skin, the starry void in the lesser intestine.

'It's the sort of feeling you don't get behind an office desk,' he said. Chalk one up to the office desk, he thought.

Allan nodded, saying nothing. His silences were always positive. When the rest of the world was talking as it never had before,

107

Allan Cunliffe remained silent. Certainly he had as many mixed feelings about the Rosks as anyone else on Earth: but he kept the lid on them. It was that quality as much as any other that had guaranteed a firm friendship between Allan and Tyne, long before the latter followed his friend's lead and joined the Space Service.

'Let's get forward and see Murray,' Allan said, clapping Tyne on the back. Undoubtedly he had divined something of the other's feelings.

*

The scout was small, one of the Bristol-Cunard 'Hynam' line, a three-berth job with light armament and Betson-Wilson 'Medmenham X' accelerators. The third member of the team, its leader, was Captain Murray Mumford, one of the first men ever to set eyes on the Rosks, four years ago.

He grinned at the other two as they came into the cabin, set the autopilot, and turned round to face them.

'Luna in five and a fraction hours,' he said. Once you had seen Murray, you would never forget him. Physically he was no more and no less than a superb specimen of broad-shouldered manhood. Five minutes with him convinced you that he had that extraordinary persuasive ability which, without a word being said, could convert potential rivals into admirers. Tyne, always sensitive to the currents of human feeling, was aware of this magnetic quality of Murray's; he distrusted it merely because he knew Murray himself was aware of it and frequently used it to his own advantage.

'Well, what's the picture?' he asked, accepting a mescahale from Allan, trying to appear at ease.

'With any luck, we'll have a pretty quiet job for your first live op,' Murray replied, as they lit their mescahales. 'The target area, as you know, is Luna Area 101. Luna Intelligence reports a new object outside one of the Roskian domes. It's small and immobile – so far, at any rate. It's outside a dome on the southern perimeter of Area 101, which means it is fairly accessible from our point of view.'

'What's the state of light there now, Murray?' Allan asked.

'Sundown in Grimaldi, which contains Area 101, was four hours ago. Intelligence suspect the Rosks may be planning something under cover of darkness; we have imposed a lot of shipping restrictions on their Earth-Luna route lately. So our orders are to slip in from the night side and investigate – obviously without being seen, if possible. Just a quick look over, personal inspection in spacesuits. We should not be out of the ship for more than twenty minutes. Then we streak for home again, heroes all.'

The starry void blossomed up again in Tyne's midriff. Action; this was what he feared and what he wanted. He looked at the lunar map Murray carelessly indicated. One small square of it, low in the quadrant covering Grimaldi, had been shaded yellow. This was Area 101. Beside it, in the same yellow crayon, one word had been written: Rosk.

Tyne noticed Murray studying his face intently, and turned away, 'Company Earth made a great mistake in allowing the Rosks a base away from Earth,' he said.

'You were the diplomat when Allan and I were just squaddies in the Space Service,' Murray said, smiling. 'You tell us why Area 101 was conceded to them.'

'The official reason given,' Allan said, stepping in to back up his friend, 'was that while we were being kind to aliens we could not expect a space-travelling race to be pinned to one planet; we were morally obliged to cede them a part of Grimaldi, so that they could indulge in Earth-Moon flight.'

'Yes, that was the official face-saver,' Tyne agreed. 'Whenever it is beaten on any point of an agenda, Company Earth declares itself "morally obliged". In actual fact, they ran rings round us. The Rosks are so much better at argument and debate than we are, that at first they could talk themselves into anything they wanted.'

'And now the Space Service sorts out the results of the politicians' muddle,' Murray said. It sounded slightly like a personal jibe; Tyne could not forget he had once been in politics; and in his present state of tension, he did not ignore the remark.

'You'd better ask yourself how fine a job the SS is doing, Murray. Human-Roskian relations have deteriorated to such an extent this last year, that if we get caught in Area 101, we may well precipitate a war.'

'Spoken like a diplomat!' Murray exclaimed sarcastically.

*

The three of them spent most of the next four and a half hours reading, hardly speaking at all.

'Better look alert. Put your books away,' Murray said suddenly, jumping up and returning to the cabin.

'Don't mind Murray; he often behaves like a muscle-bound schoolmaster,' Allan said laughing.

Not often, Tyne admitted to himself without bothering to contradict his friend aloud. Murray had drunk with them several times at the Merdeka Hotel in Sumatra; his manner then had been far from schoolmasterly. He thought of Murray knocking back carioka till the early hours, rising later to eat with a monstrous appetite, while Allan and Tyne beside him pushed away at the large unappetising breakfasts the hotel provided.

The immediate present eclipsed Tyne's thoughts as the great black segment of moon slid up at them. It was like falling into a smile-shaped hole. Radar-guided, the scout became a tiny, moving chip of a ship again, instead of a little world in its own right.

A few lights gleamed far ahead: Rosk lights shining up from Area 101.

'Strap in!' Murray said, over the intercom.

They were braking. As deceleration increased, it felt as if they were plunging through water, then soup, then treacle, then wood. Then they weren't plunging at all. They were featherlight. With a bump, they stopped. They were down.

'All change; please have your alien identity cards ready!' said Allan. Tyne wondered how he was feeling, even as Allan smiled reassuringly at him.

Murray left the cabin, walking with something like a swagger. He was pleasantly excited. For him, this was the simple life, with no cares but the present one.

'The radar-baffle's on,' he said. 'No signs of alarm from our friends outside. Let's get into our suits as fast as possible.'

They climbed into the spacesuits. The process took half an hour during which Tyne sweated freely, wondering all the while if their ship had been detected by Rosk vigilants. But there was no alternative. The spacesuit is a tool; a bulky, complex, hazardous, pernicketty tool for surviving where one is not meant to survive. It needs endless adjustment before it can be trusted. There was not a spacer in the system, who did not hate spacesuits, or envy the Rosks their immeasurably superior variety.

At last they had lashed, strapped, dogged and screwed each other into place. Three monstrous robots bumbled round slowly in the confined space, nearly filling the ship with their bulk; they made with slow, underwater gestures for the hatch. Five minutes later, they were all standing on the lunar surface in complete darkness.

In what were already regarded as the old palmy days, before the Rosks arrived in the system, Tyne had frequently been up to the moon, on pleasure and business. He was not prepared for how bleakly uninviting the place appeared now. In the Grade-A darkness, Grimaldi was a desert of frozen soot.

'We've something less than half a mile to the target dome,' Murray said, his voice a whisper in the headsets. 'Let's move!'

They saw by infra-rad extensions. Murray led them along by the crater edge, treading round spines of out-cropping debris. The alien domes became visible as black breasts against sequin-studded silk. Through the grille of his helmet, Tyne saw the world as a plaster mock-up of a reality too unreal ever to be true. He himself was a pigmy imprisoned in the iron bowel of a robot heading for destruction. Fighting off that irrational sensation, he sought the strange object they had come to investigate.

Something lay ahead. It was impossible to see what it was. Tyne touched Allan's arm. The latter swung round, and then turned in the direction in which Tyne pointed. Murray paused, making a clumsily impatient gesture to them to come on. Perhaps he feels vulnerable as I do, Tyne thought, sympathetically, pointing again through the blackness for Murray's benefit.

Next second, they were bathed in the ashy glare of a searchlight skewered neatly in mid-gesture.

The light came not from the domes ahead, but to one side, from a point by the crater wall. Tyne just stood there, blinded, knowing they were trapped.

'Drop!' Allan shouted.

'Shoot the light out!' Murray said. His great metal-claw went down pistol-fashion to the

service pistol, came up levelling the cumbrous weapon, jerked with the recoil. Allan and Tyne heard the shots only as vibrant thuds through Murray's suit mike.

He got the light. It cut off – but already another beam was striking out from the nearest dome, swerving and sending an oval across the ash towards them. Probably they were being fired at, Tyne thought detachedly; you would not know until you were hit. He had his pistol out and was firing too, rather wildly, but towards where the enemy attack would come from.

'Here they come! Make for the ship, Tyne!' Allan bellowed. As the new searchlight swamped them, Tyne caught a glimpse of moving forms. The Rosks had been lying in wait for them. A hammerblow struck his shoulder. Pain ran like a crazed neon system all through his body. His suit creaked like falling timber. He was falling with it. As he went, he had a see-sawing glimpse of Rosks, approaching fast.

*

Spring in the northern hemisphere. March, 2189 AD. Scanner satellites orbiting Mars reported back to Earth an unidentified object moving into the fringes of the solar system.

Computer-enhanced pictures of the object were soon showing on every screen in every terrestrial nation. It proved to be an icosahedron, with barrel-like protuberances on a number of its planes. It executed a tumbling motion as it approached the Sun. Mysterious as it was, more awesome was its size. With a diameter of 136 miles, its mass was in the region of 3.3×10^{19} lbs.

Another planet? A comet? A new planetoid? There were more questions than answers. But one inescapable answer emerged from the accumulating data. No kind of natural object emitted coded radio signals. No kind of natural object would slow as it approached the Sun. The news of this shedding of velocity came as a relief at first, since computers had already figured out that the object would hit Earth if it continued on its present course. This relief turned to apprehension. The object must be guided by some form of intelligence, presumably an intelligence residing within the icosahedron. The object must be an interstellar ship.

WE'VE GOT VISITORS! cried the headlines.

As with every unusual apparition in the skies, this object brought hope as well as fear. People hoped or feared according to their innate characters. Quarrelling nations united and prepared their most deadly weapons to confront a possibly hostile foe. Politicians took advantage of the chance to speak grandly of the common heritage, the common good.

Among the multitudes, polls showed that a minority were for delivering a nuclear strike against the approaching icosahedron immediately, before it fired at Earth. A majority were for waiting in preparedness, in the hope that some form of salvation was at hand. The usual percentage Did Not Know. On one thing all agreed. It was marvellous, a cause for wonder.

A two-man ship, launched from Mars, matched velocities with the mighty visitor, and was not attacked.

Mankind's time of isolation in a gigantic universe was over. No longer could people regard themselves as the only sentient creatures. Nor could they think of themselves as potentially owners of space. This visitor from the unknown manifestly came from a technologically superior civilisation. The great hope was that that civilisation had also developed a superior morality.

As the icosahedron took up a braking orbit about the Earth-Luna system, the civilisation chose to reveal itself. Speculation had run high, almost feverishly high, as 'experts' all over the world had vied with each other to explain how monstrous the aliens would appear to human eyes. Ever since the days of H. G. Wells, almost three centuries earlier, the world's imagination had been amply stocked with scientifically plausible extraterrestrials. But science! What was science beside the great unknown? The Rosks made themselves known. And they much resembled human beings. It was an anti-climax. The most marvellous anti-climax ever. No horns, no tails, no green skins, no multiple eyes, no elephantine legs.

The Rosks, as they called themselves, resembled men and women. Not so much white men and women as, say, Malaysians. Appearances varied, but generally speaking they were light brown in colour. Their noses had no bridges. Their eyes were generally brown. Only their hair colours seemed in some cases a little unorthodox. Their body temperatures, it later transpired, were 105.1 degrees – an indication, presumably, that they came from a hotter planet than Earth.

Prurient curiosity was aroused as to whether there were women on the giant ship, what they could look like, and whether the alien method of reproduction was identical with the terrestrial one. Women soon appeared on the newsscreens. They were well clothed, and presented no divergences from Earth normal. If that too was an anti-climax, it also was wonderful.

When the great ship arrived close to Earth, Tyne Leslie was the youngest secretary to an under-secretary to the Under-Secretary of the

113

British Mission of the United Nations Council. He was in a favourable position from which to witness the agitated comings-and-goings which overwhelmed every ministerial department in every nation in the world, as gradually the implications of this remarkable visit sank in. The true situation emerged gradually, as experts and their computers broke down the formidable barrier of language and inflection which rode like a shock-wave between the two sides.

The true situation was alarming and curious. The Rosks did not come on a mission of conquest. Nor did they come to offer gifts of knowledge and wisdom. They had another reason to visit Earth.

After cautious preliminaries were over, and some mutual linguistic understandings acquired, the Rosks announced the appointment of a spokesman, their ambassador to Earth, by name Tawdell Co Barr, a yellow-haired dignitary of slender build and withered aspect. Tawdell Co Barr sent down a simulacrum of himself to address the Grand Assembly of the UNC.

The simulacrum was man-sized. It was draped in an enveloping green cloth. It spoke in English, in a pleasant tone of voice.

'We greet you all, Peoples of Earth. We are astonished by your variety. We congratulate you on living peaceably together. We wish to offer you our friendship. To that end, we offer you first some information about ourselves. I am myself a creature of formulated light, but I represent living beings who, as far as we can determine, bleed and breathe like you. Therefore we hope to establish a good relationship over the years to come.

'Our mother ship now close to your planet is an interstellar vessel which has been travelling for many years. It houses four small interplanetary craft and more than five thousand of our people, women, men, and children. They are colonists, seeking a fresh world to live in. Our own planet is overcrowded. We have solved many problems, except the problem of overpopulation. What appears simple in theory is difficult in practice.

'We come from a planet orbiting the sun you know as Alpha Centauri. Ours is the first interstellar voyage made from there. We came to Sol, our nearest neighbour, convinced by stellar analysis that it harboured habitable planets. What we find is that its one habitable planet is already swarming with an intelligent species like ourselves. True, you also have colonies on Luna, Venus, and Mars, but they cannot be sustained without Earth's resources behind them.

'Although we are happy to meet with another intelligent species, our disappointment cannot be measured. Our long journey, it seems, has been fruitless. We intended Earth to be our home.'

114

The simulacrum ceased abruptly, as if there were more to come. When it said no more, the Secretary General of the Grand Assembly made brief response.

After a courteous word of greeting, he said, 'Your science is surely sufficiently advanced for you to understand that habitable planets are only habitable because they are inhabited. It is the biomass which maintains conditions favourable to life.'

'The biomass does not depend on the presence of intelligent life. That could not be detected from Alpha Centauri.'

Other speeches followed in the course of the next few days and weeks, as the summer season encroached upon Earth's northern hemisphere and the tide of green life rolled up through the latitudes, even into Siberia. Warmth and light flooded in: so did the realisation that each fresh speech by Tawdell Co Barr's simulacrum revealed a fresh awkward fact concerning the Rosk visitation.

Secretary Leslie could see the growing consternation of politicians. The ordinary people, uninformed of the difficulties piling up, regarded the space voyagers as heroes – once they had overcome a natural initial disappointment at the lack of tentacles, eyes on stalks, and green scales. Nor were they unduly concerned when Tawdell Co Barr revealed that the home political system was a dictatorship under Leader Ap II Dowl.

An uneasy civility was the order of the day. The strain of the situation spread from government into business, and from business into ordinary life. In July, the major Revenue Integrator, which had replaced the old arrangement of stock exchanges and banks, suffered a severe selling crisis. Recession set in. The icosahedron was casting its shadow. But a handful of Rosks, women and men, came down to Earth and were seen in cities and agricultural stations. Their images spread to the far corners of the round planet.

In return for this hospitality, the Rosks presented their hosts with video-system documentaries about social and natural life on their home planet. Preserved samples of exotic flora were exchanged. Politicians pressed for entry to the great Rosk vessel. This was always denied. Presidents, scientists, newsmen, celebrities, all were politely refused entry, fobbed off with a varying stream of excuses. Rancour began to enter the fragile relationship.

In August, Tawdell Co Barr made a seminal speech, which brought some enlightenment while escalating the crisis. His timing was excellent, it was generally agreed.

'We cannot allow you entry to our colonyship. You will have sympathy with our reason for this prohibition, we are sure. Our people spent two long generations on the hazardous journey to

Earth. Lifelong incarceration brings many grave problems, mental as well as physiological. There are micro-organisms better equipped to make the trip than are Rosks, we discover. Many hundreds of our people died on the journey. Many are dying now, from hitherto unknown deficiency illnesses. Our ship is no more inviting than a charnel house. You would not wish to enter.

'We have no wish to impose upon the people of Earth. But we have to throw ourselves upon your mercy, in the name of universal intelligent life. We can travel no further. We have no home. We need refuge here. All we ask of you is some small place on your planet in which we may rest and recuperate from our long ordeal.'

A small place. But what place? Tyne listened to the politicians whispering. Where could five thousand Rosks be accommodated?

'Tell them to beat it,' Tyne suggested to the Under-Secretary. He was tut-tutted. Nobody would dare tell the Rosks to beat it.

The Roskian demand challenged the foundations of the newly established Company Earth. Finally, the old brutal philosophies of capitalism and communism had been extirpated. They had been based on a partial reading of mankind, of mankind's nature, and of mankind's relationship with his environment. The Gaian philosophy had prevailed, which recognised the role of intelligent life within a complex self-stabilising biosphere; an economy of nature.

The Gaians set about reorganising the globe and reforming its governance. Nations and the petty tribalisms of nationality would take a while to die; but meanwhile, the world community was organised into one large company, with agricultural production – that great primary target – rationalised with respect to climate, transport, and human need. Crops were grown according to actual requirement, rather than to economic or political pressure. Famine was no longer even a possibility. Self-respect was within the reach of all. Reason prevailed.

The necessity to cede territory to the Rosks threatened this peaceful Gaian stability. Who would give up land? How could they be compensated? Who would want Rosks for neighbours? Old spirits of nationalism flared up in the UNC, as every politician expressed his country's determination not to allow the Rosks on or near their territory.

A year went by in argumentation and under-counter pressure. The art of blackmail flourished.

In the end, two decisions emerged. First, that the Rosks should be granted an Earth base. Second, where it should be.

Both answers were inevitable. Even Tyne, from his back seat in the debate, saw them coming. In the human attitude to the Rosks lay both fear and envy; even if mercy should permit it, it was impossible to demand of the Rosks that they leave the solar system again. Such a move might provoke them to defiance of man. They might in desperation fight for the land they required. And what weapons they might possess was unknown; indeed, what gifts their science might yield upon more intimate acquaintance was a matter for general speculation.

As for the site of the base, it had to be in an equatorial region. Earth's equatorial belt was about as warm as Alpha II's temperate zone. A site in the middle of Africa might be too inconvenient; a small island might prove too self-contained. The mighty nations of Sul-Brazil and Brazil North would tolerate no Rosks near their borders. After many squawkings, orations, protests and uses of veto, an area of eighty square miles to the east of Padang in Sumatra was finally ceded as a Rosk base.

'For this small gift our gratitude is immeasurable,' said Leader Ap II Dowl, making one of his rare personal visits. There were many who considered his choice of adjective unfortunate – or deliberate.

So the Rosks landed on Earth in their massive ship. It soon became clear that they never intended to leave again; they had had enough of space.

Earth was unwilling to play permanent host. The Rosks, multiplying behind a perimeter they had rapidly fortified, represented a threat no less ominous for being unformulated. Yet how to evict them? It seemed to Earth's statesmen that the only possible line of action was to *nag* the Rosks into leaving.

Unfortunately, the more they scratched the sore, the more it itched.

Nation after nation sent its representatives into Sumatra, to see what could be seen, and to pick up any Roskian secrets, if possible. In the big UNC council chambers in Padang, Man and Rosk haggled and talked, demanded and conceded, bluffed and argued. The situation was at once funny and tragic. That old hope of profiting other than materially by the contact of two races was quite lost to view.

Except on diplomatic errands, Earthmen were not allowed into Rosk base, Rosks were not allowed outside it – yet in practice both sides infringed these laws. Padang became full of spies; nation spying against nation, race against race. The situation became more complex still when, in an attempt to ingratiate themselves, the UNC ceded the small Lunar Area 101 to the visitors, to allow them to test out their four interplanetary ships.

'This move touches my heart,' Tawdell Co Barr declared. 'We came as strangers; you welcome us as friends. Together, Rosk and man will build a new and lasting civilisation.'

By this time, such fair words rang hollow.

Whether Tawdell meant it or not, the hopes he expressed were the hopes of many men, everywhere. Unfortunately, this was Tawdell's last public speech! He disappeared into the Rosk base and was not heard of again. It was believed in diplomatic circles that the yellow-haired Rosk had been too friendly towards man for his overlords' liking. Ap II Dowl's dictatorship, which had been formed in the harsh environs of the ship, now took the reins. His henchmen sat at the council tables, and relations between the two sides slowly deteriorated.

The spy patrol in which Murray, Allan and Tyne served was only one instance of that deterioration.

II

Something like a lemon. No, a melon. No, it was stretching; a cucumber. No, it was bending; a banana. No, curling; a slice of melon. No, a melon again. Or was it – it was all distorted – was it a face? It rippled, solidified. It took on a firm jaw and eyes staring fixedly down. It became Murray Mumford's face, seen through a haze of weakness.

'Oh!' groaned Tyne. He was in a bunk which still rippled at the edges, staring up at Murray.

'How is it?' Murray asked. 'Feeling better?'

'Drink of water,' Tyne said.

He gulped it down when it was brought. His head cleared. He remembered the incident at 101, the numbing blow on his spacesuit.

'Where are we, Murray?' he asked.

'One hour out from Luna, unpursued, heading back home,' Murray told him. 'I was too quick for the Rosks, I thought you were never coming round. How do you feel?'

'This is the best part of me,' Tyne said ironically, raising his gloved left hand. Beneath the glove were substitute steel fingers and palm: his real hand had been amputated in an accident in childhood.

'I don't think there's much more wrong with you,' Murray said, 'apart from a few bruises. The Rosks fired on us. A bullet hit your suit glancingly on the shoulder; luckily no joints split, and shock absorbers took most of the blow. How do you do it – magic rabbit's foot?'

'How did I get here? Didn't I black out?'

'You blacked out all right, went down like a felled ox. I part-dragged, part-carried you here,' Murray said. 'Fortunately, as you went down I managed to shoot out the second Rosk searchlight.'

'Thanks, Murray,' Tyne said, and only then, with a rush of guilt, remembered his friend. 'Where's Allan?'

Murray turned away, drawing his thick brows together as if in pain. 'I'm afraid Allan didn't make it,' he said quietly.

'How do you mean, didn't make it?'

Swinging back to the bunk, as though he had suddenly found the words he wanted, Murray said, 'Look, Tyne, this may be difficult for you to take. Things got out of hand back there. It was a nasty spot – you know that. When you went down, I grabbed you and got you over one shoulder. Allan shouted out to me to run for it and leave you there. It must have been a moment of panic, I suppose. He wanted to leave you for the Rosks. I told him to cover my retreat, and the next thing I knew, he was waving his gun in my face, telling me he'd shoot me if I didn't drop you!'

'Allan!' Tyne protested. 'Allan said that?'

'Have you ever panicked?' Murray asked. 'There are situations when your moorings break loose, and you don't know what you are saying or doing. When I saw Allan's gun in my face, and felt the Rosks coming up behind, I – I lost control of what I was doing, too.'

He turned his head again, his big body tensed in a way Tyne had never seen it before. The man on the bunk felt his mouth go dry as he asked. 'What did you do, Murray?'

Space slid by outside, sly, snakey, cold as time at a crisis, ignoring Murray as he said, 'I shot Allan. Right in the stomach.'

Tyne was bound down on his bunk. He could only wave his steel fist and his flesh fist, impotently.

'There was nothing else to do,' Murray said savagely, clutching one of the waving wrists. 'Listen to me, Tyne, should I have left you there, out cold? We weren't supposed to be in Area 101–we had no legal right. Would you rather have come to with a group of killer Rosks round you? I did the only thing I could. Allan Cunliffe mutinied; as captain, I dealt with it on the spot. There's no more to it than that.'

'But I know Allan,' Tyne yelled. 'How could he – he wouldn't – he's not the sort –'

'We none of us know each other,' Murray shouted back. His

face was dark, suffused with a feverish look of excitement. 'We don't even know ourselves. In a moment of crisis, something takes over from us – our id, or something. That's what happened to Allan. Now shut up, and think things over till you see I did the only possible thing.'

He strode forward into the cabin, slamming the door behind him, leaving Tyne alone.

Tyne lay where he was, churning the whole thing over in his brain. He could believe neither that his friend was dead, nor that he had lost control of himself. Yet he could not do other than believe; after all, submerged rivalry for promotion had always existed between Allan and Murray; perhaps in those frightening seconds in the dark, it had come to a head.

Once before they landed, Murray returned to the crew room, to look in at Tyne. His manner was still tense.

'How are you feeling now?' he asked.

'I don't want to see you,' Tyne said grimly. 'I'll see you at the court of inquiry. Till then, keep out of my way.'

His face setting into harsh lines, Murray came across to the bunk and put his hand over Tyne's throat.

'Watch what you're saying and who you're saying it to,' he said. 'I've told you the facts. I don't like them any better than you do. If Allan had not suddenly turned coward, he'd be here with us now.'

Tyne brought his steel left hand over, clasping the other's wrist, squeezing, squeezing. Letting out a gasp of pain, Murray pulled his arm away; a bracelet of red flesh encircled it. He allowed Tyne one look of malice, then went back and shut himself in the cabin. It was the last Tyne would see of him for a surprisingly long while.

*

When they landed, Tyne lay patiently for a time, then bellowed for Murray to come and release him. Webbed straps, fastening under the bunk, ensured that he could not release himself. No answer came to his shouts. After twenty minutes, the rear air lock opened, and two Sumatran medical orderlies entered with a stretcher.

From them, Tyne gathered that he was back at Patrol HQ. Murray had phoned straight through to the hospital, telling them to collect him from the scout for examination.

'I'll come round for examination later,' Tyne said, testily. 'Right now, I have to report to the commander.'

'Don't worry; the commander has already been informed about the state of your health,' one of the orderlies said.

Despite Tyne's protests, the man was adamant. From his replies, it seemed as if Murray had cast some doubts on Tyne's sanity. So Tyne was carted to the military hospital on a stretcher.

Procedure there was no more rapid than in any other hospital. It took the doctors a long while to decide that Tyne Leslie was sane but savage, bruised but sound. In between the examinations were periods of waiting. All this, Tyne thought angrily, smoking his way through a packet of mescahales, was Murray's doing: the scout captain had fixed this so that Tyne's report was delayed. Well, he would fix Murray. Murray was going to be in trouble.

After two hours, buttoning up his uniform, he hurried over to Squadron Office. There a surprise awaited him. Murray had not reported in from his mission. Murray had not been seen. Suspicion and curiosity brewing in his mind, Tyne hurried over to the billets where the squadron lived. Nobody there had seen Murray either; his room was empty, none of his kit disturbed. Over his bed, a pretty half-caste girl stared saucily, blankly, from her photograph. Written in babyish letters across it were the words 'Love from Mina.'

The sun was gathering its full, mid-morning glory about it. Ignoring it, Tyne ran to the main gate to question the traffic cop on duty under his concrete umbrella. Yes, Captain Mumford had left in a staff car just after breakfast, heading for town.

'Thanks,' Tyne said. He thumbed a lift into town himself, riding the five miles of dust and sunshine in grim impatience.

He knew he should have reported in properly before leaving camp; above all he should have reported Allan's death. But in an obscure way he felt time to be vital. Murray had inexplicably disappeared; it would be easier to find him while the trail was hot. The time was 10.50.

*

By now I was certain that this adventure was yet another potboiler from the hand of Jael Cracken. The vein of sadism gave the game away.

Should I go on with it? Would Sinnikka hate me if she knew I was reading something so far below her ideals? Would she not rather that I was undergoing torture?

But the copy on the jacket held a temptation for me to

121

which she would be immune. '*An egregious novel of exile –*
Harry Harrison', it claimed. However maladroitly the Rosks
had been introduced, the situation of the unwanted intruder
was one I found promising.

Which was more than I could say for my own situation.

By now, I had come to my own unwanted conclusions
regarding the death of Carol-Ann Crutchley Cracken. The
note she had written me pointed in only one direction.

She had arrived at my house with the note and encoun-
tered Sinnikka unexpectedly. Sinnikka would have been
immediately suspicious, in her infernal way. She would feel
her precious security challenged. One look at the girl, so
innocent and open, and she would have hated her, and,
hating, would have been all sweetness on the outside, inviting, smiling, coaxing, wheedling the girl indoors – 'Oh, do
stay a moment, he'll be so sorry to have missed you' – the
mole of her cheek unblinking in its regard – 'Plenty of time
before your coach' – making circles round her as if arthritis
did not exist   'He has lots of young female admirers' – soon
getting her hands, with those sharp scarlet nails, on the vital
envelope, slicing it open with a knife in the kitchen, while
pretending to make coffee for the palpitating ex-virgin
standing dewy-lipped in the living room, hastily reading the
incriminating slop – oh, what a surge of triumph through
her, pain and pleasure meeting in a heady epiphany – and
maybe not laying down that knife again until it had done its
fatal work. Then dragging the warm body to the car, driving
off savagely to dump it in a convenient ditch. Yes, yes;
Sinnikka too was only human – full of evil . . .

The question confronting me was, should I take the blame
and save her from the result of her crime? Should I seize
on this opportunity to pretend to myself to be heroic –
'good' – and surrender my useless life – that damning review!
– that failed symphony! – that miserable love-life! – in
exchange for hers? Or should I, on the contrary, take
the chance with Hakkennon to incriminate her further by
devious ways, playing up her suspiciously uncharacteristic
behaviour with the police captain, and so forth?

Did I love her most or hate her most?

The question sickened me. I longed to escape from it. It had no answer, since it comprised all the mess of my life. Throwing it back into my subconscious, I returned to my book.

*

Padang was one of the most interesting cities on Earth. The proximity of the Rosk base had brought intimations of another world, heady visions of utopia, profit, promiscuity, and other possibilities beyond computation. The allure of such vistas was summoning a great international cast to Padang. The once modest port was being reborn into a mega-city, as hectares of paddyfield and mountainside sank under gleaming new complexes, and fresh transportation systems were forged at ground level and in the air. New technologies were born to accommodate new potentials. And the prospect of acquiring revolutionary new artefacts from the Rosk civilisation kept the stock market eternally buoyant. Money was no object. Credit knew no limit.

Among native Indonesians and Chinese moved UNC delegates from all over the world, each trailing a small noosphere of expensive requirements in the form of goods and services. Prosperity brought more prosperity. Demand fed demand. Heads of multinationals, women and men, demanded their retinues, their due displays and payoffs. It was Corruption-time. A new hotel rose air-conditioned from the Earth every dawn – still there were not enough beds to accommodate the new liaisons which arose every evening. Asceticism had no chance to flourish in the equatorial climate. Prostitutes of either sex, catamites, harlots, boys, followers, swallowers: all came where the going was good. Big business was inseparable from such expense account items.

In the shadow of the rocketing buildings, broken lives still continued in wooden shanties awaiting the bulldozer. There, street vendors hawked national emblems and a thousand other geegaws. A myriad kinds of booze and dope – Rosk-juice – were traded. The veins of the city flowed with muck and diamonds.

A block from the loftiest Hilton, or in any five-star restaurant, you could buy a lawyer, a woman, a gigolo, a snort, a jab, a smoke, or a long float, face-down, in the nearest canal.

A monorail sped Tyne the final mile into one of the central zones of the city, named the Ginza after its distant Japanese cousin. Every façade flickered with light, although it was midday. Tyne stood outside a gaudy tour-operator's, temporarily blinded, before slipping through a great undercover market stashed high with an Aladdin's cave full of flash trash-jewellery. He emerged in one of the Ginza's main thoroughfares, choked with traffic, the Bukit Besar. Pushing along the sidewalk, he sweated as he walked.

He entered the old Merdeka Hotel. It seemed to him the obvious first place to look for Murray. The Merdeka had been the nearest equivalent to home for Allan, Tyne and Murray. They had grown to love its efficient service, its poor food, its constant bustle. The Merdeka was not fashionable.

The place was full now, mainly with the sort of minor diplomatic staff Tyne had once been; nervous, cheery men downing their vodkas and keeping out of the sun – and waiting, waiting and watching. Pushing through the hall, Tyne went round the back way, to the back stairs.

He thought he saw Amir at the end of the passage, looking round and then dodging out of sight, but that could not be. Amir, the brightest boy on the staff, would have no reason to hide in that way; he had become almost a personal friend of theirs.

Climbing the back stairs, fishing his key out of his pocket as he went, Tyne reached Room Six. This was the room Allan, Murray and Tyne shared. Had shared . . . Unlocking the door, he went in.

The immense influx of foreigners had caused a housing shortage in Padang. Hotel rooms were impossible to find; only by paying through the nose for this one all the time did they enjoy the privilege of using it at weekends.

A hurricane had hit Room Six.

Tyne whistled. All their kit, their civilian clothes, everything, had been flung into the middle of the floor. Someone had searched the place, thoroughly, in a hurry. Who? Why?

'I don't like it,' Tyne said aloud. He went and shouted over the banister for service.

As he waited, he stood in the middle of the room, thinking. He was involved in a mystery. Something odd had happened on the Moon – he had not heard the truth about that, he felt sure. Now something odd had happened here. Why had Murray deserted? Where had he gone? A numbing suspicion that he had murdered Allan overtook Tyne. But why?

He went back on to the landing and shouted for service again.

Hatred for Murray filled him. It reached back, embracing Murray-in-the-past. The big man's easy manner now seemed no longer likeable, but the sign of a boundless superiority. His ready, cheerful smile became false, the arbitrary grimace of a murderer. Yet supposing he had killed Allan . . . he could so easily have told Tyne that the Rosks had shot him – Tyne, after all was unconscious when it happened. Nothing was sure. Rather, one thing was sure: Tyne wanted to get hold of Murray and wring the truth out of him.

He went out on to the landing to bellow for service again, and nearly bumped into a little maid.

'Where's Amir?' Tyne asked.

'Amir has a day off today.'

'What? First time I've ever known him have a day off.'

'Amir is not so well today. Had a bad head and takes medicine. What can I get for you?'

Suddenly, he wanted nobody to see into the room. He felt weak, tired, hungry; this was his first man-hunt.

'Will you bring me some breakfast, please?'

'Breakfast is long finish, sir.'

'Make it lunch then, anything.'

Going back into the room, he locked the door on the inside. He started methodically tidying the muddle on the floor. It hurt to fold up Allan's belongings, knowing he would not want them again. Some of Murray's civilian clothes were missing, but a uniform was here. So.

Lunch came promptly, a denationalised dish of chopped sausage, cabbage and rice, followed by tasteless plankton jelly. A big new plankton plant down the coast at Semapang provided more and more food for the island; as yet, its products were more nourishing than appetising.

With the meal, Tyne's spirits rose. He had ceased to be a secretary to an under-secretary of the Under-Secretary because he wanted action. Here it came. The original instinct that had led him to Sumatra had been sound. He had been static, stale, discontented, a man without manhood, set on a career of his father's choosing that bored him thoroughly. His chief task had been minute passing: how suitable that that should be a synonym for time wasting!

But the equator is the hottest bit of the planet, the bit that goes round fastest, though that is not apparent to the senses. Now something was really starting to spin.

On his way out, he ran into the proprietor and asked for Murray.

'Sorry. I don't see him today,' Mr Niap Nam said. 'If he come, I don't see him. Now it is best for you to leave by the back way. In front is having a little trouble from the Displaced. Maybe shooting from these foolish men.'

'Thanks, Niap,' Tyne said. He had heard the noise in the street but had taken no notice of it. In a moment, one shot was fired, the shouting rose to a crescendo, then came the sound of people running. Tyne slipped out the back way, through the courtyard, under the cassia tree. The Displaced were a group of terrorists, largely formed from natives whose kampongs had been evacuated to make room for the Rosk base: their daily acts of violence–often the sticky-bombing of diplomats' limousines – added an additional spice of risk to life in Padang.

*

Tyne headed for the Roxy. If anyone knew where Murray was, it should be Mina, the little half-Dutch girl (her other half remained unspecified) who occupied most of Murray's spare time. Tyne looked at his watch. It was just after noon; his enemy, for already that was how he thought of Murray, had as much as four and a half hours' start.

The Roxy was an all-day cinema. Now the boom was on, the solids flickered in the big perspex cube for twenty-four hours out of the twenty-four. The foyer was large, deep, lush, with people coming and going, or just standing smoking.

On the ice cream counter, Mina squeaked with pleasure at the sight of Tyne. Yes, she was nice: dark, lively, animated; perhaps after Murray was out of the way . . .

'Yes, he came to see me here,' Mina said, in answer to Tyne's question. 'Is he in some sort of trouble, Mr Leslie, can you tell me? He had a look as if something is striking him not so funny.'

'Perhaps he had his shoes on the wrong feet,' Tyne said, and then waited patiently for the girl to control her shrieking laughter. He had forgotten how the silliest remark set her going.

'I've got to find him, Mina,' he said. 'The commander wants him urgently. Did he say where he was going?'

'No, Mr Leslie. All he say is not even "give a kiss" but just "hello". That is why I think perhaps something is striking him not –'

'Yes, not so funny. I know. What else did he say besides "hello", Mina? Did he ask you to meet him later?'

'Excuse a minute.' She turned, all smiles, to serve a tall Pakistani, and then continued, 'All he say to me is that he goes to the plankton plant. I can find him at the plankton plant. What for he wants to go to that place, Mr Leslie?'

126

'Perhaps to plant plankton,' Tyne suggested, turning away un-smiling as she doubled up again with fluty laughter. What the devil would Murray be going out there for? Walking blindly, he almost bumped into a fat man in a white linen suit.

'Follow me to hear about Murray Mumford,' the fat man said; speaking from the corner of his mouth and appearing to take no notice of Tyne. As Tyne stared after him in surprise, the fat man pushed through a swing door into one of the adjoining bars. For a moment, Tyne wondered if he had heard all right. Then he shouldered his way through the door.

*

A miniature solid a foot high fluttered on the bar counter. It was silent. Piped from the full-size cinema solid, it showed only half the original. As such, it was almost unintelligible: but its job was to lure bar-flies inside to see what the original was about. At present, the breasty half of Lulu Baltazar reclined on pillows gesturing meaninglessly.

Tyne flicked his gaze from the cube to the fat man. The fat man was sitting in the far corner with his face to the door, raising two plump fingers to the waiter. The waiter was nodding and smiling like an unctuous fool. Several people sat about, drinking.

'Who are you?' Tyne asked the fat man, on reaching his table. 'Sorry, but I don't remember you.'

'Sit down, Mr Leslie,' the stranger said. 'Remember your man-ners and thank your lucky stars I found you before anyone else did.'

'Who are you, I asked?' Tyne said, sitting down. 'Have you a message for me from Murray?'

'Here come the whiskies,' the other said, smiling as the waiter set the glasses down. 'Let me drink to your continued health.'

Tyne pushed his away.

'I'm in a hurry,' he said. 'How do you know I am after Murray? I suppose you overheard what I said to the ice cream kiosk girl. Are you trying to be funny or helpful?'

The fat man downed his drink and then, looking quizzically at Tyne, usurped the one Tyne had pushed away. Without troubling to answer any of Tyne's questions, he said, 'If you want to call me anything, Stobart is as good a name as any, I'm a CoE agent. I can arrest you by flicking my fingers, should I feel like it.'

A bit – a very nice bit – of Lulu Baltazar was climbing into a

127

dyno-car. The waiter was smiling and nodding like a fool to new patrons.

'You talk as if you've just popped out of a cloak-and-dagger solid,' Tyne said.

'Don't reveal your genteel background, son,' Stobart said curtly, 'I'm real enough, as you'll find out if you start playing tough. And remember – I've got no sense of humour.'

'All right. You're real,' Tyne conceded. 'Then tell me this. Why should a CoE agent reveal himself as you have done? Why should he be interested in me, or in Mumford? If you were a thick-eared MP from camp, I could understand it.'

'You couldn't understand a thick-eared hatstand. Look, son, you are dabbling on the edge of deep waters. Stay out. That's all I'm here to tell you; stay out! The finding of Murray Mumford is top priority, and you'll only be in the way of several interested parties.'

As he spoke, he slid the whisky back to Tyne, who took it and drank it. Stobart raised two fingers in the air, and the waiter doubled over, curtseying, with more drink.

'Let me in on the mystery,' Tyne said. He disliked the note of pleading he heard in his own voice. 'Why did Murray kill Allan Cunliffe? Why are the CoE and not the police or the Space Service after him?'

'You're inquisitive,' Stobart said stonily.

Tyne went red in the face. He took one of the empty glasses in his left hand and squeezed. He went on squeezing till a little pile of glittering fragments lay on the table.

'Answer my questions,' he said.

Stobart laughed. 'You've got a temper,' he said, and blew the powdered glass over Tyne's jacket. Before Tyne could move, the other had grasped his left wrist in an unshakable grip.

'Listen to me, Mr Leslie,' Stobart said. 'Stay out of this. Mumford lied to you, I don't doubt. He wouldn't let you see how big this thing was. I want to hear what he told you happened inside Area 101; then I'll tell you what really happened. Fair enough?'

Sullenly, Tyne repeated the story Murray had told him on the scout ship.

'Hogwash,' Stobart exclaimed at the end of it. 'While you were out cold on the Moon, the Rosks *caught* you and Mumford. He had no time to get back into the ship, man, not with you sleeping peacefully on his shoulder. They caught him as easy as kiss your hand, and persuaded him to carry vital information down here, to a Rosk contact in Padang who will pass it to the Rosk Sumatra base.'

'How could they persuade him? What was the information? Why couldn't he have told me the truth?'

'You innocent fool!' Stobart said. He had stopped looking at Tyne now, as if he had lost interest in him; his watery eyes slid round the other customers in the bar. 'Do you think Mumford would tell anyone the truth? He has turned traitor! He's helping the Rosks; don't bother to ask me what they offered him for the job. And don't bother to ask me what the information is; if I knew I shouldn't tell you.'

'I can't believe it! Why couldn't the Rosks carry the information themselves? They've got four small ships plying between Earth and Luna.'

'If I knew all the answers, we'd not be looking for Mumford now,' Stobart said tersely. 'And that's all I've got to say to you. On your way, Leslie, blow. Go back to camp and play spacemen before the shooting starts.'

'You're drunk, from the way you talk and look,' Tyne said quietly. 'Or does your mouth always hang down like an old red sock?'

'There's a Rosk sitting up at the bar disguised as a Sumatran business man, watching us like a hawk,' Stobart replied, without batting an eyelid.

'I'm from Neptune,' Tyne said. 'How did you get hold of all this information, Stobart?'

The fat man swore at him. 'Think I'd tell you? For the last time, get, Tyne. You're up against organisations. You'll never find Murray Mumford. Go on, on your feet, beat it! The free whisky is finished.'

A bit of someone was wrestling with a bit of Lulu Baltazar as Tyne passed the bar. He boiled inside. His face burned. He hated every cubic inch of lard in Stobart's body, but his intelligence told him the man's advice was sound. If Murray was really involved in trouble so deeply, the affair had passed out of Tyne's hands.

Avoiding Mina's eye, he strode out on to the Roxy's steps. It was raining heavily. The streets ran with water. Further up the street, two policemen stood beside the smouldering ruin of a Russian Pudenta; the Displaced had struck again. The time was 1.15.

Inside the cinema, Stobart watched with satisfaction as the Rosk agent slid from the bar and left, almost directly after Tyne Leslie. Stobart liked his job. As long as you stayed in control it was as comfortable as an old armchair. With the right psychological push, anyone could be induced to do anything. Even a random factor like Mr Tyne Leslie.

III

Tyne decided to cut through the side streets. He might dodge most of the rain that way. The sooner he got back to base, the better; there would be trouble awaiting him for failing to report in from a completed mission. He felt full of defeat. He had even forgotten to ask that slob Stobart about Allan.

Rain pelted down his neck. His light tropical suit would be soaked in no time. A taxi slowly overtook him, splashing his legs.

'Jump in for a good ride, sir,' the Chinese driver called cheerfully.

It was a sound idea. As Tyne bent to open the back door, it was flung wide. Strong hands grasped his hand, catching him off balance, pulling him into the car. He felt it gather speed even as he struggled under a heavy rug which was thrown over him. Someone was lying on top of him, pinning him down. Tyne fought to get his steel hand free. Then a blow caught him on the nape of his neck.

For what seemed like an eternity, he lay half-suffocating under the rug, in a drifting state between consciousness and unconsciousness. Lurid colours curled and coiled in his head. When the car began to bump, as if it had left the road, he took an intelligent interest in the world again. An odd hissing noise rose outside; they were driving through long grass.

The occupant of the back of the car had climbed off Tyne now, and was arguing with the driver. It was something about damage to the machine. Money was offered, the driver was refusing it.

At length the car stopped. Tyne did not struggle as his wrists were lashed behind his back. The hands that touched his felt feverishly hot. Undoubtedly their temperature was 105.1 degrees.

He was hauled unceremoniously out of the car by his shoulders, rolling over in knee-deep, wet grass. As he struggled to his knees, and then to his feet, he saw the Chinese driver accept a wad of dollars, grin and rev the engine. The Rosk took Tyne by the belt of his pants, pulling him out of the way as the car backed round and shot back up the track in the direction it had come from. It disappeared; man and Rosk were alone.

130

Tall trees, secondary growth rather than true jungle, surrounded them. The only sign of human existence was an old native hut sagging under its own weight, although in the distance came the regular sound of traffic: a highway not too far off.

'Let's walk, shall we?' the Rosk said, pleasantly, pushing Tyne ahead.

'If you've nothing better to offer.'

It was still raining, but without passion, as they started down the track. Tyne had hardly managed to get a glimpse of his assailant. He looked like a Malayan. How ironic, Tyne thought, that this race should have set itself up in Sumatra! They could pass anywhere here unnoticed. In England, they would stand out a mile.

'Fond of the country?' Tyne asked.

'Keep walking.'

The track grew worse. The rain stopped as if a celestial tap had been turned off. The sun came out; Tyne steamed. Through the trees, the ocean appeared. It lay there flat as failure, stagnant and brassy.

The cliffs were steep here, deep water coming in close. Together, Tyne and his captor slithered down a perilous slope. At the bottom, three great palms fought motionlessly for position on a minute ledge, their stony trunks canting over the water. Down below the surface, their roots extended like drowned fingers; Tyne could see fish among the fingers. Then, without warning, he was pushed off the ledge.

He went down among the roots, the water burning up his nose. He struggled frantically. He was drowning! With his hands tied, he was helpless.

There was hardly time to think. The Rosk was swimming beside him, tugging his collar. In no time, they slid into darker water under the cliff, and surfaced. Water streaming from his mouth and clothes, Tyne gasped painfully, floundering up rough steps as the Rosk dragged him out.

They were in a cavern, the mouth of which would be hardly visible even from the sea, thanks to the big palms outside. Conditions were claustrophobic in the extreme. The water came within two-foot six of the slimy roof; there was no chance of climbing out of the water – one just stood chest-deep in it. Bitterly, Tyne remembered that the Rosks had strong aquatic traditions.

In the middle of the cavern, in deeper water, floated a small submarine. It looked battered and ancient, and was streaked with rust. It might have been a veteran from the Malayan Navy, before the Gaians started slow global disarmament.

131

The conning tower was open. A dark head now appeared, exchanging a few barked words with Tyne's captor. Without delay, he was prodded aboard.

Inside, it was like crawling round an oven, both as regards heat and size, Tyne was made to lie on the bare steel lattice of a bunk, his hands still tied behind his back. When the sub began to move, the motion was barely perceptible.

Shutting his eyes, he tried to think. No thought came. He only knew that the repulsive Stobart's warning had been well founded but too late. He only knew that he coveted the life of a secretary to an under-secretary of the Under-Secretary.

'Up again now,' the Rosk said, prodding his ribs.

They had arrived.

Pushed and goaded from behind, Tyne climbed the steel ladder and thrust his head into daylight.

The sub had surfaced out to sea. No land was visible, owing to haze which hung like a steam over the smooth water. A native, low-draught sailing ketch floated beside them, a mooring line from it already secured to the sub's rail. Three presumed Rosks showed predatory interest when Tyne appeared. Reaching over, they took him by his armpits and hauled him aboard the ketch, to dump him, dripping, on deck.

'Thanks,' Tyne snapped. 'And how about a towel, while you're feeling helpful?'

When his first captor had climbed aboard, he was urged down a companionway, still dripping. Below decks, structural alterations had created one good-sized room. The ketch was perhaps a hundred-tonner. Evidence suggested it had been used as a passenger boat, probably to nearby islands, before it passed into Rosk hands.

Five male Rosks and a woman were down here. They were dressed in Rosk style, with an abundance of oily-looking cloth over them that seemed highly out of place on the equator. Relaxed here, among their own people, the *foreign-ness* of them became more apparent. Their mouths, perhaps by the quick, clattering language they spoke, were moulded into an odd expression. Their gestures looked unnatural. Even in the way they sat on the plain wooden chairs was a hint that they found the artefacts alien, out of harmony.

These were beings from Alpha Centauri II, beings like men, but inevitably always estranged from man. The physical similarity seemed merely to mark the spiritual difference. As though life on Earth, Tyne thought, wasn't complicated enough without this . . .

The Rosk who had captured Tyne in Padang was delivering a report, in Roskian, to the leader of the group, a coarse-looking individual with nostrils like a gorilla's and a shock of white hair. He interrogated Tyne's captor at length, searchingly, but in a manner that suggested he was pleased with the man, before turning to address Tyne in English.

'So now. I am War-Colonel Budo Budda, servant of the Supreme Ap II Dowl, Dictator of Alpha-Earth. We need information quickly from you, and shall use any means to extract it. What are you called?'

'My name is Pandit Nehru,' Tyne said, unblinkingly.

'Put him on the table,' Budda said.

Moving in unison, the other Rosks seized Tyne and laid him, despite his struggles, heavily on his back in the middle of the table.

'Pandit Nehru was a figure in your history,' Budda said impatiently. 'Try again.'

'Martin Todpuddle,' Tyne said, wondering just what they did or did not know about him.

Evidently they did not know his name.

'You were talking to a CoE agent,' Budda said, 'at half-past twelve by your local time, in the Roxy Cinema, Padang. What were you talking about?'

'He was telling me I should change my socks more often.'

A terrific side-swipe caught Tyne on his right ear. The world exploded into starlit noise. He had forgotten how unpleasant pain could be; when he reclaimed enough of his head to render hearing partly possible again, a lot of his cockiness had evaporated.

Budda loomed over him, gross, engrossed.

'We people from Alpha II do not share your ability for humour,' he said. 'Also, time is very vital to us. We are about to select from you a finger and an eye, unless you tell us rapidly and straightly what the Company agent spoke about to you.'

Tyne looked up from the table at their foreshortened faces. What were these aliens thinking and feeling? How did it differ from what men would think and feel, in their position? That sort of basically important question had never been intelligently asked or answered since the Rosks arrived, nearly five years ago. The great, seminal, emancipating event, the meeting of two alien but similar races, had been obscured in a fog of politics. The merging of cultures boiled down to a beating-up on a table.

Tyne had been on the talking end of politics. Now here he was on the receiving end.

'I'll talk,' he said.

'It's a wise choice, Todpuddle,' Budda said; but he looked disappointed.

This acceptance of his false name gave Tyne heart again. He began a rambling account of the murder of his friend Allan, without saying where it took place.

Within a minute, the Rosk who had captured Tyne came forward, clattering angrily in Roskian.

'This fellow says you lie. Why do you not mention Murray Mumford?' Budda asked.

Turning his head, Tyne glared at his first captor. He had had no chance until now to get a good look at him. Like a shock, recognition dawned. This was the man drinking at the bar of the Roxy, whom Stobart had named as a Rosk agent; he was still dressed as a local businessman. Then if Stobart knew this fellow, perhaps Stobart or one of his men was following, and already near at hand. Perhaps – that thought sent his flesh cold – Stobart was using him, Tyne, as bait, expecting him to pass on Stobart's tale to the enemy. Stobart, as a rough calculation, was as callous as any three Rosks put together.

His mind totally confused, Tyne paused.

At a barked command, one of Budda's henchmen began to rip at Tyne's clothes.

'All right,' Tyne said. One look at Budda, crouching eagerly with tongue between teeth, decided him. 'This is what Stobart said.'

While they stood over him, he told them everything, concealing only the fact that he had been personally involved in the affair on Luna. As he talked, Budda translated briskly into Roskian.

On one point in particular the war-colonel was persistent.

'Stobart told you Mumford had to meet one of our contacts in Padang town, you say?'

'Correct.'

'Mumford did not have to go to our base here?'

'I can only tell you what Stobart told me. Why don't you go and pick up Stobart?'

'Stobart is not so easily caught as you, Todpuddle. There is a native saying of ours that little fish are caught but big fish die natural deaths.'

'Stuff your native sayings. What you are going to do to me?'

Budda did not answer. Going over to a cupboard, he opened it and pulled out a simple-looking gadget that evidently functioned as a radio-phone. Something in his manner of speaking into it suggested to Tyne that he was addressing a superior, presumably at Sumatra Base. Interestedly Tyne sat up on the table: nobody knocked him flat again. The interrogation was over.

Replacing the instrument, Budda began shouting orders to the other Rosks.

Tyne slid his feet down on to the floor and stood up. His clothes were still wet, and clung to him. The cords that secured his hands behind his back seemed to grow tighter by the minute.

'Are we going home now?' he asked.

'You are going to your eternal home,' Budda said. 'You have served your function usefully, Mr Todpuddle, and I am grateful. Now we all go to capture Mumford in a big hurry, leaving the lady of our party, Miss Benda Ittai, to sew you in a sack and hurl you in the blue water. It is an ancient Alpha form of burial. Farewell!'

'You can't leave me like this –' Tyne shouted. But the others were already hurrying up the companionway. He turned to face the Rosk woman.

He already knew she was beautiful. That was something he had noted instinctively on entering, although his mind had been on other things. Now he saw how determined she looked. Benda Ittai was small but wiry, very graceful despite her strange clothes, and she carried a knife – an Indonesian blade, Tyne noted.

She came towards him warily, clattering brusquely in her native tongue.

'Don't waste your breath, Mata Hari,' Tyne advised. 'I can't savvy a word of it.'

He could hear the others climbing down into the sub; they'd be packed in there like kippers in a can he thought. When they had gone, he could rush this little thug, knock her over, and get free.

But the little thug knew her onions. Bringing out an old sail from a locker, she spread it on the deck. Moving swiftly, she got Tyne in a sort of Judo hold and flung him down on top of the sail. Before he knew what was happening, he was rolled into its folds. Struggling was useless. He lay still, panting, to listen. Benda Ittai was sewing him in – very rapidly, with an automatic needle. Right then, he really grew frightened.

When she had rendered him quite harmless, she went up on deck. In a minute she was back, tying him round the middle with rope and thus dragging him, bump by bump, up the narrow stair well. The stiff canvas protected him from the harder knocks. When he reached deck level, Tyne began yelling for mercy. His voice was hopelessly muffled.

He was pulled across the deck to the rail.

Sweating, kicking feebly, he felt himself being lowered over the side. This is it, Leslie, he told himself in furious despair. He was swinging free. Then he felt the blessed hardness of a boat beneath him. The girl had put him into what seemed to be a rowing boat.

Tyne was still half-swooning with relief, when the girl landed beside him. The boat rocked gently, then shot away from the ketch. So it had a motor: but the motor was completely silent.

A momentary insight into the way Rosks got away with so much came to him. The average Sumatran remained poor, despite the early advances of Gaian reorganisation. The concept of world loyalty is not beyond him, but the chance to sell a fishing boat, or a knife, or a ketch, at a staggering profit is something which cannot be forgone.

To a considerable extent, the Rosks had found themselves on neutral ground in Sumatra. The ceding of territory, despite compensation, had brought disaffection to neighbouring areas.

'I can help you in some way, Todpuddle,' Benda Ittai said, resting her hand on the sail imprisoning Tyne.

By now, the situation was so much beyond Tyne, and to hear her speak English was so reassuring, that he could only think to mumble through his sheet, 'My name's Tyne Leslie.'

'The others in my party do not know I speak Earthian,' she said. 'I have learnt it secretly from your telecasts.'

'There must be quite a bit about you they don't know,' he said. 'Let me out of this portable tomb! You really had me frightened back there, believe me.'

She cut away at the canvas with her sharp knife. She would only make a hole for his face, so that he lolled in the bows like a mummy, staring at her.

They regarded one another tensely.

'Don't look at me as if I am a traitor to my race,' she said uneasily. 'It is not so.'

'That was not quite what I was thinking,' he replied, grinning involuntarily. 'But how do you come into the picture? What are you to do with Murray?'

'Never mind me. Never mind anything! All this business is too big for you. Just be content I do not let you drown. It is enough for one day.'

The sea was still lake-calm. The mist still hung patchily about. Benda was steering by compass, and in a minute a small island, crowned with the inevitable palms, waded out of the blankness towards them. The girl cut the engine, letting them drift in towards a strip of beach lying between two arms of vegetation.

'I shall leave you here and you can take your chance,' she said. 'When Budo Budda returns to the boat, I tell him my duty is performed. Here the water is shallow enough. I will cut your binding and you will wade ashore. No doubt that a passing boat will soon see you.'

'Look,' he said desperately, as she severed the cocoon of sail, 'I'm very grateful to you for saving my life, but please, what is this all about?'

'I tell you the business is too large for you. With that, please be content.'

'Benda, that sort of talk implies I'm too small for the business. That's bad for my complexes. You must tell me what's happening. How can this information Murray has be so vital that everyone is willing to commit murder to get it?'

She made him climb overboard before she would loosen his wrists, in case he pounced on her. He stood waist-deep in water. She tossed the knife to him. As he stooped to retrieve it, glittering like a fish under water, she called, 'Your Murray carries what you would name a microfilm. On this film is a complete record of the imminent invasion of Earth by an Alpha fleet of ships. Our ship which arrived here five years ago is not what you think it is; your people were misled by our Leader. It is only a forward reconnaissance weapon, designed

137

to make a preliminary survey for those who are now coming to invade. Against the slaughter to come, you or I, whatever we feel, can do nothing. Already it is really too late. Good-bye!'

Tyne stood in the sea helplessly, watching till she vanished into the golden mist.

IV

The solar system progressed towards the unassailable summer star, Vega. The Earth-Moon system danced round the sun, host and parasite eternally hand-in-hand. The planet spun on its unimaginable axis. The oceans swilled forever uneasily in their shallow beds. Tides of multifarious life twitched across the continents. On a small island a man sat and hacked at the casing of a coconut.

His watch told him that it was 4.20, local time. It would be dark in three hours. If the heat mist held till sunset his chances of being picked up today were negligible.

Tyne stood up, still chewing the last morsel of coconut flesh, and flung the empty case into the water. In a few minutes, it drifted ashore again. He fumed at his own helplessness. Without the sun, he could not even tell in which direction Sumatra lay. There, wherever it was, the fate of man was being decided. If Company Earth could get hold of that precious spool of microfilm, counter measures could effectively be taken. Stobart had spoken vaguely of 'information'; did he know the true value of what Murray was carrying? It seemed possible that Tyne was the only man in the world who knew just what tremendous stakes were in the balance.

Or did Murray know?

Murray had killed his friend and would betray his kind. What sort of a man was he?

'If ever I get my hands on him . . .' Tyne said.

Was Benda Ittai's horrifying story of imminent invasion true?

He was determined that he would no longer be a pawn in the big game. As soon as possible, he would take the initiative. Unknown forces had hitherto carried him round, much as the revolving equator did; from now on, he would move for himself.

Accordingly, he made a tour of the island on which he had been marooned. It was not much more than ten acres in extent, probably an outlying member of the Mentawai group. On its far side, overlooking a tumbled mass of rock which extended far into the sea, was a ruined fortification. Possibly it dated from the Java-Sumatra troubles of the twentieth century.

The fortification consisted of two rooms. In the inner one, a table rotted and an iron chest rusted. Inside the chest lay a broken lantern, a spade and a pick. Mildewed shelving lined one wall of the place.

For the next few hours, Tyne was busy building his own defences. He was not going to be caught helpless again.

As he worked, his brain ran feverishly over what the alien girl had told him. He was simultaneously appalled at the naïvete of Earth in accepting as simple truth the tale the Rosks had spun on arrival, and at the mendacity of Alpha II in thus taking advantage of man's generous impulses. Yet it was difficult to see how either side could have behaved differently. Earth had no reason to believe the Rosk ship was other than what it claimed to be. And if the Rosks were truly set on invasion, then from a military point of view their preliminary survey of Earth's physical and mental climate was indeed a sound one.

Exasperation saturated Tyne, as it so frequently had done in the old days round the UNC's shiny council tables. For these damnable oppositions, it seemed useless to blame the persons involved; rather, one had to curse the forces that made them what they were.

After he had been working for an hour, a light breeze rose; the mist cleared, the sun shone. Low clouds in the horizon marked the direction of Sumatra. Tyne's clothes dried off, his mescahale lighter functioned again. He built himself a bonfire, lit it, and worked by its flickering radiance when the sun went down.

At last, his work completed, he flung himself down on the sand, overlooking the beach where Benda Ittai had left him. The lights of one or two Gaian freighters showed in the distance, taking no notice of his beacon.

The sand was warm. He had time to think, listening to the rhythms of the sea breaking on the beach.

He tried to consider what a Rosk invasion and conquest of the planet would mean. Ever since the Rosk interstellar ship had settled into the duly ceded territory, pessimists had been claiming that its mass, added to the Earth's, would affect Earth's orbit. According to astronomers, that had not happened, so far at least. But, argued the pessimists, that could be because Roskian science had developed some sort of negative-gravity force, by which the ship was rendered all but weightless.

The case for such super-powers remained unproved, though the sheer bulk of the ship had certainly rendered the local microclimate uncertain and stormy – an effect of which Gaians were well aware.

Super-powers or not, Earth was vulnerable to attack. The old nuclear arsenals were being slowly destroyed. A special act would have to be passed before more could be manufactured. It would be a gradual process: invasion was a swift one. The chances for Earth were not good.

No one could say how the Rosks would treat terrestrials as they took over the planet. But history provided enough examples of what happened to the vanquished for Tyne to make an educated guess.

His grandfather had been a butcher. Even then, butcher was a dying trade, as the Gaian movement gained strength. Nowadays, vegetarianism was commonplace. The mass-slaughter of domestic animals was a thing of the past, a phase that was over. The lean meat of wild boar, deer, goat, eland, and so forth was eaten, the animals culled from the world's great agricultural stations which covered a major part of the Earth's surface.

Civilised life on Earth was at last improving: not just for the rich, for everyone. The new harmony with and understanding of nature had bought back the vision of utopia. Men and women were working directly and successfully towards that end. It was ironic that threat of invasion should come at such a propitious time.

Everything worth living for, if not life itself, would be destroyed. Looking into himself, Tyne saw how already he was slipping back into a less civilised state. He was again quite prepared to maim and kill. The Gaian oath meant nothing in a crisis. Already the dream of peace on Earth was melting like an iceberg towed to some equatorial port. The heat was on.

He frightened himself with thoughts of the possible future.

He slept.

When he woke, it was too cold and cramp. Cool breezes blew in off the sea. It was before ten at night. Low over the surging ocean, a segment of moon had risen, aloof, superb, an ancient symbol of hope.

And a fishing boat was heading towards the island. The dim throb of its engine had wakened him.

Tyne was going to be rescued! At the sight of the reassuringly familiar shape of a local boat, he realised how much he had dreaded seeing Budo Budda's ketch instead. At once he was jubilant.

'Here! Here I am! Help!' he called in Malayan, jumping up and flinging fresh wood on to his fire. The fishing boat moved rapidly, and was already near enough for the hiss of its progress over the water to be heard.

The boat carried a dim light halfway up the mast. Three men sat in it. One of them cried out in answer as they collapsed the single sail. The boat nosed in, bumping against the sand.

On his way down to meet them, Tyne paused. These men were muffled like Arabs. And one of them – that was a weapon in his hand! Alarm seized him. He turned to run.

'Stand still, Tyne Leslie!'

Reluctantly, he stopped and turned. Of the two who had jumped from the boat, one had flung back his hood. In the moonlight, his shock of white hair was dazzling, like a cloud round his head. It was War-Colonel Budo Budda. He was aiming his gun up the beach at Tyne.

They were not twenty yards apart: Budda and his fellow Rosk standing by the lapping sea, Tyne up the narrow beach, near the fringe of trees. It was a lovely night, so quiet you could hear your own flesh crawl.

'It was good of you to light a signal to guide us,' Budda said. 'We grew tired of searching little islands for you.'

At the words, Tyne realised that their finding him was no accident. His heart sank still further as he realised that there was only one source from which they could have learnt he was still alive. Without thinking, he blurted out. 'Where is Benda Ittai?'

Budda laughed. It sounded like a cough.

'We have her safe. She is a fool, but a dangerous one. She is a traitor. We long suspected it, and set a trap to catch her. We did not leave her alone on the boat with you, as we declared we would; secretly, a man was hidden to watch her. When she returned alone, having left you here, he confronted her and overpowered her.'

Whatever they had done to her, she had evidently not revealed where she had left him. That girl was a good one, Rosk or no Rosk. Tyne thought with compunction of her returning to the ketch, only to be jumped on. He remembered her nervousness; the memory seemed to come back to him like a fresh wind.

'You're too bloody clever, Budda!' he shouted. 'You'll die of it one day.'

'But not today,' Budda said. 'Come down here, Tyne. I want to know what the Ittai woman told you.'

So that was why they did not shoot him outright! They needed to find out if Benda had passed on anything they did not know.

Without answering, he turned and ran up the beach, pelting for the trees. At once he heard the sound of firing; the unmistakable high-pitched hiss of the Roskian service gun, a big .88 with semi-self-propelled slugs. Then he was among the trees and the undergrowth, black, hunched, reassuring, in the dark.

He began immediately to double over to the left, on a course that would bring him rapidly back to the sea without leaving the shelter of the trees. As he dodged along he looked frequently over his shoulder. Budda and companion were momentarily nonplussed; after the poor performance Tyne had made earlier in their hands, they probably had not expected him to show initiative. After holding a brief confab, they took a torch from the boat and commenced up the beach at a trot, calling his name.

By this time, Tyne had worked round to their flank. He crouched on a low cliff directly overlooking boat and beach. Groping in the undergrowth, he found three hefty stones.

At that moment, the two Rosks were running to the top of the beach. Tyne held his breath. They yelled together, their torch went spinning, they crashed into the trap he had prepared earlier on. To guard against eventualities, Tyne had used the spade he discovered to dig a deep trench in the sand across the path anyone heading inland must take. Covered with the rotted shelving from the old fortification, which in its turn was covered lightly with sand, it made a perfect trap. As the Rosks stepped on the concealed boards, they pitched through into the trench. Owing to the steep lie of the beach at this point, an avalanche of fine sand immediately poured upon them.

Tyne's advantage could be only temporary, a matter of seconds at best.

As the Rosk in the boat stood up to see what the trouble was, Tyne flung the first stone at him. The man was clearly outlined against bright water, and only a few yards away. The stone struck his arm. He turned, raising a .88. A clunk of rock the size of a man's foot caught him in the stomach.

Almost as he doubled up, Tyne was down the sandy cliff and on top of him. He sprang like a leopard, knocking the Rosk over. A clout over the head with another stone laid him flat. Tyne pitched him unceremoniously on to the wet sand, jumped out himself, and pushed the boat savagely out to sea. Flinging himself after it he climbed aboard and hoisted the sail. A bullet from the shore shattered the lamp on the mast. Tyne felt oil and glass spatter his flesh, and he laughed.

Turning he saw two figures, black against the sand, climb out of his trap and run to the water. They fired again. The big bullets whined out to sea as Tyne dropped flat.

Rosks could swim like sharks. In their first year on earth, before the trouble began, they had entered the Olympic Games and won all the aquatic events with ease. No doubt they could swim as fast as a fishing boat moving in a light breeze.

Fumbling into the bottom of the boat, Tyne's steel left hand found the gun dropped by the Rosk he had overpowered. He grabbed it with a whispered word of thanks.

Budda and his companions were wading out, still firing and clutching their torch. They made perfect targets. Steadying his aim over the side of the boat. Tyne drew a bead on the war-colonel. The wind was taking the sail now, making the boat dip as it left the lee of the island. He tried to synchronise his firing with the motion, ignoring a hissing missile that slashed through a plank not a foot from his face.

It was funny to be trying to kill someone on such a grand night . . . Now!

The Rosk weapon was superb. Recoil was non-existent. Across the level waters, not so many yards from the boat, Budda croaked once like a frog and pitched forward into the sea, carrying the torch with him.

'My God!' Tyne said. He said it again and again, as his boat gathered speed, dragging him over the moon-smeared waves. After the shock of killing came the exultation of it; he was almost frightened by the savage delight of his new mood. He could do anything. He could save the world.

The exultation quenched itself as he wondered where Budo Budda was now; whether anything of the Rosk survived apart from the body peering down into dark water. Then Tyne deliberately turned to face more practical matters.

*

Midnight was an hour and a half away. Time slid away from him like the wake of the boat. Murray had to be found before the Rosks reached him – unless he had been found already. Obviously, the first thing to be done on reaching the mainland was for Tyne to report all he knew to Stobart, or to someone in authority. To think to continue a lone hunt for Murray was foolish: yet Tyne found himself longing to do just that, to confront the monster, to . . .

Yes, he wanted to kill the big, laconic space captain. Even – and it was shrinkingly he recognised the urge in himself – he wanted to feel that terrible exhilaration of killing for its own sake.

But another side of his nature merely wanted to solve the puzzle of Murray's disappearance and all that hung upon it. Merely! Tyne fumed to think he had been unconscious during those vital seconds in Area 101, of which Murray had given one account, Stobart another. The truth might lie in either or neither of them, and the truth might never be revealed. Truth was a primal force, almost

143

like gravity; like gravity, it was always there, yet some people never even realised its presence.

Pocketing the .88 gun, Tyne steadied the high, stiff tiller. One of his earliest memories, half embedded in the slit of forgetting, was of himself in his pram and certainly not more than three years old. He was throwing a toy out of his pram. The toy fell to the ground. Every time he threw it, the fool thing went *down*. He tried with other toys, with his shoes, his hat, his blankets. They all went down. He still remembered the disappointment of it. Even today, he still hated that lack of choice.

Truth had the same inevitability about it; he just had to go on throwing facts overboard and it would eventually reveal itself to him. This time it was worth preserving: the future of Earth hung upon it.

At the moment, it seemed to him almost an abstract problem. He knew he should be hating the Rosks, the five thousand of them here, the millions of them mustering back on Alpha II. Yet the hate did not work; could that be merely because he knew one of them to be both brave and beautiful?

He switched his attention to sailing. The sail was cumbersome, the boat did not handle readily. It would probably, Tyne reflected, take him longer to get back from the island to Sumatra than the scout ships took from Sumatra to Luna. Progress, as good Gaians learned, embraced stability; a thousand centuries on, and paddy fields would still be cultivated. Another hard lesson: nature always had final say. Tyne consequently, was going where the wind blew.

But he was lucky. A south-east monsoon wind had him. In half an hour, the coast was in sight. In another hour, Tyne was steering in under the dark cliffs, looking for a place to scramble ashore. On a small, rocky promontory, two huts sagged under their load of thatch; a yellow light burned in one of them. Running the boat ashore on sand and stones, Tyne climbed out and made for the dwellings.

Among the trees stood a small kampong. It smelt good: smoky and sweet. Tyne found an old man, smoking the last half-inch of a cheroot in the moonlight, who would lead him to a road. As they walked, Tyne learnt with relief that he was no more than a dozen miles south of Padang.

'Not an hour's walking from here,' the old man said, 'is a telephone in which you may speak to certain people at the capital. If you say to them to send a fast car a fast car will come.'

'Thanks for the suggestion. I'll certainly do as you say. Whereabouts is this phone? In a house or a shop?'

'No, the telephone is in the new sea water works, where sea water is turned into food.'

Tyne recognised this description; the old man was referring to the plankton plant at Semapang. He thanked him gratefully when they reached the road, asking him to accept the fishing boat as a present. Much delighted with this, the native in return produced some food wrapped in a palm leaf, which he insisted Tyne should have. Tyne thanked him and set off with a good heart. The folded leaf contained boiled rice, pleasantly spiced and with a few shreds of aswabi added. Tyne ate ravenously as he walked. Though the road was no more than a track, every rut in it lay clearly exposed in the moonlight. On either side stood the jungle, still as an English wood.

Fifty minutes passed before he gained the first sight of the plankton plant. By then, Tyne was feeling less fresh than he had done. The moon was inclined to hide behind accumulating cloud. Leaning against a tree, he paused to rest and consider. Thunder grumbled like thought above the treetops.

Mina, when Tyne questioned her in the Roxy, had said that Murray was coming here, to the plankton plant. The spy patrol captain could have only one reason for visiting this place. The plant was completely automated; at the most, it was peopled only by an odd engineer during the day and a guard at night. Murray must have chosen the spot as a hideout until he could make contact with his Rosk agent. On the face of it, it seemed a remote and unlikely spot to choose: but that in itself might be a good reason for choosing it.

Tyne's mind was made up. In his pocket was a Roskian .88 gun. He would hunt down Murray himself; if he was here, he would find him. There was a personal score to be settled with Murray. After that would be time enough to phone Stobart of the Company.

Through the enamelled outlines of the trees, the bulk of the plankton plant loomed. It looked, in the wan moonlight, like an iceberg. And like an iceberg, much of its bulk lay below water, for it stood on the edge of the sea, its rear facing on to land, its massive front thrusting out into the Indian Ocean.

Every day, millions of tons of sea water were sucked into its great vats, to be regurgitated later, robbed of their plankton content. These minute organisms were filtered into tanks of nutrient solution, fed and fattened, before being passed over to the synthesising process, which turned them into compressed foodstuffs, highly nourishing and palatable. Such plants, established at intervals round the shores of the Indian Ocean and the China Seas, had done much to alleviate dietary problems prevailing in the more populous areas of the tropics. They were as familiar a sight as nuclear plants had been once.

Tyne approached the place cautiously.

Though he had never been here before, he found it all familiar, thanks to the publicity it enjoyed. He knew that the plant was almost impossible to break into. Where, then, would a hunted man hide? One answer seemed most likely: on the seaward façade.

There, numerous arches and buttresses over the submarine mouth of the plant would afford shelter from the elements – and from all but a personal, on-the-spot-search.

Now Tyne was going to make that search.

He slid round a deserted heliport. Clouds drifted over the moon; he was happy to take advantage of them. At the end of the tarmac was a high wall. Over the wall was a narrow passage, and then the main building, rising sheer. Carrying an empty oil drum across to the wall, Tyne stood on it, crouched, jumped upwards. Clawing desperately, he pulled himself on top of the wall. He crouched and listened. Nothing. Only the murmur of the sea, the stammering call of a night bird.

The impossibility of getting on to the building now dawned on him. The white walls rose a hundred and fifty feet above him, stretching away unbrokenly on either side, and punctuated only by a dark streak some yards away. Keeping his head down, Tyne wormed along the top of the wall; the dark streak resolved itself into a steel ladder, starting some fourteen feet above the ground and going right up to the roof.

Tyne, getting opposite to it, stood up on the wall and jumped forward, across the passage below. Seizing the rungs with both hands, he got a foothold. His steel hand was nearly wrenched from its socket with the sudden exertion; he clung there motionless until the pain in his arm had subsided. The darkness grew thicker and thicker while he waited. Thunder rumbled overhead. Then he began the upward climb.

Even as he started, the rain began. Tyne heard it swishing through the jungle towards him. Next moment it hit him as if trying to squash him against the wall. He wondered grimly how long it was since he had last been completely dry and continued to climb.

Once on the roof, he squatted and peered about him, trying to see through the wet darkness. Rainclouds now obscured the moon. To his right, he saw tall ventilation stacks and heard the rain drumming against them. He was cursing, half-aloud. He was cursing the whole universe, suns and moons and planets but

146

especially planets, for harbouring freak phenomena like life and weather.

Advancing on hands and knees, he made for the seaward side. One last ridge to crawl up, one last ridge to slither perilously down, and he crouched on the top of the façade of the building. Below him were the arches and cavities in which he expected to find Murray. Below that, irritable now, lay the sea.

He could dimly see it, needled unceasingly by the downpour, sucking and slumping against the plant. Immediately below him was a patch of relatively calm water. This lay inside the plankton mesh, a vast perforated screen which ensured that nothing larger than a small shrimp would be sucked into the plant's internal processes. On the other side of the mesh, spray fountained.

In the noise about him, Tyne had lost the need for concealment. He stood up now and shouted, cupping his hands round his mouth.

'Murray!'

The cry was washed away at once into the gutters of soundlessness. He did not shout again.

With water streaming down his face, Tyne dropped on to hands and knees, to begin a crawl along the leading parapet, looking for another inspection ladder that would enable him to get down the façade.

He found one. Grinning to himself with satisfaction, he swung his legs over the edge of the drop. As he took his first foothold, a shot rang out.

Tyne froze. He crouched with his head against the streaming concrete, body tensed against pain. It was impossible to tell where the shot had come from, from above or from below. For the space of ten unendurable seconds, he lay rigid. Then he slithered down the ladder as fast as he could go, heedless of the pain in his good hand and wrist. The wind buffeted him as he went.

No more shots sounded. But in the dark, someone was trailing him.

Tyne climbed off the ladder on to a narrow catwalk. Here was shelter. The architects responsible for the elaborate artificiality of this seaward façade had arched off this layer of it with a row of small, blind tunnels. If Murray was anywhere in the vicinity, the chances were that he would be here. As Tyne entered the first arch, a startled seabird clattered past his face, squawking. He stood quite still until his heart stopped jumping.

Then he began to move from one arch to the next, fumbling, looking for Murray. It was a nerve-racking business. Underfoot, a slippery mess of bird droppings made the going doubly perilous.

He had reached the third arch along when a watery moon slid

through for a moment. Glancing back over his shoulder, Tyne saw a figure climbing down the steps he had just left. Man or Rosk? and if man, was it Murray? Acting hurriedly but indecisively, Tyne swung round to face his pursuer. His foot slid across the slippery concrete, went over the edge.

Before he could save himself, Tyne had fallen from the catwalk. For an instant, his ten fingers, five steel, five painfully flesh, scraped safety; then he was dropping freely, plunging down towards the sea.

Dark water slammed up to meet him. He hit it shoulder first and went under. As he came up gasping, he saw he was inside the plankton mesh.

Someone seemed to be calling from a long way off. The rain beat down like a solid thing, raising slashes from the sea, so that the surface was impossible to define. Tyne choked down water as he swam for the wall.

Then over all the rest of the noise came a new one. It was low and continuous, the roar of a superhumanly angry bull. Tyne felt his legs caught, his progress halted, as if the sound itself had hold of him. He was being drawn underwater. Fighting, shouting, he realised what was happening. The plant's subterranean intake gates had opened. He was inside the screen. He was going to be turned into plankton juice.

Somewhere below him, sluices swung wide. The man was dragged under, over and over, swept into the throat of the great plant, helpless as a leaf in a storm. The last shreds of light and air were torn from his world.

v

The swamping pounding liquid registered on his tousled sense as sound: sound roaring him to death.

In the blundering blackness before Tyne's eyes, pictures squirmed like worms, sharing his agony. They were images of his past life bubbling up, scum-like, to the surface of his drowning brain. Incidents from his personal history returned to him, enfolding him as if to protect him from present pain. Then they were gone.

The bubble of the past had burst. His head was above water again. Exhaustedly, gulping down air, Tyne paddled to keep afloat in the racing water. Faint, reflected lights rode on the flood round him. He was somewhere inside the huge, automated plant, which was dimly lit by multicoloured guidelights here and there. The factory was cybernetically controlled, tenanted by robot devices. No one would save him if he could not save himself.

In the relief at finding his head above water, Tyne did not for a minute realise the grimness of his new predicament. He was simply content to float at the top of a rising tide of water, breathing and snorting painfully. Beyond thick glass, he could see the interior of the plant, where a shadowy file of processing tanks, moving by jerks, slowly revolved vats of jelly; endless pipes and presses marched into the background. He could see too, negligently, successive floors of the edifice sink from his gaze as the water lifted him up and up.

His mind snapped back into something like its normal degree of awareness. Searchingly, Tyne looked about. He had come up through the bottom of, and was now imprisoned in, a great glass tube with a diameter of some fifteen feet, standing a full six storeys high.

Peering through the glass, Tyne saw other giant tubes ranged alongside his, like the pipes of some overblown organ. The tubes stretched from base to roof of the plant, through all floors, and were filling rapidly with the incoming sea water.

Tyne looked up. The ceiling was growing closer. The tube was filling right up to the top.

This was inevitable. He knew immediately where he was. These entry tubes took each intake of water. When they were filled, great filter plungers came down from the top like slow pistons, filtering through the sea water, compressing plankton to the bottom of the tube; and not only plankton, but any other solid which happened to be there. Mercifully, Tyne Leslie would be dead by drowning before he was crushed against the bottom.

Between the turbulent water surface and the underside of the plunger, only some nine feet remained; the distance was decreasing rapidly.

Groaning, treading water, Tyne felt in his trouser pocket. The Rosk .88 was still there. Tearing it free, Tyne lifted it above the surface of the water.

Six feet left between him and the plunger.

He prayed that a man who had once told him that these weapons were unaffected by water had spoken the truth. Shaking it, he turned over on his back, floated, aimed at the glass imprisoning him.

Five feet of air above him.

He squeezed the trigger. As always with this incredible weapon, there was no recoil. The big slug shattered the tube up, down and sideways, converted it in a flash into a multitude of glass shards, a foot thick and some of them a couple of stories long. Tyne was swept at this fearsome barrier by the weight of released water.

It carried him right out into the factory. For a moment, a great gulf extending down into the bowels of the plant hung below him. Then he snatched at and clung to a balcony railing. His arms creaked at their sockets but he clung there. As though for an age, Tyne hung on; as though for an age, water and glass cascaded past him, a waterfall containing death. With a great effort he climbed over the rail to safety, hardly realising himself alive.

Another sound roused him, a sound easy to identify: a siren was wailing; directly he punctured the big tube, an automatic alarm had gone off.

To be caught in here would mean the end of everything. Forfeiting his freedom would entail losing the last chance of finding Murray, even the last chance of passing the vital information gained from Benda Ittai on to the proper authorities. Tyne got up, dripping, pushing the wet hair back from his eyes. He was on a catwalk; a couple of feet away, crates of processed plankton, now disguised as steaks and pâtés and spreads, moved briskly on a conveyor belt. And rapid footsteps sounded near at hand.

The dark was penetrated by widely spaced lights, some red, some orange, some blue. Peering through the gravy blackness in which swabs of light swam, Tyne saw a figure running round the catwalk towards him. Two figures! Whoever had pursued him outside, had managed to follow him into here. Someone with keys to the place.

'Leslie! Tyne Leslie!' a voice called.

It was magnified, distorted, made metallic, by the acoustics of the building; Tyne did not think he would have recognised it, even in more favourable circumstances. With sudden fear he felt convinced that the Rosks were after him. He jumped onto the conveyor belt.

He slipped, knocking a crate off the other side; the belt was travelling considerably faster than he had estimated. In some alarm, Tyne knelt up, staring back to see where his pursuer was. At that moment, he himself was borne under an orange light. Cursing lest he had given himself away, Tyne turned to see where he was being carried.

A low entrance loomed just ahead.

Involuntarily, Tyne ducked. At once, impenetrable darkness swallowed him. He was in a tunnel. His elbow hissed against a moving side wall, and he tucked it in hastily. He dared not raise his head. There was nothing to be done but crouch between crates.

The conveyor emerged suddenly into a packing bay. A robot loader under a bright light was pushing the crates shut when they filled. That was not for Tyne. He rolled off the belt just before the robot got to him.

There was no time to choose how he was going to drop. He fell painfully flat on the floor, picking himself up slowly and wearily. His watch told him that it was nearly 3.30 a.m. He should be in bed and asleep. He ached all over.

Even as he got to his feet, the conveyor exit ejected his two pursuers. They, apparently, knew better than Tyne what to expect; as they catapulted into the packing room, they jumped clear one after the other, landing nimbly on their feet. Before Tyne could make up his mind to move, they had collared him.

'Come on Leslie; let's get you out of here,' one of them said, holding tightly on to his arm.

They were masked.

Tyne could see nothing of their faces beyond their foreheads and their eyes.

'Who are you?' he asked feebly. 'Why the yashmak effect?'

'Explanation later,' one of the men said. 'Let's concentrate on getting you out of this building before half Padang arrives to investigate that alarm.'

The siren was shrilling as the men led Tyne down a couple of floors, unlocked a door with a

special key, and pushed him into the open. At an awkward jog trot, they hurried down a slope, their way intermittently lit by lightning. Although rain still fell, its force was hesitant now; the storm had worn itself out. Water gurgled down into storm drains beside their path.

A door stood at the end of the passage. The burlier of the two men, evidently the one in authority, produced another key, unlocked the door and flung it open.

They emerged behind an almost deserted car park, not far from the point at which Tyne had first tackled the building. Trotting across the puddle-strewn ground, they ran to an ancient model of a Moeweg, a German atomicar, the production of which had been banned by Company Earth some years earlier. Burly flung himself into the driver's seat as the others bundled into the back. He jerked the dipstick and they were moving at once.

As they accelerated past the front of the plant, the first car to answer the alarm call arrived from the opposite direction. It had a searchlight mounted on the roof; it was a police car. As the old Moeweg dashed by, a uniformed man leant out of the police car and bellowed to them to stop. Burly accelerated.

'Damn it, they'll have our number,' he said over his shoulder, to the man beside Tyne. 'We'll meet trouble as sure as eggs. I'm going to turn off before we hit traffic; this is no time to play questions and answers with a bunch of local cops.'

A fire engine dashed past them. A helicopter thundered overhead. Bright headlights through the trees indicated a stream of traffic heading round a bend for the scene of the alarm. Burly wrenched the dip; they slewed across the road and squealed into a narrow lane leading into jungle.

The lane had been intended for nothing bigger than a cowcart. Foliage whipped and smacked against the windows as the car lunged forward.

'It's crazy!' Tyne thought, 'all absolutely crazy!' He had time to wonder about the respect he had held for men of action. He had seen them as people at the equator of life, in the hottest spots, going round the fastest; he saw now it was true in only a limited sense. These people merely went in circles. One minute they were hunters, the next hunted. They made decisions rapidly, yet those decisions seemed based less on a rational understanding and interpretation of their opponent's motives than on a desire to keep hopping continually in an immense, indeterminate game.

A game! That was the secret of it all! These men of action could

152

enter a contest involving life and death only because once they had plunged in, the stakes became unreal. This was chess, played with adrenalin instead of the intellect. They had got beyond the ordinary rules of conduct.

The terrible thing was, Tyne found, that although he now saw this clearly enough, he too was caught in the game – voluntarily. World events had become too grave to be treated seriously. One could escape from all their implications by sinking into this manic sub-world of action, where blood and bluff ruled. By the same token, he saw the pendulum which ruled the sub-world sliding back in his favour. These men had caught Tyne when he was unprepared; now that he was in their hands, he could be relaxed but alert; in a sense, he had no care; they had the worries. When this pressure grew to a certain pitch, they would become in their turn unprepared – and he would elude them. It was inevitable, just a rule in the crazy game. After that, of course, the big pendulum would swing the other way again.

'This is far enough,' Burly said, when the Moeweg had rocked and staggered some hundreds of yards into the jungle. The man beside Tyne never uttered a word.

The car stopped, and with an effort Tyne brought his attention back to the present. His mind had been busily elaborating his theory – even giving it some such half jocular title as Leslie's Principle of Reciprocal Action, or the Compensatory Theory of Irresponsible Activity (Leslie's Effect) – with the same attention it had once devoted to preliminary drafts of official memoranda.

Burly flicked off the headlights, so that only the dash light illuminated them. Outside, the rain had stopped, though the foliage overhead still dripped meditatively on to the car roof. It was 4.15, a numb, light-headed time of night.

'All right,' Tyne said, 'now suppose you tell me who you are, what you're doing, and why you think you're doing it?'

Removing the cloth which had covered the lower part of his face, Burly turned in his seat to look at Tyne.

'First of all,' he said, in a gentle, educated voice, 'we ought to apologise for virtually kidnapping you like this, Mr Leslie. Time pressed, and we had no alternative. I ought perhaps to add – forgive me – that none of this would have been necessary if you had waited for us to explain when we caught you up on the façade of the plankton plant. Your dive into the sea was spectacular but unnecessary.'

'I didn't dive,' Tyne said, wryly. 'I slipped.'

Abruptly, Burly burst into laughter. Tyne found himself joining

153

in. The tension eased considerably. The masked man beside Tyne never moved.

'This is the situation,' Burly said. 'My name, by the way, is Dickens – Charles Dickens. No relation, of course. I am working with the man you know as Stobart, the CoE agent; his second-in-command, as it were. You have been missing now for some hours, and we frankly were worried. You see, your role in this affair is an ambiguous one; we naturally like to know where you are.'

'Naturally. What made you look for me at the plankton plant?' Tyne inquired. 'Or shouldn't I ask?'

'We weren't looking for you,' Dickens said. 'We just happened to be searching the place at the time you came along. Like you, we were hoping to find Murray Mumford there.'

'How did you know I was still looking for Murray?'

'You called his name, remember? For another thing, Mina, Murray's woman, told you to go there. *She* told you Murray had said he would be at the plankton plant.'

Tyne suddenly fell silent. Dickens' words brought back a vital memory to him, something that he had recalled during those terrible moments of drowning in the plant. The memory gave him the key to Murray's whereabouts; he must get away from Dickens and his silent partner as soon as he had as much information as possible from them. Dragging his mind back to the present, he asked, 'How did you find out about Mina, Dickens?'

'Stobart found out. He questioned her after you'd left him. We've not been sitting down doing nothing.'

'Don't talk to me about Stobart. There's a man who should learn a few manners before he mixes with people.'

'Stobart is something of a psychologist,' Dickens said. 'He deliberately made his advice to you to stop looking for Murray so unpalatable that you would ignore it.'

Tyne smiled to himself. These boys thought they had all the answers. What they did not know was that he had, in fact, already stopped looking for Murray when the. Rosk picked him up in the taxi. Stobart could stuff that up his psychology.

'So Stobart wanted me as a stooge,' he said. 'Why?'

'You were just one of his impromptu ideas. The Rosks had him cornered in the Roxy when you arrived. You were a diversion to draw them away. Actually, you were doubly useful. After the Rosks had taken you out to their ketch –'

'What!' Tyne exploded. Suddenly he was furiously angry. The silent man beside him placed a restraining hand on his arm, but

154

Tyne knocked it off with his steel fist. 'You mean you people knew about that ketch? Yet you let it stay there? You let me be tortured – well, I was nearly tortured there. You let that thug of Ap II Dowl's, Budo Budda, come and go there as he pleased? And all the time you *knew* about the ketch and could have blown it out of the water? Isn't it infringing the interplanetary agreement by being there?'

'Don't get excited. We didn't know you were taken to the ship; the Rosks picked you up too quickly for that – you weren't half awake, Leslie! We were waiting for big game; Ap II Dowl is to visit that ketch in the early hours of this morning. By now, in fact, we should have trapped him there. If we can get him in the bag, many of Earth's troubles will be over.'

'You don't know how many troubles she's got,' Tyne said grimly. 'She's about to be attacked by an Alpha II invasion fleet. That's the cheering news Murray carried round with him.'

'We know.'

'You know! How do you know?'

'We have means, Mr Leslie; leave it at that.'

As Dickens spoke, a buzzer sounded. A radio telephone glowed on the Moeweg's dashboard, Dickens picked it up, listened, spoke into it in a low voice; Tyne caught his own name being mentioned.

'Can't you ever think of a word to say?' he asked the man sitting next to him. The other shrugged his shoulders and made no answer.

Suddenly Dickens thrust the phone down and swore luridly. He cursed with vigour and a vinegary wit, making it as obscene as possible. It was a startling display, coming from him.

'Leslie, you've properly buggered things up,' he said, swinging round in the car seat. 'That was Stobart calling. He says you were marooned on a small island called Achin Itu until about ten o'clock this evening – that is, yesterday evening. They found your monogrammed mescahale lighter on the beach. Is that a fact?'

'I'd like that lighter back; it cost me fifty chips. Tell Stobart, will you?'

'Listen, Leslie, you shot up that Rosk Colonel, Budda. Do you know what you've done? You scared Ap II Dowl away! When he got wind of Budda's death, he stayed tight in the base. Our fellows raided the ketch an hour back, while you were playing tag over the plankton plant, and got nothing but a lot of useless information.'

'Don't blame me, Dickens. Call it one of my impromptu ideas, eh? Any time one of Stobart's plans go wrong, give me the word; I find I get a thrill out of hearing about it.'

'You're coming back to Padang with me, Leslie, right away. We're going to lock you up until you learn not to make a nuisance of yourself.'

'Oh, no you don't!' Tyne said, half-getting out of his seat. Something hard pressed against his side. He looked down. The silent partner was digging in with a revolver, his eyes unwavering behind the mask. Dickens switched the car headlights on again as Tyne sat back helplessly in his seat.

'That's right, relax,' Dickens said. 'From now on, you're living at the government's expense.'

'But I've got a hunch about finding Murray,' Tyne said. 'I swear to you, Dickens, I may be able to go straight to him. You still want him, don't you?'

'We'd trade in Company Earth Building for him,' Dickens said quietly, starting the engine. 'But things are too complex for you, feller. There's no room outside for amateurs just at present; you've done enough damage. Here's another thing you didn't know. Have you paused to wonder why the Rosks couldn't slip a roll of microfilm smaller than your little finger from Luna to Earth themselves? There's a reason why they got Murray to carry it. It's stolen from the Rosks.'

'You mean the Rosks stole the film from the Rosks?'

'Yes; that's what I said and what I mean. Ever heard of the Roskian peace faction, the RPF, led by Tawdell Co Barr? They're a small and semi-illegal organisation of Rosks ranged against Ap II Dowl and pledged to work for peace with Earthmen. Their numbers are few. In Luna Area 101 there can't be more than a handful of them. But they managed to get their hands on this film, and of course they want it to reach the main body of RPF in the Sumatran base here. I fancy it'll be used for propaganda purposes, to show the Rosks what a blood-thirsty maniac Dowl is.

'I tell you this so that you can see why the situation is too complex for you; it comes in layers, like an onion.'

Even as he spoke, Dickens was wrestling with the car. The wheels spun in mud but did not move. While they waited here for the alarm on the main road to die down, the heavy vehicle had sunk into the soft track. Tyne scarcely noticed what was happening as he mulled over what Dickens had told him. It threw new light on at least one Rosk: the girl, Benda Ittai, who had saved his life.

'Have you ever heard of Benda Ittai?' Tyne asked. Speaking her name aloud filled him with an unexpected pleasure.

'We're bogged down, damn it,' Dickens said. 'Oh, how I love

Sumatra! Benda Ittai is evidently one of the RPF. Stobart's men found her on the ketch when they raided it. The Rosks were about to put her to death. Under the circumstances, our men found it best to let her go free; I tell you, Stobart has a soft heart – I'd have locked her up. Damn this filthy, soggy country! I can understand how they get volunteers for lunar duty. Yes, if I had my way, I'd clap her in prison; I'd clap all of you – look, I'm getting out to put something under the wheels. Leslie, if you try to escape, my friend will shoot you in the leg. It's painful. Do by all means try it and see.'

He climbed out, leaving his door swinging open. His feet squelched in the wet grass, and he steadied himself against the Moeweg's bonnet.

Tyne's heart thudded. He wondered if he stood a chance of overpowering the fellow beside him. Dickens was visible through the windscreen, bathed in bright light which only emphasised the sad waiting darkness of the forest on either side. The agent had produced a small sheath knife and was hacking at the thick fronds of a bush, throwing them under the car's front wheels.

Then something else was moving out there. It came swishing in from the treetops with a vibrant humming. Bushes and twigs writhed and cringed; everything seemed to turn alive at its approach.

Dickens straightened and saw it. Beautifully in control of himself, he dropped the foliage he had cut and reached for a holstered gun without a second's pause. As his hand came up, he fired two shots at the thing, then turned and leapt into the Moeweg, slamming the door shut behind him. Furiously, he made a fresh attempt to extricate the car from the mud. The flying thing charged at them, bowling in from the bending darkness.

'What the devil is it?' Tyne asked, 'One of ours, I hope.' He began to sweat. His ears jarred with the noise the thing made.

'It's a Rosk flyspy,' Dickens said, without turning his head. 'Sort of flying eye. Reports all it sees back to Rosk base. I've seen a captured one back at HQ. They're unarmed but definitely not harmless. Mind it doesn't – ah!'

They jerked forward a foot then fell back again, their wheels failing to grip. The flyspy hovered then dropped almost to ground level. Tyne saw it clearly now. It was a fat disc perhaps five feet in diameter and two feet six at its greatest width. Lenses of varying size studded its rim and undersurface. An inset searchlight swivelled a blinding beam of light at them.

Rotors probably mounted on a gyroscope powered the machine. They set up the humming note making the bushes in their vicinity move uneasily as if trying to escape observation. The rotors were set inside the disc protected by fine mesh from possible damage.

It moved forward suddenly. Even as Dickens instinctively ducked the flyspy struck their windscreen, shattering it into tiny fragments, Dickens swore ripely.

'The Rosk base isn't far from here!' he shouted. 'Just a few miles through the jungle. If this thing has identified us it may be planning to wreck the car – to hold us up till a Rosk patrol can get at us. Cover your face up, Leslie – don't let it see who you are!'

The flyspy had lifted. It hovered somewhere above the vehicle. They couldn't see it, but they could hear it, the venomous note of a hornet, amplified. All the leaves near the car waved furiously, enduring their own private storm. Tyne was tying a handkerchief round his face when Dickens flung the engine into reverse. Bucking wildly, the old Moeweg heaved itself out of the pit it had gouged for itself. At once the flyspy returned to the attack. With a slicing movement, it sped down and struck one of the rear side windows. It did not retreat, just stayed there pushing, huge through the shattered glass, its lens seeming to sparkle with malice. The car lurched, the coach-work crumpled.

The silent agent scrambled up on to the seat, taking pot shots through the broken window. His forehead was grey and patchy above his mask.

'Aim at its rotors through the mesh!' Dickens bellowed. 'That's the only way you'll knock it out!'

They were speeding recklessly backwards down the jungle track. Dickens drove looking over his shoulder, dipstick in one hand, gun in the other.

'That thing can squash you if you try to run for it,' he said. 'Squash you flat against the ground.'

'I wasn't planning to jump out,' Tyne replied. He had just been planning to jump out.

As he spoke, the silent man flung open his door, hanging out to get a better shot into the middle of the flyspy's works. The thing reared up immediately into the branches overhead – and crashed down into one of the back wheels. The Moeweg skidded sideways into the bushes and stopped, engine bellowing uselessly.

Tyne hardly paused to think. He knew they were trapped now. This thing could batter the car apart if it was so directed.

The dumb agent had been pitched onto the ground by the skid.

Leaping through the open door, Tyne jumped on to him, snatched his gun and lunged into the undergrowth. He dived into the bushes recklessly, doubled up, doing anything to get away. Moving on hands and knees, he charged forward, heedless of any cuts or tears he sustained. Shots sounded behind him; he did not know if Dickens was firing at him or the flyspy.

He travelled fast. He tumbled into a little overgrown stream and was out in a flash. The faintest light, perhaps the first light of dawn, aided him.

He knew what to do. He was heading for a belt of thick trees with low branches. The flyspy had severe limitations, for all its power. Dense foliage would stop it.

Tyne was on his feet now, running doubled up. He no longer knew which way he was running. That deep, determined humming sounded behind him. A light flickered and swam among the leaves, as the searchlight sought him out. The leaves writhed. Where were the damned trees?

Blowing hard, he pounded through chest-high vegetation. It seemed endless.

Now he bounded down a bushy slope, plunged into a line of trees, tore himself free of brambles. When he tripped a minute later, he could hardly get up. Looking wearily above his head, he saw against the dark sky a protecting network of branches. The smaller branches waved in an artificial wind.

Panting, Tyne lay there like a trapped animal.

All he could do, he had done. He hadn't imagined it would come after him; he had thought it would stay by the car and the two CoE agents. But . . . if its transmissions back to Rosk base had caused him to be identified there as the Earthman to whom Benda Ittai had spoken, then there was good reason for his being the quarry.

The leaves and grasses trembled about him. The resonant hum filled his ears. Jumping up like a frightened stag, Tyne flung himself into one of the trees. Pulling himself up, he hauled himself ten, fifteen feet above ground, hugging the trunk among a welter of stout, out-thrusting branches.

Seeing was better now. First light drifted like sludge through the trees. The slope he had run down lay in one direction, a fast river in the other. On the other side of the river lay what looked like a track.

The flyspy had seen him. It swooped in low, cutting above the ground, its light probing. It could not rise to him because of the branches; they shielded him as he had hoped. Instead, the machine nuzzled lightly against the tree bole. For the first time, looking down on it, Tyne saw its big fans, revolving in a whirl behind protective gratings. He fired at them with the agent's gun. His arm shook, the shot went wild.

The machine backed away and butted the tree. Then it circled out, seeking another way to get at him. Almost at the same time, Tyne became aware of Dickens, running down the slope. Following the flyspy's noise, the agent had followed Tyne.

Branches cracked. The flyspy was pushing through twigs and light branches on a level with Tyne. Tyne slid round the other side of the trunk. If he could only hold out till full daylight, this thing would be bound to go home or else risk detection. He squinted down below but Dickens had disappeared.

Again he changed position, to keep the tree's girth between himself and the machine. This meant slipping down to a lower branch. He must beware of being forced all the way down; on the ground he was defenceless. The thing droned angrily, like an immense spinning top, pushing persistently through a maze of twigs. It worked to one side; again Tyne worked away from it.

Suddenly there was a shout, and the sound of shoes kicking steel.

Tyne looked round the tree, peering out like a squirrel.

Dickens had jumped or fallen on to the flyspy! The agent had climbed the next tree and then launched himself, or dropped outwards. Now he sprawled on top of the disc, fighting to get a grasp of it.

'Dickens!' Tyne yelled.

The agent slithered over the rocking surface of the flyspy. His legs dangled, kicking wildly in air. Then he caught a finger hold in the machine's central mesh and drew himself into a more secure position. As the flyspy rocked among the branches, he pulled his gun out, aiming it at the rotor blades.

All this had obviously taken the Rosks who controlled the big disc completely by surprise. It just drifted where it was, helplessly. Then it moved. Its pervasive note changing pitch, it shot up like an express lift.

Dickens was knocked flat by a bough. Partially stunned, he slithered once more over the side, and his gun went flying – clatter-clattering all the way from branch to branch down to the ground.

'Jump, Dickens, for God's sake!' Tyne shouted.

It was doubtful if the agent heard a word of it. He was carried

160

up through the foliage, hanging on grimly, head half-buried in his arms. The last leaves swished by, and the flyspy was out in the open, climbing slowly.

Heedlessly, Tyne jumped from the tree to sprawl full length in a flowering bush. Picking himself up, he broke from the trees, running along below the flyspy, shouting incoherently. He dared not fire in case he hit Dickens.

In the vapid early morning light, the disc was clearly visible thirty feet up, heading fast on an unswerving course that would, Tyne guessed, take it back to Sumatran base, where the Rosks awaited it. Dickens had evidently had the same thought. He knelt on top of the thing, wrenching at the screens on its upper surface. In a moment, he had unlatched a segment of screen, a wedge-shaped bit that left the rotors revolving nakedly underneath.

He wrenched his shoe off and flung it into the rotors.

At once the dynamic hum changed into a violent knocking. From the knocking grew the mirthless squeal of metal breaking up. With a few staccato grinding sounds, the flyspy began to fall, canting sharply.

Tyne was still running when it crashed into the river he had noticed earlier, bearing its passenger with it. They disappeared with a splash and did not come up again.

VI

It was 9.15 in the morning.

Tyne Leslie sat at the back of a Chinese coffee shop, eating durian off a plastic plate. His cheeks were smooth, his head was clear; he had been to a nappi wallah who had shaved him and massaged his head and shoulders. When he had finally plodded into Padang, ninety minutes ago, after a fruitless search along the river bank for Dickens, he had felt half-dead. Now, after a shave, the massage and breakfast, he was alive again, alert, planning ahead, casting little feelers of worry into the future.

Already he had written a note to Under-Secretary Grierson, a secretary to whose under-secretary Tyne had been, outlining that threat of invasion to Earth. That note had been delivered to the British Diplomatic Mission building, and would be before the Under-Secretary himself within an hour. How long it would be before any action was taken on it was another matter.

Meanwhile time grew short. Murray had been at large in Padang for twenty-four hours. If the Roskian RPF agent had been unable to reach Murray, it would be because he had been dogged by his own people, the Rosks faithful to Ap II Dowl. Undoubtedly though, the parties interested in finding Murray were closing in: RPF, Dowl's men, the CoE, and possibly – undoubtedly, if they had wind of the affair – various nationally interested Earth groups. And Tyne.

And Tyne. He had told Dickens he was prepared to go straight to Murray. It was the truth. By a paradox, he could have done as much yesterday, before Stobart spoke to him.

The truth had lain, as so often happens, inside him, waiting for the ripe moment to reveal itself.

When Tyne questioned Mina in the Roxy foyer, she said that Murray had announced he was going to the plankton plant. She had assumed – and Tyne had unthinkingly accepted her assumption – that Murray meant the plant at Semapang, where he had nearly drowned himself. When Stobart had questioned the girl later, he had got the same answer; that was why Tyne and Dickens had met at the building.

But Murray had meant something quite different when he spoke of the plankton plant.

In those terrible seconds when Tyne was dragged drowning through the submarine intakes at Semapang, scenes from his past life had bubbled through his mind. One scene had been of Murray, Allan Cunliffe and himself breakfasting at the Merdeka Hotel after a heavy night. While he and Allan sat drinking coffee, Murray tucked in to a large breakfast, complaining all the time about the badness of the food. 'It's always synthetic at the Merdeka,' he said. 'Doesn't matter what the food resembles, it's really plankton underneath. As the Americans say, it's a plant. A plankton plant! I tell you dreary-looking couple of so-and-sos, we live in a plankton plant. Before you know it, the management will be offering us plankton women . . .'

The comments had stuck. From then on, the three of them had occasionally referred to the Merdeka as 'the plankton plant'; it had been a private joke between them, until they tired of it.

All of this had run through Tyne's drowning mind. He knew now that to find Murray he had to go to the Merdeka again; that was the place Murray had been referring to. Mina had been misled; so had Stobart; naturally enough, for they had never heard the old private joke. Tyne had been once, fruitlessly, to the Merdeka; today, he was going to ask the right questions of the right people.

Settling his bill, he left the cafe. He had already purchased a spare clip of ammunition for the stolen gun in his pocket. Now he moved through side streets, warily, alert for danger. A protest march of the displaced, complete with drums and banners ('ROSKS LEAVE OUR WORLD TO PEACE'. 'WORLD POWERS ARE DUPES OF ALIENS'. 'SUMATRA HAS BEEN SACRIFICED!'), acted as convenient cover as Tyne slipped into the foyer of the hotel.

The familiarity, at once welcome and repugnant, of the place assailed him like a pervasive fog. At this hour, before Padang's political life, with its endless conferences and discussions, was under way, the lounge was full of the sort of men Tyne had been: restless, wretched (but smiling) men who continually manoeuvred, but never manoeuvred boldly enough. Tyne skirted them, feeling as alien to them as a Rosk might have done.

He went through the building into the rear courtyard, where two very ancient Chinese ladies were combing each other's hair in the sunshine.

'Have you seen Amir, please?' Tyne asked.

'He is at the warehouse, checking the rations.'

The 'warehouse' was a rundown building beyond the courtyard, tucked between other buildings and conveniently facing a small back lane. Outside it stood a little delivery van, labelled in Malayan, Chinese and English, 'Semapang Plankton Processed Foodstuffs.' The Merdeka was getting its daily quota of nourishment.

As Tyne approached, a uniformed driver emerged from the warehouse, climbed into the van and drove off. Tyne went stealthily to the warehouse door. Amir was there alone, left arm in a sling, leaning over a box checking delivery notes. Tyne entered, closing the door behind him.

Amir had been something of a friend of Allan's and Tyne's. Now there was only fear on his dark, intelligent face as he looked up and recognised his visitor.

'What have you done to your arm, Amir?'

'I thought you were dead, Mr Leslie!'

'Who told you that?'

'You should not be here! It is dangerous here, Mr Leslie! The Merdeka is always being watched. Please go away at once. For everyone's safety, go away!'

His agitation was painful to watch. Tyne took his good arm and said: 'Listen, Amir, if you know there is danger, you must know something of what is happening. The lives of everyone on Earth are threatened. I have to find Murray Mumford at once. At once! Do you know where he is?'

To his surprise and embarrassment, the young Sumatran began to weep. He made no noise or fuss about it; the tears rolled down his cheeks and fell on to the clean floor. He put up a hand to cover his eyes.

'So much trouble has been caused my country by other countries. Soon I shall join the Displaced. Company Earth is revealed as an illusory hope. When our numbers are big enough, we shall force all foreigners to leave our land.'

'And the Rosks,' Tyne added.

'*All foreigners*. Do you know there is a funeral to be held this evening, at the Bukit Besar? Do you know whose funeral it is? The half-Dutch girl, Mina.'

'Mina! She's dead?' exclaimed Tyne.

'That is generally the reason for funerals,' said Amir caustically. 'The Rosks killed her because she slept with your friend Mumford. Perhaps you will be interested to hear that the Rosks came for me yesterday; they tortured me. Perhaps today they will come back to kill me. You came to the Merdeka yesterday and I avoided you. Today I have not avoided you, and I shall probably die.'

'Nonsense, Amir, take a grip of yourself! The Rosks won't want you again,' Tyne said. 'What did they ask you yesterday?'

Amir stopped crying as suddenly as he had begun. Looking Tyne straight in the eye, he pulled his bandaged arm from its sling and began to unwrap it. In a minute he produced it, exposing it with a penetrating mixture of horror and pride.

'The Rosks asked me where Murray Mumford is hiding,' Amir said. 'Because I did not tell them, this is what they did to me.'

His left hand had been amputated at the wrist. Grafted on in its place, hanging limply, uselessly, was a chimpanzee's paw.

Tyne's own artificial left hand clenched convulsively in sympathetic pain.

'I'm sorry,' he said. 'I'm sorry, Amir.'

'This is how they think of man.'

He turned away, clumsily rebandaging his limb, and added in a choked voice, 'But I did not tell them where Murray is. You I can tell. When he came here early yesterday morning, he said he was going to hide in the old Deli Jalat temple, down the lane. Now please go. Go and do not ever ask me anything again.'

'I'm truly sorry,' Tyne said, pausing by the door. 'This'll be made up to you one day, Amir. Wait and see.'

Amir did not turn round. 'I can tell another thing. Mina once lived with her family happily in a kampong where is now Rosk base.

164

She was Displaced, her life destroyed. So she become prostitute. Is bad, bad . . .'

*

Outside, Tyne leapt straight over a low stone wall and crouched there with his gun out. Amir had given him a bigger shaking than he cared to admit to himself. Slowly he raised his head and looked about.

One or two natives were busy about the few dwellings facing on to the little back street into which he had emerged; none of them seemed to be interested in Murray. High over their heads, over the seedy local buildings, loomed the bright steel towers of New Padang. He realised a bitter truth in what Amir had said. To the local population, the visiting nations which had descended upon Sumatra were as troublesome as the Rosks. The Rosks owed their ability to travel easily beyond their perimeter to a typically Eastern indifference to two forms of exploitation. For all Company Earth's fine words, and the compensation paid by the Sumatra Company Government, the lower members of society had suffered grievously.

As Tyne was about to climb back over the wall, a man appeared from the direction of the Merdeka. He walked slowly as befitted his bulk, his eyes guardedly casting to left and right. It was Stobart.

He was walking away from the direction in which the Deli Jalat temple stood. When he saw the road was empty, he quickened his pace. As Tyne sank back into concealment, Stobart produced a whistle, raised to his lips, blew it. No audible sound emerged; it was ultrasonic – no doubt a summoning of forces.

Directly the Company agent had gone, Tyne hopped back over the low wall and headed in the direction of the temple, where Murray had told Amir he was going to hide. The settlement with Murray was coming; in Tyne's pocket, the loaded gun felt reassuringly heavy.

Despite the hot sun on his shoulders, icy clarity seized him. He knew exactly what he was going to do. He was going to kill Murray.

Only one thing worried him, and he wasn't going to let that spoil his aim. Murray, waiting with his microfilm to meet the RPF agent, had covered his tracks well; the glimpse of Stobart (who had no doubt picked up Tyne's trail in the Merdeka lounge) was a token he was still at large, despite the none too scrupulous powers ranged against him. Yet Tyne, working alone, was on the point of finding him. Why?

165

Two pieces of information had led Tyne to Murray: Mina's information about the 'plankton plant'; and from there, Amir's about the temple. Both Company and, presumably, Rosk had got the same lead from Mina; neither had got anything from Amir. Mina's information was capable of correct interpretation *only by Tyne*; Amir had said his piece voluntarily *only to Tyne*. Why?

One answer emerged. Murray had expected Tyne to pursue him. Before going into hiding, he had left those two messages with Mina and Amir deliberately, *knowing Tyne would follow them up*. Yet Murray would realise Tyne could have only one reason for following: to avenge Allan Cunliffe's death on the Moon. And the motives a man might have for silently, deviously, beckoning his murderer towards him remained notably obscure. And seductively obscure.

Murray must be made to explain before the stolen gun and the bought bullets had their way with him. He must explain – and of course he must yield up the vital microfilm; then he could die. Tyne experienced that touch of ice-cold clarity again. Once more he was right in the torrid zone of events. The equator of action whirled faster and faster about him; yet he could not feel a thing.

'Come in, sir. I will make inquiry about your friend from the priests,' the wizened dwarf at the teak gate said. He pattered away on bare feet, crabbed and eager. Fallen women and white tuans especially welcome.

The Deli Jalat temple stood decaying in several acres of ground which were littered with past attempts to start chicken farms and scrap heaps. The central building was a not ignoble imitation of a late Hindu temple, highly ornamented, but round it had collected, like smashed cars round a road obstruction, a number of later erections, most of them flimsy affairs of lath or corrugated iron. These had never been immaculate; now they were merely tumble-down. No doubt all would be swept away next week, to make way for new high-rise offices.

Unwilling to wait where he was bidden, Tyne moved over grass-encircled stones after the gatekeeper. In the air lingered an enchantingly sweet-sharp smell, a scent that seemed to carry with it its own unidentifiable emotion. There was a spice garden – grown out of hand, no doubt! close by. Turning a corner, Tyne came on a ramshackle covered way. At the far end, a woman in a Chinese dress, with clacking wooden soles on her feet, turned to look at him, then ran through a doorway. It looked like – yes, it had looked like Benda Ittai. Instinctively, Tyne increased his pace, sunlight jogging up and down on his shoulders.

He had a sudden cheering image of taking her into the deserted spice garden, of making love to her there. It was not a picture he had intended. He turned his thoughts to Murray.

At the last door, the gatekeeper almost fell upon him with excitement, waving his arms anxiously.

'No sir, not here, sir! Stop by the gate, sir. Previously I ask you to wait. The priests will not be prepared –'

'I've not come to see the priests,' Tyne said. Pushing the man aside, he stepped in, into the shade inside the building. It was as if the sunlight had rattled up like a blind, showing the room behind it: a cool room, all wood, except for two big stone vases in the middle of the floor. Three men, priests, with that vindictive, forward-leaning air that religion implants in the elderly, came forward at once.

'Please take me to Murray Mumford. I cannot wait,' Tyne said.

'This is not a suitable hour,' one of them said, ineffectually waving his hands.

'I'm sorry I cannot wait.'

The three priests broke into a dialect, chattering rapidly to each other. They were frightened and angry. Fright won.

'Better to follow me,' one of them said, beckoning querulously at Tyne.

He led the way up broad and creaking stairs, on which a smell of cats floated. They passed down corridors of wood and corridors of stone, finally stopping by an insignificant door below another staircase. The priest unbarred this door and opened it. A short anteroom was revealed beyond, with two doors leading from it.

'Try the right door,' suggested the priest.

As Tyne stepped inside, the priest slammed the door behind him. Left suddenly in semi-darkness, he moved carefully over to the right-hand door; steadying himself, levelling the gun, he flung the door open.

It was a long, narrow room with a dirty window at one end. Occupying most of the space near the door was a wooden bed, now in use as a table and seat combined.

Benda Ittai, in a Chinese dress, stood alone in the middle of the room, her mouth slightly open in a *moue* of surprise.

'Come in, Mr Todpuddle,' she said, using the name Tyne had assumed when interrogated on Budo Budda's ketch.

He nodded to her, as if in brief acknowledgement of her beauty.

His hackles up, Tyne took one step inside the room. Murray Mumford stood behind the door, his hands raised above his head. Round his waist he wore a Space Service belt; a revolver protruded from its unbuttoned holster.

Tyne swung slowly on his heel, bringing his own revolver up to cover Murray's chest. He was aware of his face, stiff as leather, contorted into a killer's grin.

'Glad you finally made it, Tyne,' Murray said, with a fair attempt at his old manner. 'Put your gun away and make yourself at home. Welcome to my humble –'

'Move over by the girl,' Tyne said in a rasping whisper. 'And I'll have your gun. Keep your hands raised. You're scum, Mumford – a betrayer, a traitor.'

'If you hadn't got that toy in your hand I'd break your neck for saying that,' Murray said evenly, his cheeks colouring darkly.

'No, you wouldn't! Are you suggesting you aren't carrying information for the Rosks – information absolutely vital to Earth?'

Murray, keeping his hands raised, looked at Tyne straightly as he shuffled over towards Benda. His roughly handsome face looked tired and shadowy.

'If you want to discuss it, throw both the guns up on that high shelf,' he said.

The shelf he referred to ran along one wall by the ceiling. Tyne

168

never even glanced at it. He had the two of them together now, standing awkwardly by the foot of the bed.

'I don't want to discuss anything with you, Murray,' he said.

'Go ahead and shoot me, then. But you probably realise as well as I do that one fool move like that and everything is lost.'

'Give me that spool of microfilm, Murray.'

'I've not got it!'

Tyne jerked his revolver convulsively. That he had not expected.

'Stop!' Benda Ittai made a nervous move forward. Though haggard, she still looked impressively cool and beautiful. 'There is no time for quarrels, or we may be trapped here. Mr Leslie, put both of the guns on the shelf and then we can explain to you. It is really necessary.'

Tyne hesitated. He was in an awkward spot and he knew it. The vital matter was not his personal urge for revenge, but the need to get the film. The Rosk woman at least made it possible for him to back down without losing too much face. Roughly, he snatched Murray's revolver from its holster and threw it up on the shelf with his own.

'Better,' Murray said, lowering his hands and fumbling for mescahales. Tyne noted with satisfaction how those hands trembled as they lit the tube. His own hands – even his steel one – were trembling in the same way.

Taking the initiative again, he said to Benda, 'I assume from your presence here that you are the Rosk agent Murray was told to meet?'

She said: 'That is correct; as you know, I was held up.' She smiled slightly, with satisfaction at the understatement.

Murray said: 'You guess right; now stop guessing and listen to me. We may have very little time and we need your help.'

'My help!' Tyne exploded. 'I came here to kill you, Murray, by God, and now you tell me –'

Benda Ittai laid her hand on Tyne's arm. It felt soft and hot. 105.1, of course.

Suddenly he had a vision of how it would be to make love to such a woman.

'Please give him a chance to explain!' she begged. 'Don't talk so much: listen! Just listen!'

'Yes, sound advice to an ex-politician!' Murray said. He was quickly getting control of himself. Tyne also savagely, wildly, took control of himself, sat on the edge of the plank bed and took a mescahale from Murray.

'Make it good,' he said. 'Make it very good.'

'The microfilm must be handed to Miss Ittai,' Murray said, 'and she must get it to Sumatra base, to the RPF there. Remember Tawdell Co Barr, the first Rosk to speak to Earth? He's the Peace Faction leader, opposing Ap II Dowl. The RPF is weak; here is the one last chance to strengthen them to the point where they might overthrow Dowl. If they could show this microfilm, this proof of Dowl's unscrupulous methods, to a majority of the Rosks, the population would rise and rebel against the dictator.'

'Our people are as human as yours,' Benda broke in. 'Please see this terrible business as a moral struggle rather than a detective game. When their eyes are opened to what is going on behind their backs, all my people will surely rise against Dowl.'

'You're trying to tell me they don't know they're merely the advance party of an invasion?'

'Of course they don't. Can't you see,' she said desperately, 'we were all born on the ship, thinking ourselves colonists. There must have been sealed orders passed down from one generation of the officer class to the next.'

'I see,' Tyne said. He did see; this is how political manoeuvres must be carried out anywhere in the galaxy. The leaders plotted, and the rest followed like sheep – unless they could be roused to see that only muttonhood awaited them.

'You already have proof that I am no friend of Ap II Dowl and his ruffians,' Benda said, speaking quietly, probably conscious of the effect she had upon Tyne. 'Therefore trust me. Let me take the microfilm to my people, the RPF. There it will be used to more effect than if Company Earth got it. Can you see that?'

Yes, it was all clear enough, Tyne thought bitterly, knowing the other two were searching his face for a clue in advance to what he was going to say. He did not know what he was going to say. The issue – get the microfilm or bust! – had disintegrated as he approached it. Now he was faced with as ticklish a problem as ever he had met across the highly polished tables of Company Earth.

If he did nothing – say, if he were shot – Under-Secretary Grierson would start the machinery grinding. The small Rosk force on Earth would be crushed before reinforcements arrived. And when they did arrive? Why, they would presumably be merciless: nuclear bombardment from space did not bear thinking of.

If Stobart and his men arrived here, they of course would take the microfilm without delay; they would find it wherever it was concealed. It would never go near a Rosk again. That move would also entail an immediate counter-attack against the perfidious alien within the gates.

If Ap II Dowl's men arrived here first – well, that was obviously the worst alternative of all.

At present, however, the initiative was not with Grierson, Stobart or Dowl; it was with Tyne. Fleetingly, he remembered the Theory of Irresponsible Activity he had formulated; he must have been light-headed at the time. Here he was faced with the weightiest problem of all time; how was he to resolve it for what would ultimately prove the best?

Turning towards the window, he gazed irritably out through the dusty panes, to hide his indecision from Murray and the girl. In the bright landscape outside, something moved. A man – or a Rosk – had dodged from one clump of bushes to another. Tyne's time was running low.

Abruptly, he turned back into the dull room. The RPF ought to have knowledge of the invasion plans, as Benda suggested; the more dissension sown in Sumatran Base, the better. Equally, Earth must have the details; then, they could be prepared for eventualities.

'A copy must be made of the microfilm, Miss Ittai,' he said. 'The Company will keep the copy to study. You will then be given safe conduct to slip back into your base with the original, to hand over to Tawdell Co Barr.'

He turned to Murray, sitting now on the edge of the bed, stubbing out his mescahale.

'As you observed, time is short,' he said. 'Give me the microfilm quickly.'

'You don't seem to take a point too well,' Murray said. He rubbed his eyes, looking tired and irritable: it was as if he had suddenly realised that whether he personally triumphed now or not, life would ultimately triumph over him – impersonally, of course, but with as little remorse as if the issue were a personal one! 'Lord Almighty, Tyne, isn't it obvious to you what a fool you are being? As I told you, I haven't got the microfilm.'

The bent figures running behind bushes – they would be straightening up now, perhaps making a last dash for the temple. And there was Allan Cunliffe, permanently straightened up, stiff as a stick. The two images, spears of urgency and anger, struck at Tyne's mind. He flung himself at Murray.

Murray got half up, then fell back under the assault. They crashed together on to the bed. The middle of it fell through, pitching them on to the floor. Tyne rolled on top of Murray.

Doubled up, Murray ground his knee into Tyne's solar plexus. Tyne brought his steel hand chopping down on the side of Murray's neck. Blue about the lips, Murray subsided.

'That'll settle . . . your . . .' Tyne gasped. He had been badly winded. Blobs of colour waved like flags before his eyes. He shook his head to get the knocking sound out of it, before realising that someone was actually hammering on the door.

Looking up amid the ruins of the big bed, he saw Benda Ittai – but through a haze – open the door; one of the priests entered, speaking urgently to her. After a minute, she ran over to Tyne.

'The enemy are surrounding this building!' she said. 'The priests have seen them. Quickly, we must get away! I have a helicopter concealed outside. Come along!'

Seizing his good hand in her hot one, she pulled him to his feet. Murray groaned to himself as the weight shifted off him. Dazedly, Tyne allowed himself to be dragged from the room as the priest led them out. They trotted through the labyrinth of the building, Tyne gradually regaining his wits as they went. As they left the temple, he recalled that he had left his gun behind. It was too late to go back.

They emerged into a secluded courtyard surrounded by small cells once inhabited by novices. The whole place was slowly crumbling; it might have been built of old bread. Heat as choking as regret lay in the well of the mossy buildings. Under a stretched canopy of some camouflage material stood a small, trim helicopter. Benda ran across to it. She pressed one corner of the canopy and the whole thing collapsed, snapped up together like a blind. Picking it up, business-like, the girl stowed it into the helicopter and swung herself up.

She had an attractive pair of legs, Tyne thought. His powers of observation and deduction were returning. Even the sick feeling in his stomach was fading.

He pulled himself into the seat beside her as the priest backed bowing into the temple. At once, Benda started the rotors moving. They could see the disturbed heat move in whirlpools round them. Big green lizards scuttled for safety in the courtyard.

'Look!' Tyne shouted, pointing.

Over the top of a row of cells, a head appeared. Then shoulders. Then a rifle, swinging down to point into the helicopter. Rosk or man? Did Benda know? All she had said in the temple was, 'The enemy are surrounding us.' By that, she might have meant Ap II Dowl's toughs, or Stobart's. Which indicated the ambiguity of the role she played.

172

Almost jabbing her elbow into Tyne's ribs, Benda thrust her hand down into a capacious pocket. She had one of those murderous .88s there. Whipping it round, leaning half out of the cabin, she took a pot-shot at the sniper on the roof.

She missed.

Tyne saw the ridge of the roof shatter, spraying bits of tile into the sniper's face. His rifle went off wildly as he flung his hands up to his bleeding mouth. Then the helicopter began to rise.

As they began to bucket upwards, a man ran from the temple into the bright sunlight. It was Stobart, his face blistered with sweat, his great body heaving with exertion. Although he clasped a gun in one hand, he made no attempt to shoot; instead he was bellowing at Tyne, beckoning him savagely. Not a word came through the blanketing roar of the rotors above them.

'Just away in time!' Benda called.

Rising speedily above the ramshackle knot of temple buildings, they slanted eastwards and saw ant-sized men run into the open. Their shadow fled across the ants. The ants were firing upwards, fruitlessly.

VII

Mopping his face, Tyne thought hard. It was obvious enough that the charming Miss Ittai, far from having saved his life again, as he had at first believed to be the case, had tricked him into getting into the helicopter. She had wanted, for reasons of her own, to get him away from his own people. His brain was still muzzy from the effect of Murray's knee in his stomach; savagely, he shook his head. Fuzzy he might be, but on several points he was clear enough. And one of them was: this little beauty was heading in the direction of the Roskian Sumatra Base as fast as she could go.

A little, round cloud formed ahead, and another beyond that. They hit turbulence and lumped heavily up and down. Someone below had an anti-flight gun trained on them.

Tyne looked down, but could see only roads and plantations, the once-prospering stations of Company Earth. All round the outskirts of Padang, the Company Force had pockets of fortification and defence. Stobart must have worked quickly in getting on to them. In a minute, Tyne thought, interceptors would be up after them. He did not relish the idea.

The same thought had occurred to the girl. Grimly, she was

knocking every last spark of power out of the machine. Another crumpling explosion outside sent them rocking sideways. Locking the controls on a climbing course, she turned to Tyne. Suddenly, the gun was in her hand again.

'I hate to do this, but you must realise I will do anything to succeed, anything,' she said. 'This mission must be carried through at all costs. Beside it, none of us matter at all. If you so much as move suspiciously I will kill you. I will have to kill you.'

'You know, you interest me, Benda,' Tyne said. 'Why couldn't you have fallen in with the scheme for duplicating the microfilm I suggested back in the temple?'

She smiled dismissively. 'Do you really think your people would let you, me or the film go, once they had us? You are really an amateur, Tyne.'

'I've heard that said before, thanks. What do you want me to do?'

The craft bucked furiously as he asked. Hanging on, keeping the gun fixed on him, Benda said, 'It is getting rough. We are probably being pursued, so you must bail out. There is one of our mini-rotor kits behind you, which is the equivalent of your parachutes. Put it on, jump! That will be a distraction to your forces. Possibly when they see you are going down, they will cease to chase me. Also, this little flier will travel faster without you.'

'You have it all worked out,' Tyne said admiringly. 'And it can't be far to the Rosk base now. Anything else you want before I go?'

Her gun waved a little.

'Yes,' she said. 'Unlock your false hand and give it to me.'

A wave of something like triumph ran over Tyne. So at last he had guessed, and guessed rightly. Benda had 'rescued' him for the same reason that Murray had deliberately left him a trail to follow: because Tyne was absolutely essential to their plan. All the time he had seemed to be on the fringe of events, he had been at the centre.

Murray had wanted a safe hiding place for the microfilm, some-where where his contact could still get them even if he were intercepted. So when Tyne was unconscious on the trip back from Luna Area 101, it had been an easy matter for him to slip the little spool inside the cavity of one of Tyne's false fingers. Then he had played on Tyne's feelings harshly enough to ensure the latter followed him, made himself conveniently accessible! All the time that Tyne had presumed himself to be acting under free will, to be daring all in the name of action, his moves had been calculated

174

long in advance by someone else. The puppet had danced, unconscious of its strings.

Reading the anger and resentment on Tyne's face, Benda jerked the gun at him in warning.

'Fire!' he said. 'For God's sake, fire, girl! I'm less of an amateur than you think. When I thought about it, it was obvious why you left Murray behind at the temple instead of me; before I broke in on the pair of you, he told you what he'd done about hiding the film, didn't he?'

'I'm sorry,' she said. 'You were rather sweet.' Shutting her eyes she fired at point blank range. He watched her little fist contract as she squeezed the trigger.

Tyne opened his good hand, showing her a palm full of the semi-self-propelled bullets.

'I emptied your gun while you were playing with the controls. I thought you might be dangerous; I was right, wasn't I?'

Unexpectedly, she burst into tears; they looked much like any girl's tears. Tyne did not realise at the time the relief those tears expressed; relief both at having done her duty and at having been baulked of the necessity for taking life. Pulling the gun from her hand, Tyne reloaded and thrust it into his own pocket.

Now he turned his attention to the helicopter.

The anti-flight barrage had dropped behind. They were over jungle now, still gaining height. Screwing his eyes against the sun's glare, Tyne peered back into the blue sky. Scudding behind them, a V-shape moved low over the variegated cover, gaining, climbing. It was a manned interceptor, coming after them fast.

It seemed to be a case of get down or be shot down. Tyne grabbed the controls, angling the rotors, letting them slide down the sky. He felt only exhilaration at that moment.

Away ahead, blue, hazy, a huge multi-plane object stuck out of the broken wash of landscape. It was the grounded Alpha II ship. They were that near Rosk Base! At least he had saved himself a visit there. Moreover, although at the eleventh hour, he had saved the situation; Benda sat helpless beside him, suddenly drained of will. He was in control now.

He felt more than heard the interceptor come up. Tyne jogged the wheel, letting them sideslip – but not out of danger. An air-charge burst above the cabin. The controls went dead instantly, their vital elements fused.

Tyne cursed as the helicopter jerked over on to its back, clouting his head against the brace. For a moment he became detached from the scene, watching as from a long distance while the Rosk girl wrenched helplessly at the panel. Then the jungle spun up, and he snapped back into full possession of his senses. They were about to crash!

'Hang on!' he yelled.

So he was in control, was he? – And this was what being in control consisted of: hanging on!

They struck!

In the terrifying concussion, shreds of pulpy green stuff flew everywhere. The helicopter split like matchwood. Yet they were lucky. They had crashed into a thicket of giant cactus, some pillars of which reared twenty-five feet high. The stuff acted like a great pulpy cushion, breaking their fall.

Groaning, Tyne rolled over. Benda sprawled on top of him. Dragging her with him, still groaning with mingled shock and relief, Tyne crawled out of the debris, pushed his way painfully through shattered cacti, and stood up. Groggily, he looked round him.

The cactus thickets grew in an old lava bed. Rutted and furrowed, it supported little in the way of vegetation except for thorn and cactus, which crept tenaciously along fault lines. It was as forbidding a landscape as could be imagined. A quarter of a mile away stood a low rampart: the fortified perimeter of Sumatra Base. Directly he saw it, Tyne dropped to his knees. It did not do to come within range of that place.

As he was trying to drag the unconscious girl behind a cactus cliff, a shadow swooped across him. The interceptor was coming in to land. It amazed him that there was still no activity from the Rosk base; they had been known to fire on any Earth plane flying so near the perimeter. Settling Benda down as comfortably as he could, Tyne ran back to meet his pursuer.

The interceptor had made a vertical landing. Already the pilot was picking his way over the uneven ground towards Tyne: although his head was bent as he watched his footing over the lava, Tyne recognised him. Dodging behind some nearby columns of cactus, he drew Benda's gun and waited in ambush for him.

'Raise your hands!' he said, as the man appeared.

Startled, Allan Cunliffe did as he was told.

'You don't have to aim that thing at me, Tyne,' he said quietly. He bit his lips and looked round anxiously.

'I think I do,' Tyne replied. 'Until about ten minutes ago, I thought you were dead; now I want a few explanations from you.'

'Didn't Murray tell you I was still alive?'

'No, Murray didn't have time to tell me much. I worked this

one out for myself, believe it or not. As soon as I knew Murray
had tricked me into following him around, I guessed his tale about
shooting you on Luna was a lie, the carrot that kept me going like
a donkey; I had thought it unlikely to begin with. Obviously that
means you're as implicated as he. Take your belt off.'

'My trousers will fall down.'

'Keep clear of the cactus then!'

'You're not pleased to see me, Tyne; you're all mixed up.'

'So mixed up I trust no one. I regard you as an enemy,
Allan.'

Tyne took the belt and began to tie Allan's hands behind his
back. As he worked, Allan talked, protesting.

'Listen, Tyne, you can trust me, just as you always could. Do
you think I'd work for the Rosks in any way? I'll tell you this: I
was a Company agent before I ever met you – even before I joined
the Space Service. And I can prove I'm an agent. Look, the two
men who caught up with you at the plankton plant, and were in
the car when the flyspy appeared –'

'Dickens and the dumb fellow?' Tyne asked. 'What about them?'

'I was the dumb one, Tyne! I had to keep masked and silent or
you'd have recognised me.'

Allan stood there helpless now, his trousers sagging down to his
knees. In sudden fury, Tyne pushed him over and knelt by him,
grabbing his shirt in his fist.

'You bastard, Allan! *Why* couldn't you have spoken? Why've I
had to go round in the dark all the time, nobody helping me?'

Allan tried to roll away from him, his face black.

'You still had to think I was dead then, in case you gave up the
hunt for Murray,' he said. 'Time was short; we wanted you to keep
driving ahead. Don't you see that when Dickens had given you a
spot of necessary information, we were going to *let* you escape!'

'You could be lying now!'

'Why should I lie? You must have that microfilm now – you
reached Murray; all that's needed is to get it to the Company as
quickly as possible. Hand it over to me and let's get back to safety.'

*

Tyne's heart jumped. So Allan – once his friend, now (caught in
the no-man's land of intrigue) his rival – did not know how Murray
had concealed the invasion plans. Grabbing him by his shirt, Tyne
dragged him until they were behind a cactus clump, out of sight
of the Rosk base, still surprisingly silent and menacing.

'Tell me what happened on Area 101 when I was laid low,' he demanded. 'When you were supposed to have been killed.'

'It's no secret,' Allan said. 'You went out like a light when you were hit on the shoulder. Murray and I tried to carry you back to the ship and of course the Rosks caught us and disarmed us. There were only three of them – did you know that? – but in their far more efficient suits, they made rings round us. They told us that they and the fellow manning the searchlight were the only members of the peace faction, the RPF, supporting Tawdell Co Barr on Luna. But they'd managed to filch these plans; that was easy enough. The trouble was to get them to Earth – they were all three already under suspicion.

'When we heard the facts from them, Murray volunteered to take the spool to their Padang contact. To make sure he did so, they said they would hold me hostage. I watched Murray drag you back into the ship and leave.'

'How did you get away from them?' Tyne asked suspiciously.

'I didn't. They let me go of their own accord after a while. At first I thought it was for the reason they gave, that they could not keep me concealed anywhere from Ap II Dowl's secret police; but it wasn't. They wanted me loose so that I could set Company Earth forces on to Murray. I made full pelt for Company HQ Luna in the stolen lunarider they gave me, and got through to Double K Four – the agent you know by the name of Stobart. By the time he picked you up in the bar of the Roxy, he had heard from me and knew roughly what was going on. Then I got back to Padang myself as quickly as possible, meeting up with Stobart and Dickens. By then –'

'Wait a minute,' Tyne said.

He could hear a whine growing louder in the sky. He had been listening for it. Other interceptors were heading this way. Allan looked up with hope in his eyes. Tyne had less than five minutes left.

'I don't know what you're talking about,' he said roughly to Allan. 'You tell me these Roskian pacifists let you go so that you could set our people on to Murray, just when everything depended on his getting through? How do you make sense of that?'

'The whole business was staged to look as if everything depended on Murray's getting through. In fact, those RPF boys were clever; they wanted Murray caught with the film on him. They never intended anything but that the plans should fall into Earth hands. If Murray had double-crossed them, so much better. Of course,

Tawdell's agent here, the girl Ittai, didn't know that; she went to meet Murray in all good faith.'

'Why go such a long way round about? Why didn't they just post the film, once they had stolen it, direct to the Company?'

Allan laughed briefly.

'And who'd have believed it? You know how the political situation stands. If the film had been sent direct to us, it would probably have been dismissed as just another of Ap II Dowl's threats. The Area 101 RPF had even planted that strange object we had to investigate outside their dome as a bait; we happened to be the mice who came and sniffed at the cheese.'

Tyne stood up. He could see the interceptors, three of them flying low. At any minute now, they would see the crashed helicopter and be coming down.

'You've made yourself clear,' he said to Allan. 'The whole episode has been a twist from start to finish, and I've had to take most of the twisting. Only one thing isn't clear to me.'

Hopefully Allan propped himself on one elbow and asked what that was.

'I don't know who I can trust but myself. Everyone else is playing a subtle double game.'

'You can trust Stobart, even if you refuse to trust me. He should be in one of those three interceptors.'

'I trust nobody, not even that fat slob Stobart!'

Stooping, he wrenched Allan's trousers off, tied them savagely round his ankles.

'Sweat it out, feller!' he advised. 'Your pals will be down in a couple of minutes to put your pants on. And don't forget to look after Benda Ittai. She's over by the crash. Meanwhile, I'm borrowing your machine.'

Ignoring Allan's shouts, he ran across the lava bed to the grounded interceptor. The other planes were wheeling overhead. As he pulled himself into the swing seat, the radio was calling.

'. . . Why don't you answer? What's happening down there?' It was Stobart's voice, harsh but recognisable.

Puffing, assuming Allan's voice as well as he could, Tyne flipped the speech switch and said, 'Regret delay . . . fight with Leslie . . . I've got him tied up . . . Come on down.'

'Have you got the microfilm? Murray Mumford reports that it's in Tyne's false hand.'

'I haven't got it. Come on down,' Tyne said, cutting the voice off. Switching on the feed, he tensed himself and eased in the jets.

Rocking skywards, the interceptor responded perfectly; Tyne had flown these machines back in his training days.

With joy, he thought of the indecision that must be clouding Stobart's mind. Yes, Stobart would be suspicious. But Stobart would have to land to discover what was going on. Tyne found himself hoping that the guns of the Rosk base would open up. Just to give the agent a scare.

He checked the fuel; his tanks were almost full. Excellent; he could get to Singapore, centre of Company Earth, in one hop. He was not going to unscrew his steel fist for anyone less than Company Governor General Hjanderson.

VIII

It was, and the most scrupulous person must agree, a beautiful cell; commodious, with toilet and bathroom (complete with shower, jacuzzi and massage unit) attached, it was furnished in impeccable if uninspired taste, and provided with books, visicube and pictures; there was air-conditioning, there was concealed lighting, but it was still a cell.

The food was excellent and Tyne had eaten well. The couch was comfortable and Tyne had slept well. The carpet was deep, and Tyne now walked restlessly back and forth upon it.

His left hand was missing.

He had been confined for twenty hours. Arriving in Singapore shortly after two o'clock on the previous afternoon, he had been arrested at once, interrogated at length and shut in here. His questioners had been civil, removing his steel hand sympathetically, even apologetically. Since then, all his wants had been ministered to, his patience had been exhausted.

A knock came at the door. They knocked! It seemed the ultimate in irony. A slender man with a face the colour of an old pocket, dressed in a faultless suit, entered and attempted to smile at Tyne.

'Would you be so kind as to step this way to see Governor Purdoe?' he asked.

Tyne saved his wrath, until he was ushered into a large, bare room where a uniformed octogenarian rose from behind a desk. This was Prison Governor Purdoe, a watchful man with a watchful smile arranged on his apple-clean face.

'How much longer am I going to be locked up here?' Tyne

demanded, marching up to his desk. 'When am I going to see Hjanderson? What the devil do you want to talk to me about?'

'I am the governor of this institute,' the old man said reprovingly, without removing his smile.

'Let's not bring rank into this. All I want to know is am I or am I not a bloody hero? If I am, is this the sort of treatment you think I enjoy?'

'You are indeed a hero, Mr Leslie,' the governor said placatingly. 'Nobody denies it. Please sit down and smoke a mescahale and let some of the blood drain out of your head.'

Governor Purdoe came round from behind the desk. He stood in front of Tyne, looking at him until he seated himself; then he said, 'It may console you to know that your two associates in this affair, Murray Mumford and Allan Cunliffe, are also detained here. We are not sitting idly by. Your stories are being correlated.'

'All I'm saying is that there was no need to place me under lock and key to start with. I came here voluntarily, didn't I?'

The governor inclined his grey head.

'When you arrived, there was a general Company call out for you, dead or alive. You were fortunate, Mr Leslie, that we managed to get you and keep you safely before less enlightened parties reached you. An agent whom I believe you know as Stobart had reason to fear, when you tricked him yesterday, that you might have turned traitor. He merely took the precautions expected of him.'

'Don't mention Stobart to me, Governor! It brings me out in a rash. Just tell me what you wanted me for. Can I have my fist back?'

Governor Purdoe smiled a little bleakly. Seen close to, the smile was not attractive.

'Shortly,' he said: 'I summoned you here because I wanted in general to tell you that you are in the best place here – that far from being neglected, you are the prime mover in a lot of intense activity, most of which necessarily remains secret, even from you – and in particular to tell you that Governor-General Hjanderson will come to thank you personally as soon as possible. We believe you acted with excellent intentions, you see.'

Snorting, Tyne stubbed out his mescahale on the shiny desk top and jumped up. He topped Purdoe by a head, but the latter never moved.

'Governments!' he snapped. 'You people are all alike! Diplomacy and suspicion – nothing but! Nobody trusting anybody! Don't you take anything that happens at its face value? Didn't you take the Gaian oath?'

'You have run into a lot of trouble because you did just that,' the governor said. He turned away, walked round behind his desk, sat down with a hint of tiredness. His manicured right hand performed a gesture of contempt. 'There is no trust anywhere, Leslie. I regret it as much as you, but I face the fact. None of you young men are realists. These plans for the invasion from Alpha Centauri II – not a word about them must escape to the public; that is just one good reason for your continuing to stay with us. Try – please try – to think less of yourself, and reflect instead on the grave issues looming behind these plans. Sithers, conduct our guest back to his – room.'

The man with the dirty linen face came forward. Tyne shrugged his shoulders, making hopelessly towards the door; he knew he would get nothing out of Purdoe even if he squeezed him like a sponge. He had met the institutional type before.

In the doorway he paused.

'Just tell me one tiny, weeny little state secret, Governor,' he begged. 'All that tale Allan Cunliffe told me about the Rosks really manoeuvring to get the microfilm in our hands – was that true or false?'

An odd expression – it might have been another smile – passed over the governor's face and vanished.

'Cunliffe has been an excellent agent for a number of years,' he said, 'And, though I grant you it does not necessarily follow, everything he told you was perfectly correct. The RPF wanted us to get the invasion plans. However, there was one minor point he missed, because he could not possibly have known it. The invasion plans themselves are most probably false.'

*

The rest of the day passed with intolerable slowness for Tyne.

He reflected, as the governor had urged him to do, on the grave issues behind the Rosk invasion plans. One issue at least stuck out a mile. There had been no proof as yet that Alpha II's technology was far in advance of Earth's in this last decade of the twenty-second century: even the construction of a gigantic interstellar ship was, in theory at least, not beyond Earth's resources. But an interstellar invasion implied many things. It implied, surely, some form of faster-than-light communication between Ap II Dowl's force and Alpha II. It implied, too, a drive a good deal faster than the one professedly used to get the first ship here, for no invasion would be feasible between planets a two-generations' journey apart. It implied, undoubtedly, an integration of planetary resources towards which Company Earth was still laboriously working. It implied, above all, an overweening confidence in success; as vast an undertaking as an interstellar invasion would never get under way unless the powers behind it considered it a fool-proof scheme.

The picture was not, Tyne admitted to himself, anything but gloomy. The role he had played in it shrank into the mere prologue to a whole volume of catastrophe.

But if the plans were false?

What did that mean? Had the RPF been tricked, perhaps, into believing that the belligerent forces would do one thing, whereas actually they intended to do another? Tyne, sitting hour after hour in his so comfortable, so commodious cell, could invent many such unhelpful questions to ask himself.

If he disliked not knowing the answers, he disliked knowing the questions even more.

He had time to worry about Benda Ittai, and wonder if he would see her again in happier circumstances. A lascivious thought teased him: who would be the first terrestrial man to make love to an alien woman? It would be a wonderful experience. 105.1 degrees . . .

On the third day of Tyne's imprisonment, he was summoned again to the governor's presence. He appeared in chastened mood before the old man.

'I've had no news,' he said. 'What's the general situation? Are the Rosks making a move?'

'The situation has changed very radically since we last met,' Purdoe said, his face crumpling into innumerable pleats as he smiled. 'And may I say, Mr Leslie, how glad I am that you no longer come into here clamouring for release. You have been thinking, I take it?'

Tyne sighed.

'I'm not really a man of action, Governor, but that doesn't mean you have to be avuncular with me. What have you brought me here for this time?'

'Take a mescahale, young man. I should advise you to watch your tongue. Now please excuse me for a minute.'

He disappeared through a rear door with his sprightly old man's gait. To kill time, Tyne stared at the linen-faced attendant who had brought him here; the attendant fingered his tie and coughed.

His days in the diplomatic field had accustomed him to waiting.

Rooms like the one he was in were designed less for work than for waiting. Of course, the time would come when prisons would be abolished. And after that, perhaps, rooms in which human beings were expected to waste their lives away. It needed patience and another generation and a lot of hard Gaian re-education. Plus, of course, a successful outcome of the crisis with the Rosks.

Governor Purdoe returned with a functionary who bore Tyne's artificial hand on a tray. Tyne clipped it on again without a word. The perfect instrument responded immediately to the nerves in his wrist. He looked enquiringly at Purdoe.

'You are going to see the governor-general of the Company as you wished,' Purdoe said. 'He is about an hour's flight from here. Then you are perfectly free. This man here will fly you to Mr Hjanderson.'

'I'm a pilot. I can fly myself.'

'You will be taken in one of our executive jets. This man will fly you.'

As he turned to go, Tyne said, 'What did you mean by saying that the Roskian invasion plans are false?'

'I'm only a prison governor. I think you may get a better answer from the governor-general of the Company. Goodbye, Mr Leslie.'

The plane was a six-seater American Souslik. It rose into the atmosphere, and all of Singapore Island was immediately visible behind them, set in its blue sea, like a coda at the end of Malaysia's long tail. He saw once again the marvellous beauty of the world in which he lived, sensitised to it after three days in a cell.

Mankind had had to separate itself from Nature to achieve its distinctive personality, to become the one creature on the planet capable of observing itself and all other creatures. Technology and science had been its vital aids, from the first crude arrowhead of flint onwards. Through science, mankind had come finally to a realisation of the unity of all living things, of the whole biomass, of that vast and complex machinery of mindless cooperation which meant that only life sustained life over the face of the globe: without life, Earth would be sterile like Mars and Venus. For more and more people, the revelation had dawned with the force of a religious visitation. Intellect was for Earth, and for its husbandry. Yet Gaia was no religion, simply a supreme commonsense.

From that time onwards, humankind began to cease abusing its environment and itself. This technologically marvellous hand, Tyne thought, is going to turn swords to ploughshares from now on, if only the threat of invasion is lifted. No more brutality. I swear. He thought of his grandfather, the butcher, bringing his chopper down on to raw meat on the slab before him, and shuddered. Poor grandfather . . . victim of a bad dream from which, with luck, there would be an awakening. Humanity was going to change for the better, almost despite itself.

Maybe that was false uplift. Here, splitting the atmosphere with the tropical world below him, anything seemed possible.

They came down in the Highlands of Sumatra, near Lake Toba, not so far from Padang and the Rosk ceded territory.

Governor-General Hjanderson was inspecting a new eland farm. Tyne waited in the shade of some catalpa trees until the older man was ready to see him. He recognised Hjanderson from his photographs, a tall man with pronounced nose and jaw, fiftyish, with a sharp but not unkindly eye.

They shook hands. 'You have been having a bad time,' Hjanderson said. 'So have we all. I should really not be here while we have a crisis on, but this was a longstanding date. You can ride with me back to the station and we will talk as we go.'

A large afforested reservation had been established here where previously cash crops had been grown, and male and female eland, bred in captivity, turned loose in it. They would be used as a food resource, to be culled once a year.

As they climbed into the Company car, Hjanderson said, gesturing to a line of distant trees, 'We have to get rid of them. They are eucalyptus. No good for this soil, and nothing can grow near them because of the phytotoxins they spread in the soil. They are another cash crop – quick timber – we have to get rid of, to use the land more sensibly.'

'Are we going to get rid of the Rosks?'

'Perhaps they're providential, another lesson to us to value our own world.'

Tyne wasn't having any of that. 'Would you mind telling me if those invasion plans are true or false?'

'Yes, of course you were never fully in the picture, were you? But you are well aware how largely politics are a game of bluff and cunning – war by peaceful means. Those with the weakest hand risk the most. The Rosk organisation, the RPF, for instance, was a spurious front, established by Ap II Dowl and his junta on their ship. Oh, a lot of the Rosks genuinely wished for peace with us, and still do. But Tawdell Co Barr was himself simply a well-meaning puppet of Dowl's.'

'How do you know this, sir?' Tyne asked, suspiciously.

The car was rolling over a narrow road among dense trees,

through which an occasional eland could be glimpsed. Ahead lay a round glass building, the agronomy station.

'Company Earth has received a great deal of help,' said the governor-general, 'from the Roskian woman Benda Ittai, whom I believe you left for dead beside her crashed helicopter.'

'I certainly didn't leave her for dead.'

Hjanderson cocked an amused eye at Tyne, but said nothing.

'Where is Benda Ittai now?' Tyne asked.

The car slowed and stopped before the glass rotunda.

'In here,' Hjanderson said, pointing ahead.

Tyne gave a shout of delight, jumped from the vehicle, and ran forward.

He pushed through a revolving door and was in a large air-conditioned space, filled with tubs of bamboo, information displays, and a lounge with a bar. Benda was already walking towards the door, wearing a light nylon fur over her sarong-type garment. He hurried to her, kissed her, and seized her hands. They were hot. 105.1°. Alien. But she was beautiful, and smiling in a tender and delightful fashion.

'I haven't seen you since you tried to shoot me,' he said.

'How happy I am the situation has changed since then,' she said.

The governor-general came towards them, looking rather displeased – envious perhaps, Tyne thought, or annoyed that Tyne had so far forgotten protocol as to enter the station door in front of him.

'I can see you have lost interest in the political situation,' Hjanderson said, rather stiffly, trying to pass off the remark as a joke.

'Not at all, sir. I think I have shown my concern sufficiently. May I ask you again about the threatened invasion of Earth, or will you again change the subject?'

But there was a stir and a bustle from the other side of the chamber, and a group of five people came forward to surround the governor-general with an official welcome. A lot of official smiling went on, accompanied by various empty social remarks.

Finding that they were outside this charmed circle, Tyne said to the girl whose arm he held, 'I would prefer to ask you this over a restaurant table, but what has been happening I ought to know about?'

'Maybe the table can be arranged later. But I can tell you immediately that I am now on . . . what's that expression? – on your side of the fence. It has to be. I cannot go back to my people, or I shall be killed. That is why I have told everything I know to your Company staff. This man Hjanderson and so on.'

'The invasion?'

'The invasion threat was false. Maybe you also heard that the RPF was another ruse of Ap II Dowl's – we were taken in by it, and no doubt we should all have been wiped out by the time we had served our purpose. Some day I will explain how awful circumstances are, trapped inside that great hunk of our insane technology . . .'

'Budo Budda was out to kill you.'

She nodded. 'I was nothing. I was expendable. But even Budo Budda would not have known that the RPF was a false front organisation, designed to trap dissidents. Otherwise he would not have been after Murray, your friend.'

As he thought about it, he guided her away from the governor-general and his little coterie, towards the bar. In a diorama tank, minute images of eland herds moved among standing timber: one shape of things to come for Sumatra.

'My diplomatic training forces me to believe all this, but how did you find out?'

She shrugged her shoulders under the fur. 'Many little events on our ceded territory made me suspicious. The intention to get whatever concessions we could out of Company Earth was always clear. But Ap II Dowl was just as happy to get what he could out of us. I really realised what was going on that time when we crashed near the base and they did not open fire on us or send out a party to pick us up. You remember, Tyne?'

Of course he remembered. 'It was odd.'

'Certainly it was. Their silence could mean only one thing. Those vital little plans causing you so much trouble had to stay outside the base. In other words, they were intended for Company eyes. The Company had to seem to get hold of something it was not meant to get hold of, eh?'

'Because they were fake?'

'Because their objective was simply to throw a scare into Earth, to win concessions.'

'They certainly did that as far as I was concerned. Still do, fake or not. Let's get a drink.'

He summoned a waiter. His thoughts ran ahead. So there were no more ships launching out from Alpha Centauri? He still could not get the terror of a conquest of Earth from his mind. Just supposing that Benda Ittai was lying even now? Then another piece of the puzzle dropped into place.

'That fits with something I could not understand. Now it's clear. What was that spool of microfilm doing on Luna in the first place? That always rang curiously false. Obviously it had to be planted there, far from base, where its journey would attract maximum attention.'

She made no answer. They were sitting together at a bamboo table, and she was shielding her eyes with her hands, her elbows on the table. He realised that she was weeping without making a sound.

As the drinks came, she wiped her eyes on a handkerchief. Without speaking, she brought a microcassette from her purse and laid it on the table before him. Switching it on, she made a few adjustments, then looked up searchingly at Tyne with her dark eyes.

'I will play you something. This is after I told everything to the Council. You will hear Hjanderson's voice.'

A voice recognisably Hjanderson's said, evidently to his colleagues, 'It is sad for this young woman to find herself so at odds with her own kind. We must not allow her to feel too much in exile. The invasion plan was Dowl's last grand bluff. They're all dying in that damned interstellar vessel. If we had confronted him with a knowledge of the plan, Dowl would probably have said that he would call off the invading fleet, provided we ceded him all Sumatra. Maybe he would have asked for all Africa as well. Who knows what he would have demanded? . . . No, whatever threats he makes, he has nothing to back them with. It was unfortunate that Leslie and those other men got mixed up in the deception . . . We are awaiting word from our Astronomical Unit which may help us further.'

She switched the little instrument off.

'That was two days ago. You see what a traitor I am.'

'No. No. I see your courage. I see what pain you've been through. And I'll do what I can about that, I promise.'

He leaned towards her but, as he did so, the governor-general of Company Earth, together with his coterie, advanced towards their table. Hjanderson held a flimsy piece of paper in one hand. Tyne flashed the man a glance of pure anger at the interruption, but Hjanderson ignored it and gestured to Tyne to stand up.

'Leslie, you'd better be allowed to see this. I have to confess that you and the girl are both under observation at this minute. I'll call the agents off now. We had to be absolutely certain that Ittai wasn't yet another Dowl trick. This communiqué makes the situation clear, I'm glad to say.'

Tyne took the flimsy and read it, at first with caution, then with growing excitement.

The message read: 'Circulation Double Restricted. Govt. Levels A-C only, List 566. Text begins: Sagan Observatory, Luna, confirm readings indicate Alpha Centauri unstable. According new radio spectra analysis, Alpha about to go nova. Increase in apparent magnitude visible shortly. Life on its planets calculated untenable within century end.

'Confirm local Alpha observers would have detected unusual solar activity three generations ago. Rosk ship is therefore escape ship in all probability. Chance of invasion regarded as highly improbable, repeat highly improbable.

'Suggested course of action: Submit announcement of text of this message, coupled with warning to Ap II Dowl to resign leadership or else his people expelled from Sumatra and Earth. Text ends.'

Tyne's excitement died as it was born. His instinctive reaction was to put an arm protectively about Benda Ittai. He saw exactly what this information – with which she must be already familiar – meant to her and the surviving Rosks.

A flash of memory illuminated him. He was playing in his grandfather's butcher's shop, aged five. His grandfather had gone out to the cold store. Tyne seized the meat chopper and started to imitate his grandparent's actions on the wooden block. What excitement, burying the blade into the wood. Then he was staring in an eternal moment of pained dismay at his severed hand.

In his life until now, he had known of no greater severance.

The cruel personal image dissolved into visions of Alpha's oceans steaming, of volcanoes erupting across the land, of babies cooking slowly in underground refuges, of whole planets turning slowly to ashes. He hid his head on Benda Ittai's shoulder, as if it was he, not she, who needed comforting. As a Gaian, he found the news of any destruction of life a reduction of his own life-energy.

Hjanderson's response was far less complex. He strode about, calling to the Sumatran manager of the rotunda to serve everyone drinks. Tyne looked up once, to see why he was making so much noise. Beyond the massive face of the governor-general, little bright finches hopped among the bamboo stands. Whether they had been introduced there or had found their own way in through an open window, they were thoroughly at home, flitting among the foliage, unconcerned with human affairs. He put an arm about Benda Ittai, as she wrapped hers about him.

Hjanderson paused before Tyne, staring down angrily. 'Leslie

189

– I had you marked out as a brash and impertinent young man. How typical of you and your generation that you should not be moved by this marvellous news. That all you think of is fondling this alien woman. Here we are –'

'Jesus, sir, I was simply thinking how –'

The governor-general was red in the face. 'I don't wish to know what you were thinking. I know what you were thinking. I can read your kind like a book. I guess you don't care that we can now squash these Rosks without fear of retaliation and –'

Tyne stood up. 'Another generation, and we'll be rid of your kind, sir.'

'Get out. And take that woman with you. We don't want you here, spoiling our celebrations.'

He wanted to say so much to Hjanderson, but anger confused his thought. He wanted to say that it would be impossible to understand a Rosk as long as it remained so easy to misunderstand a man. That centuries of peace were needed in order for inner understandings to grow. That bullies and butchers would have to become extinct. There were no words forthcoming. He could comprehend Hjanderson no more than the man could understand him.

He took Benda Ittai's arm. 'Let's go.' Here at least was someone, at present lost, worth trying to understand.

'Let's go and find that restaurant table you were talking about,' she said.

She smiled at him. It was a very comprehensible smile. 105.1 degrees.

THE MANNERHEIM SYMPHONY (III)

After finishing this agreeable diversion, I fell sound asleep in my police cell. That much I owed to Jael Cracken – yes, I was convinced he was also the author of *Equator*. Surely that final line about smiling was a covert reference to his earlier story, a signal to a private fan club, perhaps, over the heads of the general reading public. How Sinnikka would disapprove of such playfulness. Rightly so.

And both novels concerned alternative worlds which had never happened. Sumatra harboured plenty of aliens, but not of the Rosk variety. Sumatra submitted to a gritty and corrupt regime which remained in power only because of an external threat: the ever-spreading influence of the Japanese Global Co-Prosperity Sphere. No wonder Cracken had written so many books. He had found a simple formula which could be liberally applied; change some vital hinge factor in the past and you have an intriguingly different world to write about in the present.

I found myself looking for hinge factors which might be changed in our real world – just one seemingly trivial event which, if its outcome had been different, would alter history. 'The Cracken syndrome', I labelled it, sarcastically.

An instance came to mind. I recalled how, in the days of our old tyrannous and brave leader, Mannerheim, he had sought for international recognition. As I have mentioned, he invited five English politicians to Helsinki in 1935. Three of the politicians were assassinated by foreign agents – the OGPU at work, many said – including a man called Winston Churchill. Churchill was speaking out about the perils of Communism when he was killed.

The media of the time, briefly reporting Churchill's death, referred to him as a trouble-maker. This was the case particularly in the isolationist United States of America. I thought differently. Churchill seemed to me, and to many others, to be a courageous and far-sighted man. Supposing he had not visited Finland, but lived on in England and become, through some freak of politics, Prime Minister of Britain. Supposing he had then infused enough of his spirit of defiance into the English-speaking peoples for them to stand up against the tyrant Hitler. Supposing by his example he had inspired the USA also to join against the Nazis, and the two nations had vanquished fascism entirely . . .

It was an enjoyable thought. But too utterly unlikely to be contemplated as a probability by anyone but makers of Maybe-Myths like Cracken.

I sat bolt upright in shock. A reindeer was staring through the reinforced glass in the cell door, its morose contemplation a parody of human physiognomy.

The image dissolved into the face of Captain Hakkennon.

I had almost forgotten him and my present predicament, so unfocused had my mind become. In part, Cracken was to blame. But there was another factor. While I slept, I had decided how the murder charge must be answered. I had decided whether I should send my poor maltreated wife or my poor misjudged self to the electric chair.

Hakkennon unlocked the door and looked at me with an expression I could not read. Slowly he took his service revolver from his holster and raised it. Such are the fears of even short-term prisoners in our nation that I believed he was going to shoot me in cold blood.

'Come out,' he said, motioning with his long grey head.

Leaving the paperback on my bunk, I followed him out of the cell into the neon-lit passage. No one was about. Hakkennon unlocked another door and ushered me in before him.

I walked into an interrogation room, sparsely furnished, spotlessly clean. Unlike my cell, this room had a window, set in a reinforced door to the outside. Night lay beyond the window. Looking at my watch in surprise, I saw that it was near one o'clock. One in the morning, I realised, not one in the afternoon as I had previously supposed. My time-sense was badly adrift.

He came close to me, raising the gun to my temple. The hammer rose as he began to squeeze the trigger.

'Are you prepared to die?'

'My old friend Colonel H!' I exclaimed, in surprise – a literary reference which naturally eluded Hakkennon. Reindeer don't read.

'You admit guilt?'

Guilt? It was my stock-in-trade. I had such an over-surplus of guilt that only a bullet could discharge it. Why, then, did I try to summon telepathy to my aid at that moment, as if I were Conrad Wyvern? Nothing happened. At such moments, one finds oneself preferring popular fiction to life. I strained, but it did not work.

He squeezed the trigger. Click. Fortunately, the mechanism didn't work either.

'Must have forgotten to load it. Dash! We reindeer sometimes have problems with hand-weapons, as you can imagine.'

'I imagine the hooves get in the way of the trigger-guard.'

He kept hold of the gun, not particularly perturbed, as if the little charade held some meaning I did not fathom.

'You must understand that police work is a matter of obeying orders. My first priority is not to solve crime but to obey orders. Generally, those orders are to solve crime, of course. But not always. Yours is a special case.'

He gave me one of those side-glances from that old grey head of his.

'There have been phone calls in the night. I can't say from whom. I wonder if you would accept that, just as there are higher levels of authority, so there are higher levels of crime? Hierarchies of guilt?'

'Are you about to lecture me on infidelity?'

'The crime of Carol-Ann Crutchley Cracken, for example, might be wiped out – purged – by a higher crime. A crime of state, let's say. You follow me?'

'Wait.' An awful hope came to my heart with his words.

The very caution with which he approached his subject suggested that some dreadful major evil was working on my behalf. 'You're going to tell me that two blacks – at last, in this year of Our Lord – make a white, yes?'

He showed me his yellow teeth in a brief smile. They were the broad molars with long crowns and short roots of a grazing animal.

'Let's just suppose that you and your naked wife back home are playing out some little drama of your own that just happens to appeal to you. You think it's a private drama, don't you? Just between you and her, plus the fancy women you pick up and the fancy men she picks up.'

'Sinnikka doesn't pick up men. She has no feeling for the other sex. Besides, she suffers badly from arthritis. The gymnastics of the bed are painful to her.'

He felt in a tunic pocket, and produced a strip of news-print, a clip from *Tanaan*. He proffered it to me. I would not take it. I saw what it was. The headline stood out. BLATANT PAN-REICH SYMPHONY DISAPPOINTS.

'A criticism written by Alius Jalkirouka,' said Hakken-non, stuffing the clip back in his pocket. 'Your wife's lover. He has a personal interest in destroying your reputation.'

'I don't believe it. That's not Sinnikka. She called Jalki-rouka a fat little prig only yesterday – the day before yesterday. She wouldn't do that to me.'

His head went to one side. Surveying the floor sceptically, he said, 'She may not be doing it to you. She could be doing it to herself.'

'Leave psychology out of this, Hakkennon – stick to your lichen.'

'The point I'm making is that you think you have some sort of a private life-game going. You haven't. Private life is no longer available in the modern state. It's been banished as a luxury.'

I went to gaze out of the window. Crude shapes of buildings stood out against a low, swelling hillside, bathed in moonlight. I heard no sound from that world of freedom.

Hakkennon said, 'I'm alone in the station just now, and have other matters to attend to, so I'll come to the point.

195

Let's suppose that certain of my phone calls established that Carol-Ann Crutchley Cracken was not the innocent American young lady of her passport. Suppose that she was in fact an illegitimate daughter of President Mannerheim – notorious for his liaisons – by a well-connected – no pun intended – a well-connected Russian lady with friends in the Kremlin. So her national allegiances were divided, even when her parents fled to the USA.'

'As mine did, many years ago.'

'Irrelevant.' He shot me one of his guarded glances. Although his face was designed to conceal expression, I saw in his eyes a real hatred of me, and knew – in part by his body language – that he was going to enjoy telling me something I would greatly dislike. 'You're not an easy man to explain anything to, are you? So I will simply say that I have learned that Carol-Ann's initial contact with you was planned. Not an accidental encounter, as you in your pride assumed. When you missed that rehearsal of your symphony, the girl was picking *you* up, and not vice versa.'

Preferring not to think back to a pleasant interlude which had cost me so dear, I scowled at him and said, 'You don't believe in sexual freedom, do you?'

'Listen to what I'm telling you, man. She was an enemy agent. We know now who she was working for. Her orders were to ensnare you and persuade you to defect. Which you would be more ready to do when your musical career was in ruins. As it is.'

When I said nothing, he added, 'It appears you were easily hooked.'

My fury and bafflement must have burst from me. I managed to say only, 'Even reindeer don't mate for life.'

'Most reindeer end up on the butcher's block. That is what was being prepared for you. Your downfall and defection would be one more slur on the good name of our country. That's what we care about – not about you.'

'You are telling me a tissue of lies to make me confess. Put me back in my cell with my Maybe-Myths.'

He shook his head as if his antlers weighed heavy upon

196

him. Again a look of weary hatred; I fancied I could smell it, ancient and arctic.

'With each eminent man who defects from Finland, the easier it becomes for our friends in the East to take us over, lock, stock and barrel, with no protest from America and the Free Nations. Our Security forces got on to Carol-Ann Mannerheim just too late. She flew up to Kuusamo airport to be ready to meet you off your plane after the concert – another assignation. The idea was to comfort you after Jalkirouka's adverse review was printed.'

'How did she know the review would be adverse?'

'Oh, critics always have their price.'

'Not Jalkirouka!' I could not believe it of the man, however much I resented him.

'Why not Jalkirouka? He was once your wife's lover.'

I could say nothing.

'It's a corrupt world. Isn't that *your* favourite theme?' He allowed a sneer into his voice. 'Anyhow, we got one of our agents to her before she got to you. That agent met her, volunteered to give her a lift to your house, and *neutralised* her along the road – where you found her body.'

Waves of nausea overcame me. I could feel the pallor of my face. 'Could I have some coffee? My mouth is dry. I'm convinced this is all lies, isn't it?' I searched about in my confusion for some shred of evidence to prove or disprove what he was saying. There remained only the fact that Hakkennon had told me earlier that the distinctive stab-wound which caused the girl's death had been made by a Service knife. That had been before he planned to tell me this monstrous story. His unease while speaking, with all the undertones of evil, served to convince me that he was delivering something more or less resembling the truth.

'Wait!' I had it. 'The note. The girl's note. You say she never visited my house. Yet she left the note there.'

He ran his hand through the scanty hair of his head, sighing. 'That note was a forgery. Carol-Ann never wrote a word of it. It was designed to allay your suspicions, in case you were sharp enough to have any, regarding her disappearance. You had agreed to meet again, hadn't you?

197

So the note said she was off to Sweden. I'll get you some coffee. You may need it before your journey. I'm all alone here, so I'll get it myself. I believe that the outer door's locked so that you don't escape.'

'Her letter was forged?'

'Carol-Ann cared nothing for you.'

It was worse than reading Cracken. I could not believe it was happening. When I raised my hands to my dry lips, they were trembling uncontrollably. Where had my sense of fun gone?

'Who forged it?'

With a sick smile, he said, 'The agent who eliminated her. Disguised handwriting is an agent's business.' Then he left me alone.

He returned after a minute with two steaming cartons of coffee. And I had not even tried the outer door. My mind was blank.

The liquid restored some of my senses.

'Suppose all this to be true.'

'I am not saying it is true or it isn't.'

'Then this agent. Picked Carol-Ann up at Kuusamo airport, killed her on the road, smuggled a forged note into my house. How could he do that without Sinnikka knowing?'

'Sinnikka is the agent involved.' The sentence was like the death of a world.

He went over to the outer door. It was not locked. He stepped outside. I heard him breathing deep of the cool night air, snuffling it at his nostrils like an animal. I sank heavily on a chair. Something had ceased within me.

'She was getting her revenge and doing her state duty at the same time,' he called in. 'Well, this can't be too pleasant for you . . . Why not come and get a breath of fresh air? You'll feel better. Believe me, if men breathed properly every day of their lives, ran and breathed deep as we do, many of their psychological problems would disappear. They'd be transformed, as I have been.'

With heavy limbs, I went over and stood in the doorway.

'Sinnikka a security agent. It's hard for me to believe.'

In a harsh tone, he said, 'I find it hard to believe that you

198

have had contacts with our enemies to the East, but we know for a fact it is so, on your trips abroad.'

'Are you going to pin a murder charge on me, Hakkennon?'

'I was coming to that. I herewith charge you formally with the murder of Carol-Ann Mannerheim, alias Crutchley Cracken. Tomorrow, I shall fly you to Helsinki Prison – provided, of course, you don't escape first. After all, your trial would be an embarrassment to the State, and further dishonour the government.'

Only then did I realise what he wanted me to do, how his higher-ups had ordered him to act. This was why he had taken care to demonstrate earlier that his revolver was unloaded.

'Look . . .' But for once I could not formulate anything coherent to say.

He stood by me quite placidly, half-leaning against the outside wall of the building, his mild gaze turned up towards the Moon. The Moon was almost full, and sailed in a clear deep blue sea of sky.

When Hakkennon spoke, his voice was low. 'We reindeer people know why the Moon is silver and grey. Once it was all green, long ago, before man and Lapps came into being. And the reindeer herds grazed on the Moon for many generations, always happy and sportive, as is our true nature.

'Unfortunately, we did not control ourselves. God – who is a reindeer too – had given us one extra gift which was too much. That gift was sexual pleasure. We reindeer indulged it too avidly. We were unable to resist it. So more and more reindeer were born on the Moon, and eventually all those lush pastures were badly over-grazed. Finally, nothing was left but bare mud, trampled down by many hooves. Then all the reindeer in the Moon died.

'To punish us, God took away the gift of sexual pleasure from the reindeer of Earth. We still perform the act, but the pleasure is gone. That is why we always look a little melancholy. God gave that joyous gift to men and women instead. Now we see you abusing it just as we did. We await

199

the inevitable result. Meanwhile, as I have suggested, the cure for your problems is to RUN.'

I started out through the long grass, not looking back, with the Moon above me and a broad lane winding ahead over the low hills towards the East.

I breathed deep, as Hakkennon had done.

I was going to be an exile again.

It was my natural element.